力得文化
Leader Culture

Lead your way. Be your own leader!

力得文化
Leader Culture

Lead your way. Be your own leader!

Banking English

力得文化
Leader Culture

證照是基本條件，英語溝通力是**勝出關鍵！**
全方位國際化銀行人＝專業能力＋業務能力＋語言能力

一開口就會的銀行英語

『到銀行櫃檯存錢』的英文是 make a deposit，不是 save money！
『國際匯款』為什麼叫 wire transfer？
你知道 nest egg 的意思是「積蓄」嗎？

◎精彩單元

- **實境對話** 菜鳥寫履歷表到變身業務經理
- **日常用語** 常用會話簡單一句搞定
- **好用句型** 提升業務能力，從容得體處理各種狀況
- **職場需知** 如何介紹雙方認識、怎麼將客戶抱怨轉化成銷售契機、說話扼要的藝術

季薇‧伯斯特 ／ Paul James Borst ◎著

- 銀保科、金融財經系所英語會話最佳輔助教材
- 現職櫃台員加薪、升遷提升職場核心競爭力不可不看
- 投考外商銀行、轉調外國分行加強英語溝通力自學首選
- 留遊學、打工換宿、背包沙發衝浪客、常住國外凡需用英語與銀行打交道者實用參考

Chi's Preface
作者序

如果可以重新回到九年前，九年前當保羅遞給我那張空白的工作申請表時，我還會做一樣的選擇嗎？

在寫到這本《一開口就會的銀行英語》的倒數第三章時，我坐在舊金山灣區的家中，問了自己這個問題。九年來的各種回憶裡，有很多很多的挫折，有一些笑聲，有突然感到異常驕傲的時刻，也有百般無聊瞪著電腦的下午…而我知道我的答案是什麼。

一是的，我會。再回到九年前，我會選同樣的銀行，做同樣的事，我會想要相同的經歷，再次體會挫折後帶來的領悟，再次把事情搞砸所以下次就知道該怎麼做；喔，還有再次與我那些可愛的同事相遇（當然也不能忘記那些討厭鬼…），感謝老天把他們帶到我身邊，真的不知道為什麼我總是如此幸運，能跟這群聰穎、善良、慷慨的人們一起工作？我實在從他們身上學到太多太多了。

在銀行任職一年多後，也就是二○○六年時我和保羅到泰國作半自助旅行。兩人一句泰語也不會講，在旅程的途中到處碰壁、吃了許多虧；然而有一天，我們走進一間當地的銀行，含蓄有禮的櫃員操著簡單易懂的英文，十分有效率地幫我們處理事務。突然間我緊繃了十多天的情緒就這麼抒解下來，在那短短的幾分鐘內，我覺得回到了一個熟悉的地方，這個地方叫做「銀行」；在那短短的幾分鐘內，我有了一個新的觀點：在這個世界上，不論你到哪個國家，銀行都像從同一個模子裡打出來的一樣，在裡面工作的人似乎都呼吸著同一種空氣、照著幾乎一模一樣的程序來處理交易，對我來說，他們似乎在說一種共通的語言，這種語言無形也無聲，它叫作「銀行的語言」。

同時，這個世界上還有另外一個強大的語言—跟銀行語言不同，這種語言有形也有聲—叫做「英文」，今天各種深淺膚色、來自各式文化背景的人們都使用著這個語言互相溝通、了解，我十分有幸地能接觸並學習到如何每天在這兩種語言之間穿梭。在美國工作了這些年之後，我衷心地希望能藉由這本書，把這兩種世界共通的語言結合在一起。僅容我邀請你，我親愛的讀者，一起進入這個令人歎為觀止的「銀行英語」世界…Have fun！

Paul's Preface

Welcome. It is my hope that you enjoy our book. Banking is a small niche; however our experiences in the field are deep. Banking is a dynamic environment so you may have some similar and different experiences. However, the key thing to remember is to always remain flexible to the needs of your branch. Be willing to try new things and adapt quickly as issues arise. My wife and I have taken the time to give you a general insider's view of the daily ins and outs of everyday banking. Take it and learn from our successes and mistakes. In conclusion I would like to thank our readers for taking the time to be a part of our world. We love sharing our stories and we will continue to seek out new adventures to write about … so stay tuned … we've got a lot more to talk about.

歡迎，我希望你會喜歡我們的書。銀行的市場獨特而不大；然而我們在這個領域內的經歷卻相當深入。銀行業的環境是動態的，所以你或許會有一些相似，以及一些不同的經驗。不過，關鍵是記得永遠要保持彈性、隨時根據你分行的需要做調整、樂意嘗試新的事物，以及當問題出現時快速地應變。我太太跟我花了許多時間，由內部人的角度，將銀行的日常情形呈現在你眼前，請吸收這些經驗，並從我們的成功及錯誤中學習。最後，我想感謝我們的讀者，謝謝你們願意花時間參與我倆的世界，我們熱愛與大家分享我們的故事，而我們也將繼續從事更多嶄新的冒險，並把它們寫下來…所以敬請期待…我們還有很多要談的喔。

Contents 目錄

Chapter 01

Application and Interview

應徵與面試

1.1 Greener Pastures

Title Note:

Pasture 發音為[`pæstʃɚ]，指「牧草地」。Greener pastures 的意思是「更好的機會或環境」。

對話 Dialogue

Paul: How was work? You look tired.

保羅：上班上得怎樣？妳看起來很累的樣子。

Chi: I AM tired. My whole body is **sore**. I think I made more than two hundred burgers tonight. And I have to open the store tomorrow morning.

季薇：我的確很累。整個身體都好酸。我想今晚我大概做了超過兩百個漢堡吧，然後明天一早我還要負責開店。

Paul: (Gives a blank form to Chi) I want you to fill this out.

保羅：（遞給季薇一張空白表格）我要妳填這張表。

Chi: What is it?

季薇：這是什麼？

Paul: It's a job application to be a bank **teller**. Earlier today I went to the bank to make a deposit and I saw that they were hiring. I think you would be perfect for the job.

Chi: Me? Working in a bank?

Paul: Yes, YOU. You are one of the most **detail-oriented** people I know. Plus, you're already doing the **cash register** and managing the accounting files for the store. You'll be fine.

Chi: That bank is across the street from the University. They **literally** can have hundreds of graduates majoring in financing and business management every year. Why would they hire me?

Paul: You are more intelligent and capable than you give yourself credit for! Now shut up and fill it out. I'll bring it back to the bank manager tomorrow. The worst they can say is no. You lose nothing for trying and gain everything

保羅：這是應徵銀行出納員的申請表。今天我到銀行去存錢的時候，我看到他們在徵人，我認為妳是這份工作的完美人選。

季薇：我？在銀行上班？

保羅：對，就是妳。妳是我認識過最細心的人之一。加上妳現在已經在店裡經手收銀機的工作跟管理會計的檔案，妳沒問題的啦。

季薇：那間銀行就位在大學的對面，說實在的他們每年都能招到數百個財金系和商管系的畢業生，怎麼可能考慮我？

保羅：妳比妳想像中的還要聰明跟有能力得多了！現在，閉嘴把這張表填好，我明天會拿回去給那位銀行經理。他們頂多說不，妳即使沒被選上也沒損失，但是如果被選上，一扇

if a new door of opportunity opens.

新的大門就會為妳開啟。

Chi: **Ok.** I'll give it a shot.

季薇：好吧，我會試試看。

Paul: There is an interview and a math test, so <u>bone up on</u> your skills this weekend. I'll help you with the **drills** and I'll show you what you can expect during the Q and A.

保羅：接下來會有面試與數學能力測驗，所以這個週末妳必須重新溫習妳的技能。我會幫助妳練習，以及提醒妳在問答的過程中可能會出現的情況。

Chi: I am a little **rusty**. I'll take all the help I can get.

季薇：我好久沒被面試了，很多事都忘了怎麼做，你能怎麼幫我我都好。

Paul: Get a good night's sleep tonight. We'll start practicing after work tomorrow.

保羅：今晚好好睡一覺。我們明天等妳下班以後開始練習。

單字 *Vocabulary*

- **sore** [sor] **adj.** 肌肉痛的、酸痛的
- **teller** [`tɛlɚ] **n.** 銀行出納員
- **deposit** [dɪ `pɑzɪt] **n. v.** 存款、存錢
- **detail-oriented** [`dɪtel `orɪ ˏɛntɪd] **adj.** 注意細節的、細心的
- **cash register** [`kæʃ `rɛdʒɪstɚ] **n.** 收銀機
- **literally** [`lɪtərəlɪ] **adj.** 實在地、不折不扣地
- **drill** [`drɪl] **n.** 反覆練習、演練

- **rusty** [ˋrʌstɪ] **adj.** （因長時間未使用而）生鏽、衰退

片語 Phrases

make a deposit（到銀行）存款

（作者按：注意不要說成 "save money" 喔！To save money 指的是「儲蓄的行為或習慣」；to make a deposit 才是至銀行櫃台存錢的動作。）

give someone credit for something 承認某人在某件事上做得很好

bone up on something 複習、把以前學過的再重新溫習

好用句型 Useful Sentences

I'll give it a shot. 我會試試看。

你還可以這樣說

I'll give it a whirl.

I'll give it a try.

I'll give it a go.

例句

A: Do you know that you can deposit checks into your account with your smartphone?

你知不知道你可以用智慧型手機存支票到帳戶裡？

B: That sounds so cool. I'll give it a shot!

聽來超酷的，我會試試看。

01 Chapter

02 Chapter

03 Chapter

04 Chapter

05 Chapter

06 Chapter

做銀行，我？

　　數年前，當保羅提議要我試著應徵銀行出納的時候，我第一個問題就是：我的英文夠好嗎？在工作環境裡別人聽不懂我說的話怎麼辦？對於我的質疑，保羅的回答為：即使是美國人，每一個人都擔心別人可能聽不懂自己講的話！

　　聽到他這麼說，我心想既然是這樣，大家的問題都一樣，那我不是孤獨的，我並沒有落後人家太多。這麼一想通，我就勇敢地去參加面試了。

　　許多人把做銀行出納員當作是一個職業生涯起頭的踏腳石；的確，成為一名出納，尤其是在美國，銀行只要求新人具備高中畢業的文憑，有沒有工作經驗是其次，所以很多在銀行工作的人，經常十八歲開始就在分行上班了；銀行對新進人員的訓練非常仔細且完整，有些銀行甚至從如何數錢給客人開始教！出納這項工作，由於牽涉到金融系統的多層面向，而且天天會接觸到各形各色的客戶與專業人才，會為你未來職業上的發展，奠立下十分穩固的基礎，真的是一個很好的入門工作。我永遠也不會忘記在新生訓練上，一位講師這麼跟所有在場的新進出納說過：

　　I have had the honor of working with talented and devoted senior tellers, many of whom have remained in this position until retirement. They have rightfully taken great pride in the knowledge that they have served the numerous needs of their customers well.

　　（我很榮幸地曾經與許多有天份、對工作深具熱忱的資深出納員一起工作過，其中很多人在這個職位上一直做到退休。他們對自己成功地服務過無數客戶感到相當驕傲。）

　　不論你對進銀行上班的期望如何，也許你立志有天成為集團的總裁，也許你喜歡銀行安定的工作形態、優渥的員工福利及退休金制度，做出納都是一個很棒的開始！

01
Chapter

02
Chapter

03
Chapter

04
Chapter

05
Chapter

06
Chapter

對話 Dialogue

Paul arrives home.

保羅剛回到家。

Chi: Babe! They called. THEY CALLED!

季薇：寶貝！他們打電話來了，他們打電話來了！

Paul: Who called?

保羅：誰打電話來了？

Chi: The bank!

季薇：銀行！

Paul: I knew they would. When's the interview?

保羅：我就知道他們會打電話來。什麼時候面試？

Chi: This coming Friday. I'm so **psyched**! What am I going to say? What are they going to ask? What should I wear?

季薇：這個禮拜五。我好興奮喔！我應該說什麼？他們會問我什麼問題？我要穿什麼樣的衣服？

Paul: First of all, regardless what kind of questions they may ask, keep your answers short, clear, and to the point. Listen, and let the interviewer talk. In other words ...

Chi: No **babbling**.

Paul: Exactly. A lot of people make the mistake of talking too much. It is easy to get off track when you are trying to fill a seemingly uncomfortable void of silence. Avoid doing this at all costs, otherwise the interviewer may think that you can't focus. If you become distracted, you will be rejected. Banking is filled with **minutia**. You must project direct and sincere honesty. They need to know that they can trust you.

Chi: Should we practice?

保羅：第一，不管他們會妳問什麼樣的問題，妳的回答都必須保持簡短、清晰並且說重點。聆聽，讓面試官有機會講話，也就是説...

季薇：不要廢話一堆。

保羅：沒錯。很多人犯了太多話的錯誤。當妳拼命地想避免令人不舒服的沈默時，妳就容易偏離主題；盡一切能力不要這麼做，否則面試官會認為妳無法集中注意力。如果妳在面試的時候分了心，人家就不會錄取妳。銀行這份職業裡充滿各種瑣碎的細節，妳必須表達出一種直接和出自真心的誠實感，他們想確定他們能夠信任妳。

季薇：我們是不是應該來練習？

01
Chapter

02
Chapter

03
Chapter

04
Chapter

05
Chapter

06
Chapter

Paul: Of course. Now, I'm the interviewer. Show me how you would approach me when I call your name.

保羅：當然。現在，假裝我是面試官，做給我看，當我叫妳名字的時候妳會怎麼做。

Chi: Hi, I'm Chi. Pleasure to meet you. (The two shake hands.)

季薇：嗨，我是季薇，很高興認識你。（兩人握手。）

Paul: Good. Remember to look at the interviewer. Be pleasant, confident and smile. 99% of the interviews start with the question: "Tell me about yourself." Think about what you're gonna say. Keep the story brief and relevant. Write it down and PRACTICE.

保羅：不錯。記得眼睛要看著面試官，展現妳愉悅、自信的一面並微笑。百分之九十九的面談過程第一個問題是：「請妳做個自我介紹。」想好妳接下來要說什麼，確定內容簡短而且跟新工作有關，寫下來，然後練習。

Chi: Got it.

季薇：知道了。

Paul: They will hit you hard with questions like: "Why do you want to work here?" "Why do you want to leave your current job?" "What do you not like about it?" "Have you had any disagreements with your boss?" "What did you do when this occurred?" and the **trickiest** one of all "What are your weak-

保羅：他們還會投下一些難題例如：「妳為什麼想來我們公司上班？」「為什麼妳不想繼續在妳現任的公司做事？」「妳不喜歡妳現在工作的哪些地方？」「妳跟妳的上司間發生過任何意見不合的情形嗎？」「當這種情況發生時，

nesses?" How do you answer those questions?

妳怎麼做？」而其中最狡猾的問題是：「妳的缺點是什麼？」妳怎麼回答這些問題？

Chi: I ... I think I would tell them that I am looking for career advancement. I enjoy my current job, however the room for growth is limited. AND, I like my boss. Mark and I have always managed to work **collaboratively** towards achieving the company's goals.

季薇：我…我想我會告訴他們我離職的原因是希望能在個人職業生涯上晉級。我喜歡我現在的工作，只是成長的空間有限。還有，我喜歡我的老闆，馬克跟我總是能齊心協力地工作，達到公司預定的目標。

Paul: Good. Remember, stay positive. Even when the question seems to have a negative **connotation**. Never ever say anything negative about a prior employer or staff member. Companies do not want to hire potential **naysayers** should the relationship end abruptly.

保羅：很好。記得，保持積極的態度。就算問題聽起來帶有負面的意味，也絕對不可以講以前老闆或公司員工的壞話。若是雇傭關係突然終止，公司不希望招到日後可能會反過頭來批評他們的人。

Chi: Got it. Remain positive and energetic. Turn every negative back into a positive.

季薇：知道了，保持積極和活力，把所有的負面轉成正面。

Paul: The force is strong with this one.

保羅：我感到這一個的原力很強大。

01 Chapter

02 Chapter

03 Chapter

04 Chapter

05 Chapter

06 Chapter

單字 Vocabulary

- **psyched** [saɪkt] **adj.** 興奮的、情緒高昂的
- **babble** [`bæbl] **v.** 喋喋不休地講、說廢話
- **minutia** [mə `njuʃə] **n.** 細節（常當作集合名詞使用）
- **tricky** [`trɪkɪ] **adj.** 狡猾的、帶有陷阱的（文中的 trickiest 為形容詞的最高級）
- **collaboratively** [kə `læbə ˌretɪvlɪ] **adj.** 合作地、共同協力地
- **connotation** [ˌkɑnə `teʃən] **n.** 含意、暗示
- **naysayer** [`neˌseə] **n.** 持負面或消極意見的人

片語 Phrases

<u>get off track</u> 偏離主題

好用句型 Useful Sentences

Pleasure to meet you. 很高興認識你。

你還可以這樣說

Pleasure.

Pleased to meet you.

Nice to meet you.

Honored to meet you.

例句

A: I've heard so many good things about you. It's a pleasure to finally meet you!

久仰大名，很高興終於有機會認識你。

B: The pleasure is all mine.

這是我的榮幸才對。

面試囉！

　　許多人對於參加面試感到恐懼，更不要說是用英文面談了！我在學習英語的過程裡，其中一項對我啟發最深遠的建議是來自親愛的保羅先生，他說：*"Think about what you want to say and how you want to say it before you speak. And then say the whole sentence!"*（在開口講話之前，先想好妳要說什麼，以及怎麼說。然後整句地說出來！）以前在臺灣我背過大量的單字及片語，但是到了美國跟別人講話時，從嘴巴出來的句子都破破碎碎的，因為我想要複製過去講國語的習慣：想什麼就說什麼。這種講話的方式，我發現，只適合用在跟家人朋友間的聊天上，在工作面試和其他的正式場合裡，尤其你又是使用非母語的英文說話，更需要先於腦中打好草稿，架構出文法正確的句子後，再清楚地開口講出來。

　　另一個對我學英文影響也很大的建議則是來自某位久居美國的網友，她說：記下一些常用的句子，背起來。我認為這項建議也適用於面試的情況（註）。你可以在網路上或書籍裡參考別人應對面試問題的答案，然後按照自己的實際情形加以修改，寫出符合自己語氣的一篇講稿，跟朋友互相練習。記住，即使是美國總統歐巴馬，在他上台演講前也是經過再三的反覆練習，才能創造出那副流暢自然、侃侃而談的模樣。

註：面試基本上是兩個人從陌生到認識的一段過程。常用的句子除了首次見面用的招呼語外（見本篇的好用句型），結束面試時所說的話，像是 "Thank you for the opportunity. When can I expect you decision?" 或 "I really enjoy the interview. How soon will I hear back from you?" 都是值得記起來的句子。

Preparing for Battle

1.3

對話 Dialogue

Paul: Your interview is tomorrow. Make sure you bring an extra copy of your resume.

保羅：妳明天面試，記得要多帶一份妳的履歷表。

Chi: Uh, about that.

季薇：呃，有關我的履歷表。

Paul: What's the matter?

保羅：怎麼了？

Chi: I was thinking maybe you should take a look at it before I print it out. I am not very confident about my resume.

季薇：我在想也許在列印出來之前，你應該先看一下。我對我的履歷表不是很有信心。

Paul: Show me.

保羅：給我看看。

(Chi locates the file and turns her computer screen towards Paul.)

（季薇找到檔案後，將她的電腦螢幕轉向保羅。）

Paul: What is THIS?

Chi: Well, I basically translated my Chinese version to English.

Paul: You're kidding me, right?

Chi: Is it that bad?

Paul: We're gonna need to do a major **overhaul** on this. You can't take this to your interview. First of all, you don't need to put your gender or date of birth on your resume ... Height, weight, and BLOOD TYPE? Are you going to a hospital or a bank?

Chi: It seems all right to me.

Paul: No! That information is personal, private, and irrelevant to the job you're applying for. Plus it's illegal to judge a potential candidate by these standards. Your resume should always start with the most important thing: your name

保羅：這是啥米？

季薇：嗯，我基本上把我的中文履歷表直接翻成英文。

保羅：妳是在開玩笑，對吧？

季薇：真的有那麼糟嗎？

保羅：看來我們要把妳這張履歷從頭到尾改過。妳不能把這份帶去面試。第一，妳不需要在妳的履歷上註明性別或生日…身高、體重和血型？妳是要去醫院還是銀行？

季薇：照我看來沒什麼問題啊。

保羅：不！那些是屬於妳隱私的個人資料，跟妳應徵的工作沒有關係。加上雇主若是按照這些標準來評判候選人是違法的。妳的履歷表應該從最重要的一項資料開始：妳的名字跟

and contact information. Put it on the top, centered or to the left depending on what format you prefer.

連絡方式。把這份資料放在表格的最上面，然後按照妳偏好的格式置中或靠左。

Chi: Okay.

季薇：好。

Paul: Second, list your education, **certifications**, past work experiences, and additional skill sets. Start with your most recent job and work your way backwards. Don't forget to list your duties in each position, such as accounting, **inventory** management, and employee training. Your cover letter should include a brief introduction and life goals.

保羅：第二，列出妳的學歷、資格證書、過去的工作經驗，以及其他的技能。從最近的工作開始寫，然後反推回去。別忘記要列出在每個職務上妳負責的事情，如會計、庫存管理與員工訓練。妳的求職信應該包括簡單的自我介紹和生涯目標。

Chi: **Aye**, Captain.

季薇：是，船長。

Paul: Be very specific and honest. Don't ever lie on a resume. If you know how to speak other languages or know how to use a kind of accounting software then say so. List anything you think might help you do your job better. Companies are looking for **well-round-**

保羅：每一項都要條列清楚，而且誠實填寫，絕對不要在履歷表上撒謊。如果妳會講其它的語言，或者知道如何使用某種會計軟體，就寫出來。列出任何妳認為對新工作有幫助的技能或經驗。公司企業希望找

ed, flexible, and adaptive employees eager to collaborate and serve. Once you're done, bring it back to me to review again before I **finalize** it.

的是全方位、彈性、適應力強，並表現出強烈合作與服務意願的員工。妳重寫好了以後，拿給我全部看過一遍，我覺得可以了妳再印出來。

01 Chapter
02 Chapter
03 Chapter
04 Chapter
05 Chapter
06 Chapter

單字 Vocabulary

- **overhaul** [ˌovɚˈhɔl] **n.** 大幅地修改、翻修
- **certification** [ˌsɝtəfɪˈkeʃən] **n.** 執照、資格證明書
- **inventory** [ˈɪnvənˌtorɪ] **n.** 庫存、存貨
- **aye** [aɪ] **adv.** 是、好、贊成
- **well-rounded** [ˈwɛl ˈraʊndɪd] **adj.** 全方位的、通才的
- **finalize** [ˈfaɪnḷˌaɪz] **v.** 作最後決定、全部完成

好用句型 Useful Sentences

You're kidding me, right? 你是在開玩笑，對吧？

你還可以這樣說

You're joking, right?
Are you serious?
You can't be serious.

例句

A: I have to pay five dollars to cash my check if I don't have an account here? You're kidding me, right?

如果我在這裡沒帳戶，兌現支票就得付五元？你在開玩笑，對吧？

B: Unfortunately I'm not, sir.

不幸地，我並不是在開玩笑，先生。

美式履歷表怎麼寫？

美式和中式履歷表間的不同之處有幾點：

一、美式履歷表不像中式履歷那樣畫表格。在不同的項目之間，例如工作經驗、學歷及特殊技能等，只要用空行或簡單的一條直線區分就行了；而在項目標題下的內容，一概以簡單的符號如圓點等標示起頭。

二、美式履歷表不放個人照片。此外，種族、膚色、性別、年齡（生日）、體重... 任何描述你的外表或族裔背景的項目都不需要寫進去。

三、美式履歷表不附「自傳」，取而代之的，是「求職信（*cover letter*）」。求職信的內容，應包括人事部主管的姓名（如果找不到那人的姓名，亦可用 *Dear Hiring Manager at* （公司名稱），盡量避免使用 *To Whom It May Concern* 這種概括化的稱謂）、向新公司求職的理由、自己的個性、工作態度、目標、或過去優異的業績表現等。求職信是你在跟面試官真正見到面之前，唯一可以用像人的語氣一而不是制式的表格或問答一來表達自己想法的機會，所以也是求職過程中非常重要的一環。

01
Chapter

02
Chapter

03
Chapter

04
Chapter

05
Chapter

06
Chapter

1.4 The Long Goodbye

對話 Dialogue

At Speedy Burger.

在快速堡。

Patricia: You wanna take a break?

派翠西亞：妳想休息一下嗎？

Chi: Sure.

季薇：好。

Patricia: And, um, could I ask you a question?

派翠西亞：還有，呃，我可以問妳一個問題嗎？

Chi: Okay. (The two walk to the back of the store.)

季薇：可以啊。（兩人走到店後方。）

Chi: What's up?

季薇：什麼事？

Patricia: Are you ... leaving?

派翠西亞：妳... 是不是要離職？

Chi: I just gave Mark my **two weeks'** **notice** yesterday. I'm going to work at a bank. Isn't it great?

季薇：我昨天才剛給了馬克我的辭職聲明。我接下來要去銀行工作，妳說這是不是很棒呀？

Patricia: (In a trembling voice) You're leaving? What am I going to do without you? (Tears **well** up.)

派翠西亞：（以顫抖的聲音說）妳要走了？沒有妳我要怎麼辦？（眼淚湧出來。）

Chi: Oh, Patty, don't cry.

季薇：噢，派蒂，別哭。

Patricia: I'm gonna miss you.

派翠西亞：我會想念妳的。

Chi: I'm going to miss you too. (The two hug.) I love working with you. Every time I see you, you're always happy and cheerful. You're strong and hardworking. You'll be fine.

季薇：我也會想念妳。（兩人互擁。）我喜歡跟妳一起工作。我不論何時看到妳，妳總是一副快樂又開心的模樣。妳很堅強，工作又努力，妳沒問題的。

Patricia: I suppose the pay is better. And they offer insurance and employee benefits?

派翠西亞：我想銀行工作的薪資比較好，他們也提供保險和員工福利，對嗎？

Chi: Mhm, they do.

季薇：嗯嗯，對。

01 Chapter

02 Chapter

03 Chapter

04 Chapter

05 Chapter

06 Chapter

Patricia: Plus, you won't have to work on Sundays anymore. Oh, those crazy hours! I'm so happy for you, Chi. You're going to do great. (Wipes her tears.)

派翠西亞：還有，妳再也不用在星期天上班了。噢，那些瘋狂的工作時數！我真為妳感到高興，季薇。妳一定會成功。（擦拭眼淚。）

Chi: (Smile.) I hope so.

季薇：（微笑。）希望如此。

Patricia: <u>Don't be a stranger</u>, okay? Come back and say hello every once in a while.

派翠西亞：要保持連絡，好嗎？偶爾回來跟大夥兒打招呼。

Chi: I will.

季薇：我會。

Patricia: We're gonna give you a **farewell party** on your last day. I'll make a cake.

派翠西亞：妳在這裡上班的最後一天裡，我們會幫妳舉行歡送會。我會烤個蛋糕。

Chi: Thank you Patty, I look forward to it. I guess I should go tell everyone else that I'm leaving.

季薇：謝謝妳派蒂，我很期待參加這個歡送會。我猜我應該開始通知其他人我要離職的消息了。

Patricia: It won't be a surprise, but it'll be big. I promise.

派翠西亞：它不會是個驚喜派對，但我保證，它一定會很盛大。

單字 Vocabulary

- **two weeks' notice** [ˋtu ˏwiks ˋnotɪs] **n.** 員工準備辭職時，在離開公司兩週前給雇主的通知
- **well** [wɛl] **v.**（常與up連用）湧出、流出
- **farewell party** [ˏfɛr ˋwɛl ˋpartɪ] **n.** 歡送會、惜別會

日常用語 Common Expressions

Don't be a stranger. 要保持連絡喔！

好用句型 Useful Sentences

Every once in a while. 每逢一段時間、偶爾

你還可以這樣說

Every now and then.

From time to time.

例句

A: These figures don't match! I can never seem to balance my checkbook.

這些數字對不起來！我似乎永遠都沒辦法保持一份正確的收支紀錄。

B: I suggest that you log on to your online bank account and check your balance every once in a while.

我建議你每逢一段時間就上網，登入你的銀行帳戶查看存款餘額。

幾種說再見的時刻

在美國，員工辭職一般都是在兩個禮拜前告知雇主，英文講 *to give someone my two weeks' notice* 或更簡單就講 *to give someone my two weeks'*（註）。這兩週的期間，一方面可以讓公司有緩衝的時間找尋代替的人員，準備離開的人可以完成工作的交接、訓練新人必要的技能等；另一方面，也可以讓離職的員工，特別是與客戶互動頻繁的銀行業務人員，有機會跟客人道別、並向他們介紹未來接手的同事。

情況反過來，若是公司要遣散（*lay off*）員工，則按照法律公司必須將他們尚未使用的病假時間，以及未休完的假期，換算成薪資付給員工。此外許多公司還會付給離職人員遣散費（*a severance check*），以幫助他們渡過找到下個新工作前的這一段時期。

最慘的離職方式是被炒魷魚（*being fired*）。被炒魷魚跟被遣散（*being laid off*）不同，銀行炒人魷魚的原因可能是員工業績不良，或發現操行出問題、有監守自盜的情形；銀行遣散人員則是由於公司縮編規模、裁減部門等情形。不管是這兩種哪一種，美國人一律稱非自願的離職情況為 *getting the pink slip*（原因是過去的離職證明文件有三部份，白色正本跟正本底下的黃色複本由公司留存，被解雇的員工則拿到第三張粉紅色的複本）。

註："To give two weeks' notice" 可分為兩種形式，一種是口頭聲明，另一種是書面通知。像文中的餐飲業，員工一般都是直接口頭告知老闆自己要離職的意願；白領階級的員工則多會正式遞辭職信。

01
Chapter

02
Chapter

03
Chapter

04
Chapter

05
Chapter

06
Chapter

Chapter 02

New Employee Orientation

新進人員訓練

2.1 Training Day

對話 Dialogue

Paul: How was training today?

保羅：今天的訓練課程上得如何？

Chi: It was fun! The instructor showed us different kinds of bills and who's picture is on them. Let me see if I can **recite** them without looking: Benjamin Franklin is on the hundred, Grant's on the fifty, Jackson's on the twenty, Hamilton's on the ten, Lincoln's on the five, and Washington's on the one.

季薇：非常有趣！今天講師跟我們展示幾種不同的紙鈔，以及鈔票上的肖像。讓我試試如果不看，我能不能把這些人物背出來：班傑明•富蘭克林在一百元上面、格蘭在五十元上、傑克遜在二十元上、漢彌爾頓在十元上、林肯在五元上，而華盛頓在一塊錢上。

Paul: Very good. Now can you tell me, who among them was never president of the United States?

保羅：非常好。現在，妳能不能告訴我，在這些人之中誰沒做過美國總統？

Chi: I know, I know! Hamilton and Franklin.

季薇：我知道，我知道！漢彌爾頓和富蘭克林。

Paul: Do you know why?

保羅：妳知道為什麼嗎？

Chi: Um, Lauren told us Hamilton was the first Secretary of **the Treasury**. So he's very important with regard to US currency. I am not sure about Franklin.

季薇：呃，蘿倫告訴我們漢彌爾頓是首任的財政部長，所以對於美國的貨幣而言他具有很重要的地位。關於富蘭克林我不是很確定。

Paul: Franklin was one of the Founding Fathers. He helped draft the Declaration of Independence and he convinced France to fund the American Revolution. If not for him, we wouldn't have "the dollar" to fight the war for independence.

保羅：富蘭克林是美國的開國元勳之一。他曾協助起草獨立宣言，並說服法國投資美國的獨立戰爭。如果沒有他，我們就不會有「錢」來打那場為獨立而戰的仗。

Chi: Now I feel much closer to Uncle Ben. He's not just a face on the largest bill in circulation. He's a man with a fascinating life story.

季薇：我現在對班叔叔感覺距離拉近了許多。他不再只是目前流通的最大面值紙幣上面的一張臉孔而已，他這個人其實有著一段令人讚嘆的人生故事。

01 Chapter

02 Chapter

03 Chapter

04 Chapter

05 Chapter

06 Chapter

Paul: Good, but do you know why Andrew Jackson is on the twenty dollar bill, other than the reason that he is a popular former president?

保羅：很好。另外，妳知不知道為什麼安德魯・傑克遜，除了由於他是一位相當受歡迎的前任總統外，會被印在二十元的鈔票上面呢？

Chi: I don't know.

季薇：我不知道。

Paul: When he was in office, Jackson managed to shut down the central bank and pay off all U.S. debt. He didn't like the idea of having a national bank. And his **opposition** to paper money may have been the exact reason why he is on our currency. On his death bed, he said killing the bank was his greatest accomplishment.

保羅：當他擔任總統時，傑克遜曾關閉過中央銀行，並還清了美國所有的債務，他不喜歡美國有國家銀行的這個想法。而他反對使用紙幣的立場，可能正是他會出現在我們貨幣上的原因。在他臨終時，他說殺死中央銀行是他畢生最大的成就。

Chi: Is that ironic then that he is now on currency?

季薇：那他現在在鈔票上面會不會有些諷刺啊？

Paul: A little bit. Aside from that, money is always changing. New inks, colors, and security features. It'll be interesting to see if any other figures from American history will ever <u>make the cut.</u>

保羅：有一點。此外，錢幣不斷地在改變外貌，新的墨水、顏色，以及防偽設計，我滿好奇會不會還有其他美國歷史上的名人被選中。沒理由我們不

There is no reason why we shouldn't try some new faces.

能試一下其他新面孔。

Chi: People like their traditions.

季薇：人們喜歡傳統的事物。

Paul: True, but gradual changes can ease that transition. With a enough time and promotion, you can actually get people excited about the new designs. As much as we love our traditions, we also love "new" things.

保羅：沒錯，但是逐漸的改變可以幫助減輕轉換過程中的不適。只要配合足夠的時間及宣傳活動，你其實能讓人們對新的設計感到興奮。我們不但喜歡傳統的事物，我們也喜歡新鮮的玩意兒。

單字 Vocabulary

- **recite** [rɪ `saɪt] **v.** 背誦
- **the Treasury** [ðə `trɛʒərɪ] **n.** 財政部。文中the Secretary of the Treasury 即為財政部長。
- **opposition** [ˌɑpə `zɪʃən] **n.** 反對、抵抗

片語 Phrases

make the cut 因表現優異或得到足夠的分數而被選中

01 Chapter

02 Chapter

03 Chapter

04 Chapter

05 Chapter

06 Chapter

好 用句型 Useful Sentences

with regard to 關於

你還可以這樣說

regarding

with respect to

in regard to

例句

A: I am calling with regard to a recent transaction on my credit card. Who should I talk to?

我打來是想知道有關於我信用卡上最近一筆交易的細節。我應該跟哪位談？

B: I'll be happy to assist you with that. This is Cindy. How may I help you?

我很樂意幫您。我叫辛蒂，能為您服務嗎？

01
Chapter

02
Chapter

03
Chapter

04
Chapter

05
Chapter

06
Chapter

真鈔？假鈔？

　　知道哪位歷史名人的肖像在什麼面值的鈔票上，是幫助你辨識真或偽鈔的第一步。不法份子製作偽鈔的方式有的極為高明，也有些相當粗劣，其中一種粗糙的假鈔，是將面值低的紙鈔四角上的數字剪下來，接貼上高的數字，譬如說把一元美金的鈔票改成二十元，這種偽鈔我們稱作 *"raised notes"* 或 *"raised bills"*。很多人在算錢的時候，尤其是一疊一疊地算時，只看角落上的數字，所以如果有這種偽鈔混雜在其中，很容易就被忽略了。但是你若將整張鈔票拿出來看，你會發現中間的人像錯了。

　　另一項防偽設計是浮水印（*watermarks*），美鈔正面印著什麼人的肖像，右方的空白處裡就是那個人像的浮水印。所以你要是拿張紙幣對著燈光看，如果中間的人像是富蘭克林，但浮水印顯示林肯的臉，你肯定是拿到了一張偽鈔。

　　銀行裡會提供許多工具以便出納人員分辨假鈔，譬如驗鈔筆、紫外線照明器、電子點鈔機… 等；如果你沒有這些設備的話，還是有些基本的方法能讓你看出真假，第一是顏色。許多偽鈔是使用複印機翻印出來的，其顏色跟真鈔有程度上的分別，有些使用劣質的墨水，一碰水還會渲染開來；第二是紙張的材質、觸感和大小。真鈔所使用的紙較偽鈔來得光滑，而且如果你仔細看，在這種特殊的紙張裡，參雜了一絲一絲紅色與藍色的纖維；偽鈔的尺寸也經常比真鈔要來得小一些；最後第三點是刻印的技術。美鈔採用了所謂 *"raised printing"* 的方式，因此如果你用指甲在人像中的衣服上刮一刮，會感覺到細緻的條列狀突起。

　　要是銀行在收取現金時發現了偽鈔，他們必須依法沒收（也就是說他們不會把偽鈔退還給客戶！），行員必須紀錄下客戶的姓名和連絡方式，填表並將假鈔送到當地的特勤局（*secret service*）去進行進一步的辨識與建立檔案。

Attention to Details

 對話 Dialogue

At the training center.

在訓練中心。

Lauren: So yesterday we practiced using several different kinds of US currency. Today we are going to look at another instrument people use to **render** payments: checks.

蘿倫：昨天我們用了幾種不同的美國錢幣來練習，今天我們要來看看另外一種人們用來付款的工具：支票。

(The instructor signals one of the trainees to dim the lights. She turns on the projector and an oversized image of a check pops up on the screen.)

（講師指示其中一位受訓的員工把燈光調暗。她將投影機打開，一張放大的支票影像躍於螢幕上。）

Lauren: As a teller, you're going to see a lot of checks every day. When you take a check from a customer, there are five things you need to look for in or-

蘿倫：作為一名出納，你每天都將會看到許多支票。在你從客人手中取得一張支票之後，你必須根據五樣東西，來判斷

der to determine if it is **negotiable**: the date, the **payee**, the written amount, the numerical amount and the signature. Your **focal point** will follow a **zigzag** line like this. (Indicating with a laser pointer, a red dot moves from the upper right hand corner across the middle and back to the lower right.) If any of the five items are missing, you have to return the check to the customer, and the customer then would have to go back to the check issuer and either get a new check or have the error corrected. Any questions so far?

Trainee#1: What if the written amount is different from the numbered amount?

Lauren: In general we would go by the written amount. But if the customer who received the check doesn't agree, or the **discrepancy** is sufficiently large, then we wouldn't accept the check and the customer would have to take it up

這張支票能不能兌現:日期、受款人、以文字表示的金額、以數字表示的金額,以及發票人的簽名。你的目光焦點會按這樣子的鋸齒狀路線來走。(以雷射筆在支票的影像上指示,一個小紅點從右上角,跨過中間,再回到右下角。)如果這五樣東西中任何一樣有遺漏,你就必須把支票還給客人,而那位客人必須回過頭去與發票人連絡,或取得一張新的支票,或將支票上的錯誤改正。到目前為止有任何問題嗎?

受訓員工一:要是用文字表示的金額跟數字表示的金額不一樣怎麼辦?

蘿倫:大體說來,我們會按照以文字表示的金額來付款。但是如果取得這張支票的客人不同意,或者兩者間的差異太大,則我們不會接受這張支票,而這位客戶必須向原來寫

with the person who wrote the check. Next question.

支票的人諮詢。下一個問題。

Trainee#2: Can you tell us more about the payee line on a check?

受訓員工二：妳可不可以跟我們多講一點有關支票上受款人欄位的部份？

Lauren: Absolutely! A check may be made payable to either a business or a person. When the payee is a business, then the check must be deposited into the account with the same business title. When the payee is an individual, that person can either choose to cash the check or deposit it into his or her account. Which, brings us to the next subject: **Endorsement**. If a check is made payable to John Smith and Mary Smith, whose signature should be on the back of the check?

蘿倫：當然可以！支票的受款人可能是一間公司，也可能是個人。當受款人是公司時，這張支票必須存入與公司名稱相符的帳戶內。當受款人是個人時，那人可以選擇兌現這張支票，或者存入他或她的帳戶裡。這一點，正好帶出我們接下來的主題：背書。如果一張支票是寫給約翰‧史密斯和瑪麗‧史密斯，支票的背面應該有誰的簽名？

Trainee#3: The check should have both John Smith's and Mary Smith's signatures.

受訓員工三： 這張支票應該要有約翰‧史密斯和瑪麗‧史密斯兩個人的簽名。

Lauren: Correct. Or, if John Smith and Mary Smith have a joint account at the bank, the check can be stamped—with neither signature—and be deposited as a whole into the said account. On the other hand, if the check is made out to John Smith "or" Mary Smith, then either one of them can endorse the check.

Trainee#4: Can a business owner sign a check that's made out to his business?

Lauren: Only when the title of the business says DBA: Doing Business As. This title is structured as a **sole proprietor** which is common among small business owners. A business title like John Smith DBA Happy Bakery, can be endorsed either by the owner's name or the businesses name. All right, let's move on to operating systems.

蘿倫：正確。或者，如果約翰‧史密斯和瑪麗‧史密斯在銀行有共同帳戶的話，這張支票背後可以蓋章—不需要任何一人的簽名—然後整張存到那個帳戶裡。另一方面，如果這張支票的受款人寫的是約翰‧史密斯「或」瑪麗‧史密斯，那麼兩人中不論那一人都可以在這張支票上背書。

受訓員工四：如果支票的受款人寫的是某家公司，公司的所有人可以在支票背面簽他的名嗎？

蘿倫：只有當公司名稱註明「商號為」的時候。這種公司名稱是屬獨資企業的結構，常見於小型企業的所有人。公司名稱像是約翰‧史密斯商號為快樂麵包店，支票上的背書可以是公司持有人的簽名，或是公司的名稱。好了，我們接下來要談操作系統。

單字 Vocabulary

- **render** [`rɛndə] **v.** 使... 發生、提供
- **negotiable** [nɪ `goʃɪəbl̩] **adj.** （支票等）可兌現的
- **payee** [pe `i] **n.** 受款人
- **focal point** [`fokl̩ `pɔɪnt] **n.** （目光、鏡頭等的）焦點
- **zigzag** [`zɪgzæg] **adj.** 鋸齒狀的
- **discrepancy** [dɪ `skrɛpənsɪ] **n.** 不一致、差異
- **endorsement** [ɪn `dɔrsmənt] **n.** 背書、（在支票背面）簽署
- **sole proprietor** [`sol ˌprə `praɪətə] **n.** 獨資企業主、一人老闆的公司

片語 Phrases

take something up with someone 與某人就某事提出討論

好用句型 Useful Sentences

(The check) is made out to (name of person / company)
（這張支票上）寫的受款人是（某人／公司的名字）

你還可以這樣說

(The check) is payable to (name of person / company)
(The check) is made payable to (name of person/ company)

例句

A: If I want to cash my own check, who do I make the check out to?

如果我想兌現自己的支票，受款人應該寫誰？

B: You can either make it out to yourself or "cash."

你可以寫給你自己或寫「現金」。

支票怎麼寫？

　　臺灣人在付款時，一般不是使用現金，就是使用信用卡；相較之下，美國人付款的方式花樣就多了些，其中一種就是開立支票。支票的用途相當廣泛，舉凡發工資、付房租、繳水電費、購物（大至買車小到買牛奶）、小孩子打破鄰居窗戶的賠償費用、甚至從自己的銀行帳戶裡領錢出來，都可以用一張支票來搞定。今天讓我來教你怎麼寫支票：

　　假設你現在拿出一張空白支票，第一步是寫日期。大致説來，這個日期是你希望付給受款人這筆錢的日期，譬如說今天是西元 2014 年 1 月 1 日，如果你想在十天後付款，就寫 1 / 11 / 2014（註一）。特別要説明一下的是，這個日期通常只是給發票人自己當參考用，如果拿到這張支票的人在 1 月 10 日去銀行兌現，按照目前的趨勢，許多銀行也都會接受，所以一般人多用開票當天的日期，若你想在1月11日才付款，就11日當天再將支票交給受款人。

　　第二步，在字樣*"Pay to the order of"*（註二）後面，也就是受款人的欄位裡，寫下受款人的名字。寫之前要先跟對方確認姓名的拼寫方式，不要寫人家的綽號；如果受款人是公司行號，要確定公司名稱後接的是 *LLC* 還是 *Ltd*（這是兩種不同企業形態的有限公司）。如果受款人的名字寫得有一點不對，就有可能會造成對方在銀行無法兌現的困擾。

　　第三，以阿拉伯數字在支票右上方，標有$符號的空格中寫金額。美金裡有角有分，例如二十元整寫作 20.00，二十元八角三分就寫 20.83。

　　第四，以英文將金額寫在受款人欄下方的那條長長的空白處。絕大多數的支票在這個欄位的尾端都已預先印有 *DOLLAR*（美元）的字樣，所以你不用在金額裡再寫一次 *DOLLAR*。如果金額為一百五十元整，即寫：

One Hundred and Fifty 或 *One Hundred Fifty and 0/00*；如果是一百五十元又六分，就寫：*One Hundred Fifty and 06/00*。寫完後在金額的尾巴畫條線，一直拉到DOLLAR這個字的前緣，這樣別人才不能擅自加金額進去。

最後，一定要記得在支票的右下角簽名。支票上要是缺少了發票人的簽名，絕對會被視為無效而被銀行退回，搞不好還可能造成罰款的情況！另外，如果在支票上有任何塗寫或修改，要在修改的地方旁邊寫上自己名字的縮寫（目的跟臺灣人蓋印章確認文件上修改處一樣），這樣才完成了開票的程序。

註一：這種填寫了較實際為晚的日期的支票，我們稱之為 postdated check。注意美國人寫日期的順序為月→日→年，除了文章中以斜線分隔月日年的寫法外，你也可以用短橫線分隔，像這樣：1-11-14。另外很多人習慣將月份以英文清楚地寫出來，如 January 11th, 2014 或簡略的 Jan. 11, 2014 皆可。

註二："Order"這個字有「指示」、「命令」的意思。在支票上的這句"pay to the order of（payee）"即是帳戶持有人，也就是發票人，「要求銀行機構按照其『指示』支付某筆特定的金額給（受款人）」。中文可翻做「憑票支付」。

01
Chapter

02
Chapter

03
Chapter

04
Chapter

05
Chapter

06
Chapter

2.3 Operating System: Chi 2.0

對話 Dialogue

Lauren: You are going to love our new processing system! Tellers used to type in account numbers, check numbers, amounts and sometimes internal ticket numbers. It was a **tedious**, time-consuming and error-**prone** process. Now the machine reads all the numbers for you. Once you've verified the information on your computer's screen, simply click on the "next" button. It's both user-friendly and paperless. With that being said, let's take another look at our check.

(The image of the oversized check reappears on the screen.)

蘿倫：你們一定會愛上我們新的操作系統！以前出納人員必須鍵入帳號、支票號碼、金額，有時還加上內部作業用的票據號碼，這種程序不但冗長、費時，而且容易出錯。現在機器會幫你讀取所有的號碼。一旦你確認電腦螢幕上的資訊無誤後，你所需作的只是用滑鼠點「下一步」，兼具容易使用和無紙化的優點。承接以上所言，讓我們再看一次先前的那張支票。

（加大版的支票影像再次顯示在螢幕上。）

Lauren: Notice on the bottom that there's a line of numbers. This is called the MICR line. **MICR** stands for Magnetic Ink Character Recognition. MICR technology uses a specific font and magnetic ink to aid our machines in reading these numbers. On a typical check there are normally three sets of numbers: the **routing** number, the account number and the check number. Routing numbers have a nine-digit code and it tells us which bank the check was drawn from. Lengths of account and check numbers may vary. The other two numbers indicate whose account the funds will be withdrawn from and what check number the account owner is using.

Lauren: Every transaction consists of two parts: a **credit** and a **debit**. Deposit tickets, credit card payment coupons, and cash out tickets are classified as credits. While checks, withdrawal tickets, and cash in tickets are your debits. Now, everyone please take out of your

蘿倫：注意底下有一行數字。這排數字叫做**MICR**行，**MICR** 代表的是磁性油墨字元辨識 。磁性油墨字元辨識技術使用了一種特殊的字型與帶有磁性的油墨來協助機器解讀這些數字。一張典型的支票上通常會有三組數字：銀行代碼、帳號跟支票號碼。 銀行代碼由九個數字組成，它告訴我們這張支票是由哪家銀行開出來。帳號和支票號碼的長度則不一定，這兩組號碼表示這筆金額將從誰的帳戶裡扣款，以及帳戶持有人所使用的支票號碼。

蘿倫：每一筆交易都包含了兩個部份：一是金額上的增加，一是金額上的減少。存款單、信用卡付款單和出款傳單被分列為金額上的增加，而支票、領款單和入款傳單則視為金額上的減少。現在，請所有人從

01 Chapter
02 Chapter
03 Chapter
04 Chapter
05 Chapter
06 Chapter

practice kit the first deposit ticket, along with the check after it.

你的學習套裝裡拿出第一張存款單，以及附在它後面的支票。

(Trainees begin to open the envelopes at their desks and take out sample tickets.)

（受訓員工一一打開在他們桌上的信封並取出樣本單據。）

Lauren: Facing the right, place them into the scanner, together.

蘿倫：正面朝右，把它們一起放在掃描器裡。

(Students comply. Machines run.)

（學生們依照指令作。機器運作。）

Lauren: Notice the scanner automatically read the MICR lines on both the deposit ticket and the check. Now, on your computer screen, you should see that you have a credit and a debit. Let's look at the check's debit first. Is all the information, including routing number, account number, check number and the amount correct?

蘿倫：有沒有注意到掃描器自動地讀取存款單和支票上的 MICR 行。現在，在你的電腦螢幕上，你應該會看到你有一個金額上的增加，跟一個金額上的減少。我們先來看金額減少的部份，也就是支票，請問所有的項目，包括銀行代碼、帳號、支票號碼和金額都正確嗎？

Trainee#1: The routing number is missing a digit.

受訓員工一：銀行代碼少了一位數字。

Lauren: <u>Good catch!</u> Move your mouse over to the routing number, enable it, and make the necessary correction. Now look at the green box on the bottom of your screen. Does it say that your credit and debit are balanced?

蘿倫： 好眼力！把你的滑鼠移到銀行代碼上，將它反白，並做必要的修改。現在看到螢幕底下的綠色格子，請問它顯示你金額上增加的部份跟金額上減少的部份一致了嗎？

Trainee#2: No. The machine read the deposit amount wrong. The six should be an eight.

受訓員工二：沒有。機器把存款金額讀錯了，六應該是八才對。

Lauren: Click on it and change the number. (Pauses.) OK, it's almost ten o'clock. Let's take a break and afterwards we'll do some independent practice!

蘿倫：在金額上按一下，把數額改過來。（停頓。）好了，現在差不多快十點了，我們休息一下，之後我們會作一些獨立的練習！

單字 Vocabulary

- **tedious** [ˋtidɪəs] **adj.** 冗長乏味的
- **prone** [pron] **adj.** 有... 傾向的
- **MICR** [ˋmɪkɚ] **n.** 磁性油墨字元辨識
- **routing** [ˋrautɪŋ] **adj.** 指定走... 路線的、經... 路線的
- **credit** [ˋkrɛdɪt] **n.** 帳戶金額上的增加
- **debit** [ˋdɛbɪt] **n.** 帳戶金額上的減少

01 Chapter
02 Chapter
03 Chapter
04 Chapter
05 Chapter
06 Chapter

日常用語 Common Expressions

<u>Good catch!</u> 好眼力！（讚賞或感謝對方指出錯誤的用語）

好用句型 Useful Sentences

With that being said 承接我剛才說的

你還可以這樣說

That said

That being said

Having said that

例句

A: Studies show people who have their payroll set up as direct deposit tend to stay with their bank longer than those that don't. With that being said, whenever you see a customer come in to cash his paycheck, you should always encourage him to set up a direct deposit.

研究顯示，將薪資直接轉帳存入帳戶的客戶，比那些不使用這種功能的客戶待在同一家銀行的時間要久。承上所言，每當你見到有客人到銀行來兌現薪資支票，你都應該鼓勵他設立薪資自動轉帳。

B: We should print out some blank forms to keep at our desk in case customers need it.

我們應該印一些空白的表格出來放在手邊，客戶要是需要的話就可以拿來用。

A: Good idea. Let's do that!

好辦法。就這麼辦！

什麼是credit和debit？

在英文的對話中，蘿倫提到銀行內的每一筆交易都包含了兩個部份：金額上的增加（*credit*）和金額上的減少（*debit*），以及這兩部份應該相等。這是銀行流程中非常重要的一個概念，要了解它實際上如何運作也不難，就讓我舉個簡單的例子說明：

假設史密斯先生開了一張美金五十元的個人支票，他把這張支票交給王先生。王先生隨後把支票存到自己的帳戶裡。這時，以下這兩件事情會發生：

史密斯先生的帳戶金額會減少五十元。

（*Mr. Smith's account will be debited by fifty dollars.*）

王先生的帳戶金額會增加五十元。

（*Mr. Wong's account will be credited with fifty dollars.*）

在銀行的世界中，如果有一個地方產生了某個數額的*debit*，則必然在另一處會出現相同數額的*credit*，兩者互相抵消，也就形成了我們說的平衡（*balanced*）的狀態。要注意的是銀行界對*debit*跟*credit*這兩個名詞的定義跟會計學中的定義稍有出入，從銀行的觀點來看，debit 和 credit指的是帳戶金額上的減少和增加，與會計的借方及貸方不太一樣。

最後再提一點，*debit* 和 *credit* 的另外一組定義，是兩種相對的銀行單據：任何代表金錢、或者可以拿到銀行換取金錢的憑據，我們都叫做*debit*；而任何能夠告訴你如何處置 *debit* 的單據，我們就稱之為 *credit*。

現在假設王先生來到你的窗口存款，他拿給你那張五十元的支票與一張寫著存入五十元的存款單。記得，我們剛說過，任何代表金錢或者可以拿到銀行換取金錢的憑據，就叫做 *debit*，因此這張五十元的支票即為

debit；而任何能夠告訴你如何處置 *debit* 的單據我們叫做*credit*，所以五十元的存款單就是你的 *credit*。

　　好，讓我們再練習一次，這次把五十元的支票換成五十元現金：王先生拿給你五十元現金與一張寫著存入五十元的存款單，按照同樣的道理，任何代表金錢或者可以拿到銀行換取金錢的憑據叫做 *debit*，所以五十元的現金就是這筆交易中的*debit*，但是銀行出納員不能直接把現金送到交易處理中心去作處理，所以現金留在分行，出納把現金換成一種內部作業用，稱為入款傳單（*cash in ticket*）的單據，於是，入款傳單就是這裡的 *debit*，而五十元的存款單就是跟它相對的 *credit*。

2.4 How May I Help You?

對話 Dialogue

Lauren: Welcome to the last day of training! Today's topic is customer service, and I'm gonna kick off the day by showing you a short film. (Puts a DVD into the machine and switches off the lights.)

蘿倫：歡迎進入員工訓練的最後一天！今天的主題是客戶服務，我要用一段短片開始這天的課程。（把DVD放入機器內並關燈。）

On the screen, a teller is staring at his cell phone, thumbs moving.

螢幕上，一位出納員正瞪著他的手機，移動著大拇指。

Customer: Excuse me, are you open?

客人：不好意思，你的窗口開放營業嗎？

Brian: (Puts his phone aside.) Uh, yes. How may I help you? (**Tucks** in his shirt.)

布萊恩：（將電話放在一旁。）嗯，是的。我可以為妳服務嗎？（把襯衫塞進褲子裡。）

Customer: I would like to make a deposit, please.

客人：我想存款，麻煩你。

Brian: Uh-huh. Do you have a **slip** filled out?

布萊恩：嗯哼。妳單子填了嗎？

Customer: No, I didn't find any slips at the counter. I think you guys need to refill those tickets.

客人：沒有，我在櫃台那邊找不到任何單子。我想你們需要添加那些單據。

Brian: You can use this one. (Takes out a form.)

布萊恩：妳可以用這張。（拿出一張表格。）

Customer: (Starts writing. When she turns the slip over, she pauses briefly and returns it back to Brain.) Can I have another one? This ticket has someone else's writing on it.

客人：（開始填寫。當她將單子翻過去時，她暫停了一下，把它退回給布萊恩。）我能用另外一張嗎？這張單據上有其他人寫過。

Brian: Oh, <u>my bad</u>. That's from the last customer. (Pulls out a new slip.)

布萊恩：噢，我的錯。那是上一位客人的。（取出一張新的單子。）

Customer: Thank you. (Finishes writing. Hands Brian her ticket and a couple of checks.) Just a **straight** deposit, please.

客人：謝謝。（寫完後將她的單據和兩張支票遞給布萊恩。）請你幫我全部存到帳戶裡。

01 Chapter

02 Chapter

03 Chapter

04 Chapter

05 Chapter

06 Chapter

Brian: Sure. (Processes the transaction.) Was that everything for you today, Ma'am?

布萊恩：當然。（進行作業手續。）今天還需要辦其它事嗎，太太？

Customer: Yes, that's all for today.

客人：沒有其他的事了。

Brian: Here's your **receipt**, Ma'am. Have a good day.

布萊恩：這是您的收據，太太。祝您有個美好的一天。

（作者按：目前美國絕大多數的銀行皆已停止發行存摺本，因此顧客在進行存款時，不再以傳統的方式登摺，取而代之的是向出納員領取印有交易日期與金額的收據。）

Customer: You, too.

客人：你也一樣。

(Lauren stops the video. Light fills the room.)

（蘿倫停止影片。燈光充滿室內。）

Lauren: Can anyone tell me what Brain did in the movie was inappropriate?

蘿倫：有人能告訴我電影中布萊恩做的哪些事情是不恰當的嗎？

Trainee#1: He was **texting** on his phone at work!

受訓員工一：他在上班的時候傳簡訊！

Trainee#2: I noticed that he was untidy and unprepared.

受訓員工二：我注意到他儀容不整，而且沒有準備好接待客戶。

Trainee#3: He didn't clear his work space before helping the next customer.

受訓員工三：在協助下一位客人之前，他沒有清理他的工作空間。

Lauren: Yes. All of your answers are correct. As you've all noticed, Brian demonstrated a series of behaviors what a teller should NOT do. I want to add a few things that Brian could have done to better help the customer: One, he could have offered to fill out the deposit slip for her; two, he could have repeated or summarized the transaction to ensure that's what the customer wanted; three, he should have asked the customer if she needed her account balance printed on the receipt; and last but not least, when it's not busy, he could have walked around the branch in order to make sure that all of the forms were well-stocked in the lobby.

蘿倫：對，你們這些答案全都正確。如同你們注意到的，布萊恩做出一連串出納員不該做的行為。我還想加上幾件布萊恩其實可以做的事，以提供客戶更佳的服務：一、他可以幫客人填寫存款單；二、他應該要重述或總結交易的內容，以確認客人的需求；三、他應該詢問客人是否需要將她的帳戶餘額印在收據上；最後一點是，在不忙的時候他應該在分行裡四處走動，確定大廳中所有的表格都裝滿。

01 Chapter

02 Chapter

03 Chapter

04 Chapter

05 Chapter

06 Chapter

單字 Vocabulary

- **tuck** [tʌk] **v.** 把…塞進、把…的末端折進
- **slip** [slɪp] **n.** 一小張的紙片，常見於小型的表格，如存款單、收據等
- **straight** [stret] **adj.** 純粹的、不攙雜的
- **receipt** [rɪ`sit] **n.**（注意 p 不發音）收據
- **text** [tɛkst] **v.** 發傳簡訊

片語 Phrases

kick off 開始

日常用語 Common Expressions

My bad. 我的錯、我的不是。
Have a good day. 祝你有個美好的一天。

好用句型 Useful Sentences

How may I help you? 請問我能為您服務嗎？

你還可以這樣說
May I help you?
How may I be of service?

例句

A: Welcome to Best Bank. How may I help you, sir?
歡迎光臨倍斯特銀行。請問我能為您服務嗎，先生？

B: I would like speak to someone about opening an account.
我想與貴行人員談開立帳戶的事宜。

A: I can definitely help you with that. Please have a seat.
我絕對能幫您這件事。請坐。

客戶服務的重要性

　　有一句商業界中頗為流行的話是這麼講的：*"It costs 5 times more to acquire a new customer than to retain an existing customer."*（開發一個新客戶的成本是維繫一個舊客戶的五倍。）尤其是現在金融機構百家爭鳴的時代，大部份銀行提供的商品都類似，當客戶走進你的大門，他/她能不能感受到與眾不同的服務品質，就成了公司是否能繼續於這個競爭激烈的環境中生存的關鍵。

　　另一項被商管人士視為金科玉律的理論則說：*"80% of your company's revenue comes from 20% of your existing customers."*（你公司百分之八十的收入來自你百分之二十的顧客。）這些百分之二十的客戶，通常都是安安靜靜地購買、使用你的產品，這些人極少發出不滿的聲音，因此維繫這群顧客的成本費用相當低。但是一旦他們發覺自己受到了不良的對待，申訴問題後仍然沒有獲得應得的補償，他們則會選擇安安靜靜地離開，等到你發現進帳少了那一部份的時候，通常時機已晚。

　　對於一名出納人員來說，把焦點專注在眼前的客人，以及目前正在處理的工作上，是提供優質客戶服務的第一步。即使因為是新手的關係而出了錯，也不要驚慌失措，弄得心情大壞，而造成所謂的骨牌效應（*domino effect*）連後面其他客戶的交易也搞錯，那就不好了。遇到做錯事的情況時，我的建議是一次專注在一件事上（*focus on one thing at a time*），就算沒辦法立刻把錯誤更正，也不要讓它干擾到你手邊正在做的事，把那件需要修改的交易用筆寫下來，或利用任何能幫助你記憶的物品如在單據邊緣插上顏色鮮艷的便利貼或迴紋針等，到有時間的時候再去處理。

01 Chapter

02 Chapter

03 Chapter

04 Chapter

05 Chapter

06 Chapter

Chapter 03

First Week

上班第一週

3.1 Greetings and Salutations

 對話 Dialogue

At the bank.

在銀行裡。

Robert: Welcome Chi, we're all so excited to have you here. This is Michelle, she's our **head teller**.

勞勃：歡迎，季薇，我們大家都好興奮妳能來這裡上班。這是蜜雪兒，她是我們的出納主任。

Michelle: (Smile.) Hi.

蜜雪兒：（微笑。）嗨。

Chi: Michelle.

季薇：蜜雪兒。

Robert: In the next few days you're going to observe Michelle. I have been working with Michelle for over ten years and she is a **seasoned** professional. She will show you how to use the system and operate a cash drawer.

勞勃：接下來幾天妳將從旁觀察蜜雪兒。我與蜜雪兒共事已超過十年，她是一位經驗充足的專業人士。她會教妳如何使用作業系統以及操作現金櫃的方法。

Michelle: This is my station. I'm teller number one. Once you have your own drawer, you will become teller number three. Until then we'll do everything together. When I take my breaks and lunches, you will do the same. If you have any questions just ask. Ah, there is Mr. Donegan!

蜜雪兒：這是我的櫃台，我是出納員一號。等妳有自己的現金櫃以後，妳的出納員號碼就是三號。在那之前我們不論作什麼事都要在一起，我去吃午飯跟休息的時候，妳也一樣去吃飯跟休息。如果有什麼問題儘管問。啊，唐尼根先生來了！

Michelle: Hi, Mr. Donegan. I'd be happy to help you here.

蜜雪兒：嗨，唐尼根先生。我有幸能為您服務，請您過來我的櫃台。

Mr. Donegan: How are you today Michelle?

唐尼根先生：妳今天好嗎，蜜雪兒？

Michelle: I'm good! Let me introduce you to Chi. She is going to be our new teller. Chi, this is Mr. Donegan, he is our favorite customer, he comes in here all the time.

蜜雪兒：我很好！我要為您介紹季薇，她是我們新來的出納。季薇，這是唐尼根先生，他是我們最喜歡的客人了，他常來這裡辦事。

Mr. Donegan: Hahaha ... Only when I behave myself. How are you, Chi?

唐尼根先生：哈哈哈…只有當我乖乖守規矩的時候。妳好嗎，季薇？

01 Chapter

02 Chapter

03 Chapter

04 Chapter

05 Chapter

06 Chapter

Chi: I'm well, Mr. Donegan, pleasure to meet you.

季薇：我很好，唐尼根先生，很榮幸認識您。

Mr. Donegan: **Likewise.** You're gonna do well here. Michelle is the best.

唐尼根先生：也是我的榮幸。妳在這裡會一定做得很好，蜜雪兒是最頂尖的。

Michelle: Mr. Donegan, how may I help you today?

蜜雪兒：唐尼根先生，您今天想辦什麼事？

Mr. Donegan: I'd like to cash a check please.

唐尼根先生：我想要請妳幫我兌現一張支票。

Michelle: Sure. How would you like it?

蜜雪兒：當然好。您想要什麼面額？

Mr. Donegan: Twenties would be fine, thank you.

唐尼根先生：二十元的就好，謝謝。

(Michelle processes the transaction and counts out the money.)

（蜜雪兒處理這筆交易並算錢給客戶。）

Michelle: Is there anything else I can help you with, Mr. Donegan?

蜜雪兒：還有其他我能為您服務的事情嗎，唐尼根先生？

Mr. Donegan: No thank you, that's all. (Begins to walk away, but then turns around.) Good luck, Chi.

唐尼根先生：沒有了謝謝，就這樣。（開始走遠，但中途轉過身來。）祝妳好運，季薇。

Chi: Thank you, Mr. Donegan.

季薇：謝謝您，唐尼根先生。

Michelle: Thank you for coming in. And next time I'll have Chi help you.

蜜雪兒：謝謝您的光臨。下次我會讓季薇為您服務。

Mr. Donegan: (Laughs) It's a deal!

唐尼根先生：（笑著）一言為定！

單字 Vocabulary

- **head teller** [`hɛd `tɛlɚ] **n.** 櫃員主管、出納主任
- **seasoned** [`siznd] **adj.** 有充分經驗的、經過歷練的
- **likewise** [`laɪkˌwaɪz] **adj.** 同樣地、（我）也一樣

好用句型 Useful Sentences

How would you like it? 您想要什麼面額的鈔票？

你還可以這樣說

What denominations would you prefer?
How do you like your cash?
Would hundreds/ fifties/ twenties be okay?

例句

A: So your total is three hundred and forty dollars. How would you like it?

所以您的總額是三百四十元。 您想要什麼面額的鈔票呢？

B: I would like two hundred-dollar bills and the rest in twenties, please.

我要兩張一百元的鈔票，剩下的金額就麻煩你給我二十元的。

01
Chapter

02
Chapter

03
Chapter

04
Chapter

05
Chapter

06
Chapter

知道怎麼叫人很重要！

　　基本上，新人進公司的前三個月算是「蜜月期」，在這段期間內，周遭同事對你偶爾犯的錯誤都大致可以用「啊她/他是新來的！」的藉口來加以包容，對你提出的問題也會比較有耐心來解釋。但是我以過來人的身份奉勸你要準備兩本筆記本，最好是那種三孔式的檔案夾（可以隨時加新頁進去），一本用來記錄新學到的銀行業務知識，一本則用來記人名，包括同事和客戶的名字。熟悉並快速掌握你的工作內容，不容置疑地對新人而言是最最重要的事，但是如果同時能記得別人的名字，並以適當的禮貌稱呼對方，則可讓你更順利地融入工作環境。

　　記錄人名的時候，順道也寫下對那人的大概描述，與你曾幫她/他做過的事或談過的話題，以幫助記憶。在初次見面、互相介紹的時候，對同事可以直接叫名字，對客戶一律則必須使用對方的姓，男性顧客的話，姓前面冠 *Mr*，女性則可評估對方年紀，看來大約在三十五歲以上的就冠 *Mrs*（通常這個年齡以上的女性已婚，並使用夫家的姓），以下的冠 *Ms* 或 *Miss*，如果客人對自己怎麼被你叫有任何偏好的話，他們會很大方地指出來，譬如 *"Just call me Jim."* 或者 *"I am not married, please call me Ms. Smith."*（註）

　　至於對不認識的客戶，跟對方談話時，男性一概尊稱為 *sir*，女性稱為 *ma'am*（發音為 *[mæm]*）。如果那人不在場，而你要跟別人描述那個人時，指男性可用 *gentleman*，女性用 *lady*，若是年紀大的老人家，前面加 *older*，如 *"that older gentleman"*；年紀輕的少男少女，則前面加 *young*。

　　註：Ms（發音為 [mɪz]）是最普遍、對女性的冠稱，如果你不知道對方是否已經結婚，或你確知她目前的身份為離婚或寡居，則一概用 Ms。

3.2 Ring Ring

 對話 Dialogue

On Chi's second day at work.

季薇上班的第二天。

Michelle: Chi, today I want you to answer the phone. You will practice and eventually memorize the bank's standard greeting. For now, you can practice it by reading from this. (Hands Chi a piece of paper.) Feel free to tape it on the counter next to the phone if you want.

蜜雪兒：季薇，今天我要讓妳開始接電話。妳將練習銀行的標準問候語，直到妳把它記熟為止。現在呢，妳可以照著這個來唸（遞給季薇一張紙。）如果妳想要的話，可以把它貼在電話旁邊的櫃台上。

Chi: (Slowly reads the content.) Thank you for calling Best Bank University office ... This is Chi ... speaking. How may I help you?

季薇：（慢慢地唸著內容。）感謝您致電倍斯特銀行大學分行…我是季薇…請問我能為您服務嗎？

Michelle: Not bad. Next time, when you hear the phone ring, answer it. Think you can handle that?

蜜雪兒：還不差。下一次，當妳聽到電話鈴聲響的時候，就接起來。認為妳應付得來嗎？

Chi: I think so. (Phone rings.)

季薇：我想應該可以。（電話鈴響。）

Michelle: <u>That's your cue.</u>

蜜雪兒： 那是你的暗號，準備上場囉。

Chi: (Picks up the **receiver**.) Thank you for calling Best Bank University office. This is Chi speaking. How may I help you? ... Okay, a hundred in **singles**, two hundred in **quarters**, fifty in **dimes**, ten in **pennies** ... And what business did you said you are calling from? ... Starbucks. Got it. How long? Um, one moment, please. (Cover the **transmitter** while tips her head up.) Steve from Starbucks wants to know how soon can he pick up his change order.

季薇：（拿起聽筒。）感謝您致電倍斯特銀行大學分行，我是季薇，請問我能為您服務嗎？…好的，一元的要一百塊、兩角五分硬幣的要兩百塊、一角的要五十塊、一分的要十塊... 您剛才說您是從什麼公司打來的？…星巴克，知道了。要多久？嗯，麻煩稍等一下。（手蓋著話筒，同時抬起頭來。）星巴克咖啡的史提夫想知道多久他可以來拿那些零錢。

Michelle: It'll be ready in fifteen minutes.

蜜雪兒：十五分鐘內就會準備好。

Chi: Thank you. (Returns to the phone.) Steve? Fifteen minutes. So, the total amount of your requested change will be three hundred and sixty dollars, is that correct? Excellent, so we'll see you in a bit. Thank you for calling. (Hangs up.)

季薇：謝謝。（回到電話上。）史提夫？十五分鐘。所以，您所需零錢的總額是三百六十元，對嗎？太好了，我們一會兒見。感謝您的來電。（掛上電話。）

Michelle: Good job!

蜜雪兒：做得好！

Chi: Phew, good thing I had your cheat sheet. I'll need to practice some more before I feel completely comfortable.

季薇：呼，幸好我有妳這份小抄。我得多加練習直到我覺得安心為止。

Michelle: Next time, you can use the "hold" button when you need to talk to other staff members. Also, if you need to transfer a call, you will press "hold" first and then "**intercom**" plus the extension number. For example, Robert's extension is twenty-two, so you will first press "hold," then press "intercom," finally press "2" "2."

蜜雪兒：下次，當妳必須與其他同事交談時，可以使用這個「等候」鍵。還有，如果妳需要轉分機，先按「等候」鍵，然後再按「內部通訊」加分機號碼。舉例來說，勞勃的分機是二十二，所以妳會先按「等候」鍵，再按「內部通訊」，最後「二」、「二」。

Chi: May I write that down? I don't want to forget.

季薇：我能把它寫下來嗎？我不想忘記這些步驟。

Michelle: Sure. And the other staff members' extension numbers are listed here.

蜜雪兒：當然可以。另外，其他辦公室成員的分機號碼都列在這裡。

Chi: Okay... (**Jotting** down instructions.) Is there anything else I need to know?

季薇：好的...（快速地寫下作法。）還有其他我需要知道的事情嗎？

Michelle: Yes, deal with only one customer at a time, otherwise you will confuse yourself, and don't forget to smile.

蜜雪兒：是的，一次只處理一位客戶的事務，要不然妳會容易搞混。此外別忘了要微笑。

Chi: Why? I'm on the phone. They can't see me.

季薇：為什麼？我人在電話上，他們又看不見我。

Michelle: True, however when we smile, it is reflected in the tone of our voices, and the smile is heard on the other end of the line.

蜜雪兒：沒錯，然而當我們微笑，這種動作會反映在我們說話的聲調中，對方在電話線的另一頭上會聽到妳的微笑。

單字 Vocabulary

- **receiver** [rɪ`sivɚ] **n.** 收話器、電話聽筒
- **single** [`sɪŋgl̩] **n.** （口語，通常用複數形 singles）一元紙幣
- **quarter** [`kɔrtɚ] **n.** （美國的）兩角五分硬幣
- **dime** [daɪm] **n.** （美國的）一角硬幣
- **penny** [`pɛnɪ] **n.** （美國的）一分硬幣

01 Chapter

02 Chapter

03 Chapter

04 Chapter

05 Chapter

06 Chapter

- **transmitter** [træns`mɪtɚ] **n.** （電話的）發話筒
- **intercom** [`ɪntɚ͵kɑm] **n.** 對講機、內部通訊系統（intercommunication system 的簡稱）
- **jot** [dʒɑt] **v.** 快速地記下

日常用語 Common Expressions

That's your cue. 那是給你的暗號，準備上場囉。

（意指「暗示你做某種動作的信號出現了。」）

Good job! 幹得好！

好用句型 Useful Sentences

This is Chi speaking. 我是季薇。（在接電話時）

你還可以這樣說

Chi speaking.

Chi Borst. (Your full name)

This is Chi.

例句

A: This is Chi speaking. How may I help you?

我是季薇。我能為您服務嗎？

B: I would like to check on my account balance.

我想查詢我的帳戶餘額。

A: Your name and account number, please.

請提供您的姓名與帳號。

電話上如何應對？

　　學會如何以英語與外國人士在電話上適當地溝通，是一門相當重要且實用的技巧。由於對方只能聽到你講話，不能藉由臉部表情或肢體語言來了解你想表達的意思，因此你聲音裡的情緒，甚至連口音，這時都會被放大，而變得異常地明顯。

　　要克服這個問題，第一步是告訴自己盡量放鬆，不要霹靂啪啦地很快講一大堆，這樣只會令聽者疑惑，所以在講電話時，可以稍微放慢說話的速度，並注意斷句，表達出一個完整的意思後稍微停頓一下，讓對方的大腦有時間吸收。有件很值得我們臺灣人注意的事情是，美國人在唸電話號碼時，會按照這種模式：*"Area code XXX, XXX*（停頓）*XXXX."* 也就是三個號碼、三個號碼，然後最後四個號碼地唸，所以在詢問電話號碼的時候，他們都預期你會照這種斷句的方式來講，如果你用了其它形式，對方會感到不太適應。譬如 *(888) 123-4567* 這個號碼，你要說：*"Area code eight eight eight, one two three, four five six seven."*

　　第二步，是把一些常用的電話用語記起來，這些用語包括了你的開場白，以及如何結束對話的結尾語。許多人一接到電話時只說 *Hello*，這當然不能說錯，但是如果你能加上自己的名字（上班期間內的洽公電話前面要加上公司的名稱），就能省了對方確認打對電話的時間。在結尾語的部份，最普遍的說法是跟對方確認所有要講的重點都已經提到了，你可以說：*"Was there anything else I can do for you today?"*（還有其他我今天可以為您效勞的事嗎？）以及重複一次對方交代你辦理的事項，譬如*"I will relay your message to John. Thank you for calling."*（我會將您的留言轉達給約翰，謝謝您的來電。）或*"So I'll see you at two on Thursday.*

Good-bye."（那我們就星期四兩點見，再會。）等。若是你必須緊急結束目前的對話，可以禮貌地解釋你的理由，但盡量使用和緩的語氣，不要讓對方覺得你在趕人，例如*"I have another customer on the line, may I call you back in thirty minutes?"*（我有另外一位客戶仍在線上等候，能不能容我在三十分鐘後回電給您？）或是用這種很圓融的講法：*"I know you are busy, so I'm gonna let you go."*（我知道您很忙，所以我就不再耽誤您了。）確認對方可以接受後，再結束電話。

01
Chapter

02
Chapter

03
Chapter

04
Chapter

05
Chapter

06
Chapter

3.3 Nighthawks

Title Note: 《夜遊者》，或譯《夜鷹》，是美國寫實派畫家愛德華・霍普（Edward Hopper）的一幅名畫，描繪顧客（也就是「夜遊者」）光顧一家二十四小時營業的美式餐廳。

對話 Dialogue

Michelle: This morning we're going to do a **night drop**. Do you have your keys?

蜜雪兒：今天早上我們要來開夜間金庫。妳帶了妳的鑰匙嗎？

Chi: Right here. (Takes out her key ring.)

季薇：在這裡。（拿出鑰匙圈。）

Michelle: Let's go.

蜜雪兒：我們走吧。

(The two approach the night drop box.)

（兩人來到夜間金庫所在的位置。）

Michelle: Put your key in and turn to the right to unlock it. (Chi complies.) Does it feel loose?

蜜雪兒：把妳的鑰匙插入並往右轉，把鎖打開。（季薇照做。）感覺鬆鬆的了沒？

Chi: Uhuh.

季薇：嗯哼。

Michelle: Good. Now I am gonna put my **combo** in. (Michelle blocks Chi's view with the her left shoulder while turning the dial. She then cranks the wheel. The vault opens.)

蜜雪兒：好。現在我把我的密碼放進去。（蜜雪兒一邊用她的左肩擋住季薇的視線，一邊轉動刻度盤。接著她旋轉曲輪上的把柄，金庫開了。）

Michelle: This procedure is called "**dual control.**" Tellers have the key while managers have the combination. Never let a manager "borrow" your key regardless of how harmless the situation may seem. Vice versa, managers should never share their combo with tellers. The purpose of dual control is to **deter** criminal activity. Not a single bank employee should be able to open the vault by him or herself. It's dangerous and against the bank's security policy.

蜜雪兒：這道程序叫做「雙重控管」。出納員持有鑰匙，而經理人持有密碼。絕對不要讓經理跟妳「借用一下」鑰匙，就算表面看來不像是什麼大不了的情形。反過來說也一樣，經理人員不應該與出納分享他們的密碼。雙重控管的目的是阻止犯罪的行為。沒有任何一名銀行職員自己一個人就能夠打開金庫，這不但危險，而且違反了銀行的安全政策。

01 Chapter

02 Chapter

03 Chapter

04 Chapter

05 Chapter

06 Chapter

Chi: What would happen if dual control is compromised? What if I accidentally see the numbers?

季薇：要是這個雙重控管被打破了怎麼辦？如果我不小心看到密碼了怎麼辦？

Michelle: Should that happen, we would have the vault **contractor** change the locks. The Diebold company can change combinations and keys as needed, however correcting errors on this scale is tedious. Do your best to avoid this by intentionally looking away. By doing so you are protecting not only yourself, but the interests of all parties involved.

蜜雪兒：若是這種情況發生，我們會通知金庫的承造商來換鎖。迪堡公司能按照我們的需求來更換密碼組合與鎖匙，但是這類程度上的變更是相當繁瑣耗時的。妳可以特意往旁邊看來盡量避免這種情形，如此妳不但保護了妳自己，也保護了所有涉及人士的利益。

Chi: Understood.

季薇：了解。

Michelle: Let's see what we've got. (Peeks her head into the vault.) One, two, three ... we have three bags and ... one envelop. Did you get that?

蜜雪兒：我們來看看今天有什麼。（把頭探進金庫裡看。）一、二、三…我們有三個袋子跟…一個信封。妳聽到了嗎？

Chi: Three bags and one envelop. Got it.

季薇：三個袋子跟一個信封。知道了。

Michelle: Now you verify my observation by looking inside the vault yourself.

蜜雪兒：現在妳要親自進金庫看一看，以確認我觀察的沒錯。

Chi: (Complies.) That's it. I don't see anything else.

季薇：（遵照指示做。）就那些了，我沒看見有任何其他東西。

Michelle: All right. There are numbers on each bag and we will record them together on the **log** sheet. If you agree that the numbers are accurate then write down your initials next to mine.

蜜雪兒：好的。每一個袋子上皆附有號碼，我們將一起把那些號碼記錄在簿子裡。如果妳同意它們是正確的，就將妳名字的縮寫填在我名字縮寫的旁邊。

Chi: Where do I put my **initials**?

季薇：我要在哪裡填我姓名的縮寫？

Michelle: Here (points) as the receiving employee. Later, you will process these deposits as a "night drop." If for any reason you can not finish these transactions, you will re-assign them to another teller and they will record it in the system. Any questions?

蜜雪兒：這裡（指出位置）在收取人員的地方。稍後，妳將把這些存款標示為「夜間金庫」輸入交易系統。若是由於某種原因妳無法做完這些交易，妳必須將它們轉交給另外一位出納，而他們會把這些交易記錄到電腦系統裡。有任何問題嗎？

01 Chapter

02 Chapter

03 Chapter

04 Chapter

05 Chapter

06 Chapter

Chi: Nope. I think I've got it. Thank you showing me, Michelle.

季薇：沒有，我想我懂了。謝謝妳教我這些，蜜雪兒。

Michelle: No problem!

蜜雪兒：沒問題！

單字 Vocabulary

- **night drop** [ˋnaɪt ˌdrɑp] **n.** 夜間投遞服務、夜間金庫
- **combo** [ˋkɑmbo] **n.** 密碼組合（非正式用語，為 combination 的簡稱）
- **crank** [kræŋk] **v.** 扭轉、轉動（器具的把柄或轉軸）
- **dual control** [ˋduəl kənˋtrol] **n.** 雙重控管、雙重內控
- **deter** [dɪ ˋtɚ] **v.** 使（某人）打消主意
- **contractor** [ˋkɑn ˌtræktɚ] **n.** 契約工、承造商
- **log** [lɔg] **n.** 日誌、記錄
- **initial** [ɪ ˋnɪʃəl] **n.** 名字跟姓的第一個字母、姓名縮寫（注意通常使用複數形+s。這個字也可當動詞用，例句如："Where do I initial?"（我要在哪裡填我姓名的縮寫？））

好用句型 Useful Sentences

Understood. 了解。

你還可以這樣說

Got it.
I understand.
Yes, sir. / Yes, ma'am.
Affirmative.

例句

A: I would like to get Sarah, our new store manager, a key to the drop box.

我想給我們新來的店經理莎拉一副夜間金庫的鑰匙。

B: Understood. We can definitely arrange that for you. When can Sarah come in?

了解，我們當然可以幫您安排這件事情。莎拉什麼時候能過來？

01 Chapter

02 Chapter

03 Chapter

04 Chapter

05 Chapter

06 Chapter

夜間金庫

夜間金庫是提供一般店家在銀行營業時間結束後，依然能存錢的服務。這種小型金庫設立在銀行外部的牆面上，構造有些類似郵筒；店家使用專門的鑰匙從外面打開，將裝有現金與存款單的包裹丟進去後，關上門，包裹就會順著內部傾斜的角度掉入金庫裡，店家確認其完全落下後，再用鑰匙把門鎖起。

客戶可選擇使用普通的袋子、信封、防篡改的特製塑膠袋（*tamper-evident bags*，封口上有強力黏膠，一旦封住，除非剪開才能取得內容物，每個袋子並印有不同的編號）或附鎖的厚尼龍袋。行員在隔天早晨從銀行內部打開金庫後，將取得的包裹一一記錄下來，交由出納確認金額後輸入電腦；如果是有鎖的尼龍袋，行員會使用客戶預先交付的鑰匙打開，完成存款動作後，將收據放入尼龍袋，等待客戶有空的時候再來銀行取回袋子。

夜間金庫裡面的特殊傾斜構造，使得即使歹徒能打開外部的門，用長鉤子也勾不到客戶的存款。銀行提供了這種服務，不但方便店家不用趕在銀行營業結束前來存錢，也不須擔心把大量金錢留在晚上沒人看管的店裡，可能招致宵小侵入的危險，可說是一舉數得。然而，數年前有位老顧客告訴我，某家銀行曾發生這樣的竊盜案件：不法份子在夜間金庫外面貼上"*out of order*"的紙條，並在旁邊地上放了一個箱子，標示"*Night Depository*（夜間金庫的另一種講法）"的字樣；由於時值週末，許多商家將額外的現金丟入這個假金庫，結果造成了總值數萬元的損失。所以，若是你看見銀行附近有任何不尋常的擺設或額外的裝置，千萬不要貿然使用，以免受騙上當！

01
Chapter

02
Chapter

03
Chapter

04
Chapter

05
Chapter

06
Chapter

3.4 Day One

對話 Dialogue

Michelle: Are you excited? Today you're going to have your own cash drawer!

蜜雪兒：妳興奮嗎？今天妳要開始有自己的現金櫃了！

Chi: Please stop **teasing** me, Michelle. You know I'm nervous.

季薇：拜託別再鬧我了，蜜雪兒，你知道我很緊張的。

Michelle: Don't worry, I'll be right here. I'll watch over ya today. So, you ready?

蜜雪兒：別擔心，我人就在這裡，今天我會看顧妳。所以，妳準備好了嗎？

Chi: I am!

季薇：準備好了！

Robert opens the bank's door.

勞勃開啟銀行大門。

Michelle: Call the customer over.

蜜雪兒：招呼客人到妳這邊來。

Chi: Ma'am, I can help you here.

季薇：女士，我可以為您服務。

Michelle: A bit louder.

蜜雪兒：大聲一點。

Chi: MA'AM, I can help you here! (Grins and waves her arm.)

季薇：女士，我可以為您服務！（露齒微笑並搖動著她的手臂。）

Mrs. Robinson: Oh, I didn't see you there.

羅賓森太太：噢，我沒看見妳在那邊。

Chi: How are you, ma'am?

季薇：太太，您好嗎？

Mrs. Robinson: I'm fine, you?

羅賓森太太：我很好，妳呢？

Chi: Good, thank you for asking. How may I help you today?

季薇：我也很好，謝謝您的關心。今天您想辦什麼事呢？

Mrs. Robinson: I would like to deposit my check and get three hundred dollars back, dear.

羅賓森太太：我想把我這張支票存進去，並取三百塊出來，親愛的。

Chi: Absolutely. May I see your ID, please?

季薇：當然。請問我能看看您的身份證嗎？

01 Chapter

02 Chapter

03 Chapter

04 Chapter

05 Chapter

06 Chapter

Mrs. Robinson: Why?

羅賓森太太：為什麼？

Chi: Sorry for the **inconvenience**, Ma'am. But since you asked for cash back, I will need to make sure I'm giving the money to the right person.

季薇：太太，抱歉造成您的不便，但是因為您要求取回一部分現金，我必須確認我把錢交給的是本人。

Mrs. Robinson: I've been coming to this bank for over thirty years, no one has ever asked me for my ID! I want to speak to your supervisor.

羅賓森太太：我來這間銀行辦事超過三十年了，從來沒有人跟我要過我什麼身分證！我要求見妳的上司。

Michelle: (Approaches Chi's window.) Sorry, Mrs. Robinson, I overheard your conversation. Please bear with us, Chi is new here. She doesn't know who you are yet and she has been taught to verify IDs to protect our customers' assets. Chi, it's okay, I'll visually verify Mrs. Robinson for you.

蜜雪兒：（走到季薇的窗口。）抱歉，羅賓森太太，我聽見您倆的對話。請您多多包容，季薇是我們的新進人員，她還不認識您，而我們教她為了保護客戶的資產，她必須確認客人的身份。季薇，沒關係，我可幫妳以目視的方式確認羅賓森太太是本人。

Chi: Thank you, Michelle. (Turns to the customer.) Mrs. Robinson, would you like me to put the cash in an envelope for you? (Finishes the transaction.)

季薇：謝謝妳，蜜雪兒。（轉向客戶。）羅賓森太太，您希望我幫您把現金放入信封裡面嗎？（完成交易輸入。）

Mrs. Robinson: Yes, please. (Pauses.) I **suppose** you were doing your job asking for ID, I think I overreacted.

Chi: Thank you for your understanding, Mr. Robinson. May I help you with anything else?

Mrs. Robinson: No, that's all. I wish you good luck, Chi. And thanks Michelle. I'll see you **folks** next month.

羅賓森太太：是的，麻煩妳。（暫停了一下。）我想妳問我要身分證其實是項盡忠職守的行為，我反應過度了。

季薇：感謝您的體諒，羅賓森太太。還有其他要辦的事嗎？

羅賓森太太：不，就這些了。祝妳好運，季薇。還有謝了，蜜雪兒。下個月再見啊。

單字 Vocabulary

- **tease** [tiz] v. 戲弄、挑逗
- **ID** [ˌaɪ ˋdi] n. 身分證（口語，identity card 的簡稱）
- **inconvenience** [ˌɪnkən ˋvinjəns] n. 麻煩、不便
- **suppose** [sə ˋpoz] v. 猜想、假設
- **folk** [fok] n. 人們、伙伴

片語 Phrases

bear with someone 寬容某人的行為、耐心地等待某人（做某事）

好 用句型 Useful Sentences

May I see your ID, please? 請問我可以看一下您的證件嗎？

你還可以這樣說

May I have (borrow / take a look at / have a quick peek at) your ID, please?

Do you have your ID with you?

ID, please.

例句

A: I would like to cash this check.

我想兌現這張支票。

B: May I see your ID, please?

請問我可以看一下您的證件嗎？

01
Chapter

02
Chapter

03
Chapter

04
Chapter

05
Chapter

06
Chapter

做為新人的藝術

　　對於一個初進銀行的新人來說，最大的挑戰之一就是如何從容且有禮貌地應對客人的質疑和不安。從客戶的角度，他們已經在同一間銀行，跟相同的櫃台人員，辦同樣的事情辦了許多年，他們期待每次進來你的辦公室，程序永遠都是一樣：稱名道姓地互打招呼、大略解釋一下待辦事宜、然後就等著拿收據。結果你這新來的一出現，又要檢查證件、又這個不懂、又那個做錯的，一下打亂了老顧客原來建立好的秩序；有耐性的客人還好，沒耐性的很容易就會對你發火，這時，你一定要控制自己的情緒，不要因為對方表現出不滿而驚慌失措，你可以說：*"I apologize, sir / ma'am. I'm new to the system. Let me get my colleague to help us with the transaction."*（先生 / 太太，我道歉。我才剛開始學會用這套系統，讓我找我的同事來幫我們做這項交易。）或*"I'm sorry. I'm new here and I am not familiar with who you are. Let me get someone else to ID you for me."*（我很抱歉，我剛來沒多久，還不認識您，讓我看看有沒有其他人能幫我認證您的身份。）

　　堅守你的原則，但是同時態度要和緩，不要緊張地用一大堆話解釋，這樣反而讓對方也跟著不安起來；只要你以清晰、慎重的語氣，用簡要的幾句話解釋公司的政策，多數的客人在你重複同樣的意思兩三遍後，應該就能理解了，如果還有問題，你可以客氣地說：*"Let me get my manager to look into this."*（讓我找我們經理來看這怎麼辦。）有時候客戶對接受單一職員的意見會有遲疑，但是只要聽到另一位有經驗的經理人也講出相同的話語，他們的立場就比較容易軟化，對你接下來做的事也會比較有信心。

Chapter 04

Daily Routines

日常例行程序

4.1 Bonnie and Clyde

Title Note:

男子名 Clyde 唸作[klaɪd]。邦妮和克萊德是美國三〇年代著名的鴛鴦大盜，兩人與其同夥曾犯下多起銀行搶案。

 **對話** Dialogue

At the branch's annual security meeting.

在分行的年度安全會議上。

Debra: Thank you all for being here. This evening I'm going to focus on our opening and closing procedures. I know most of you have been with the bank for quite some time and are familiar with the rules. But it's essential that we keep reminding ourselves and each other to be mindful of what's going on around us and to not fall into

黛博拉：感謝各位到場。今晚我要把焦點放在我們早上開門和下午結業關門的流程上。我知道這裡大部份人都已經在銀行做事有很長一段時間，並且熟知那些規則；但是持續提醒自己以及其他人留心周遭發生的狀況，以及避免掉入「每天都是同樣那一套」的陷阱是十

"the routine" trap. Also, I see we have a new face today. What's your name, and how long have you been with Best Bank?

Chi: I'm Chi. I've been here since May.

Debra: So, you're two-month "new" here! Welcome. I am sure Robert and Michelle have shown you how we open the branch. Will you please tell us how you normally start a day?

Chi: I was taught that in the morning we should always have at least two branch members open the office. One member is to go into the office while the other waits outside. The person inside will lock the door behind themselves before verifying the branch is clear. They will then signal the rest of the staff that it is safe to enter.

分重要的。此外，我看到今天現場中有一個新面孔，請問妳的名字是什麼，還有妳在倍斯特銀行上班有多久了？

季薇：我叫季薇。我是五月開始來這裡上班的。

黛博拉：所以說妳是「兩個月大」的新人囉！歡迎。我確信勞勃和蜜雪兒都已經向妳示範過開門的過程，可以請妳告訴大家在正常情況下妳如何開始一天的作業？

季薇：他們教我早上的時候一定需要至少兩名分行的職員來開啟辦公室。其中一位成員先進入辦公室，另一位則在外面等候。在裡面的人把門重新鎖上，在確認室內空無一人後，再放出信號讓其他的同事知道這時可以安全地進入銀行。

01 Chapter

02 Chapter

03 Chapter

04 Chapter

05 Chapter

06 Chapter

Debra: What if the first person never puts out the **all-clear** signal?

黛博拉：要是首先進去的人一直都沒有放出安全通行的信號呢？

Chi: We are required to immediately drive to the pre-designated area, contact corporate security and call **911**.

季薇：我們就必須立刻開車到事先指定的地點，連絡公司的保全中心，並打九一一報警。

Debra: Excellent. This procedure is to prevent the "**Morning Glory**" robbery. Thieves have been known to either hide inside the branch overnight, or wait by the **entrance** to force their way in when the first bank employee unlocks the door. On top of what Chi has stated, I would like to add a few more things: First off, when you arrive at the parking lot, if the all-clear signal has not been put up, DRIVE AROUND the building to scan for any unusually signs, such as broken windows, or any unidentified persons lingering nearby. Second, know what kind of cars your co-workers drive to work. Be extremely cautious if you see an unfamiliar vehicle parked in front of the branch. And three, keep

黛博拉：非常好。這項程序的目的是為了避免清晨期間發生的搶案。根據我們過去的經驗，竊賊有時會通宵躲藏在分行裡，或是等在入口旁，當第一個銀行工作人員開門時，以蠻力強行進入。除了季薇提到的部份，我還想再加上幾點：第一，當你到達停車場時，如果還沒看見安全的訊號，開車繞建築物一圈，掃描看有無任何不尋常的跡象，譬如被打破的窗戶，或不明人士在附近徘徊等。第二，要知道你同事開什麼樣的車來上班；如果見到陌生的車子停在分行前就要特別提高警戒。還有第三，當你在等待信號的時候，要保持引

the engine running while you're waiting for the signal. This way, if you spot any signs of danger, you can drive out almost immediately. Pay attention to what's going on around you and the building at all times, do not look down at your phone, talk on the phone, or do anything that may distract you from this task. Next, let's talk about closing. Chi, I don't mean to <u>pick on you</u> (smiles), but can you tell me what needs to be done before we close?

Chi: We would check all of the rooms and under desks in order to make sure no one is hiding anywhere inside the building. Then staff members should leave in groups of two or more.

Debra: Very good. I think we've covered the basics on daily openings and closings. Next, let's talk about security routines on shipments.

擎持續轉動，如此一來，若是看到任何危險的跡象，你就能幾乎立刻開離現場。隨時注意你自身，以及建築物周圍正在發生的情況，不要低頭去看你的手機、講電話、或做任何可能分散注意力的事。接下來，讓我們來談談關門的流程。季薇，我不是故意要一直挑妳出來講話（微笑），但是可不可以請妳告訴我們在關門前需要做哪些事？

季薇：我們會檢查所有的房間和桌底下，確定沒人躲在建築物內的任何一個角落。然後職員結成兩人以上的隊伍離開。

黛博拉：很好。我想我們已經講完日常開門和關門的基本步驟。接下來我們要談談運鈔的保全程序。

01 Chapter

02 Chapter

03 Chapter

04 Chapter

05 Chapter

06 Chapter

單字 Vocabulary

- **all-clear** [`ɔl ˏklɪr] n. 指示危險已不存在（或障礙已清除）的信號
- **911** [`naɪn `wʌn `wʌn ] n. 美國的報警電話號碼，相當於台灣的 110 報警台（不要唸成 [ `naɪn ˏɪ `lɛvən]，若是這麼唸，指的是發生於年紐約市的九一一恐怖攻擊事件，英文中間會加一條斜線，寫做 9/11。）
- **morning glory** [`mɔrnɪŋ `glɔrɪ] n. 牽牛花（其開花的習性為清晨綻放，下午閉合）；銀行界一般借用此植物的名稱來指在銀行尚未開門營業前發生的清晨搶案。
- **entrance** [`ɛntrəns] n. 入口、門口

片語 Phrases

<u>pick on someone</u> 特別挑選某人做討厭的事、故意欺負某人

好用句型 Useful Sentences

Excellent. 非常好。

你還可以這樣說

Very good.

Great.

Outstanding.

Fantastic.

例句

A: From what I understand, you are looking for ways to save interest and consolidate your debts. Is that correct?

據我所知，您正在尋找節省利息並把幾項債務合併起來的方法，對嗎？

B: Yes.

是的。

A: Excellent. I believe we have a couple options for you.

非常好。我相信我們能夠提供您數個選項。

01
Chapter

02
Chapter

03
Chapter

04
Chapter

05
Chapter

06
Chapter

三種搶劫形態

　　一般來說，歹徒搶劫銀行的方式可分為三種：第一種是本篇對話中提到的清晨搶劫模式：*morning glory*，不肖份子可能在前一天偽裝成客戶或維修人員，藉口使用洗手間而跑到隱蔽的房間內躲藏，甚至在夜間結束營業、職員離開後，破壞門鎖或從屋頂打洞進入銀行，等到早上行員進入辦公室，再趁其不備，現身恐嚇職員打開金庫。

　　第二種叫做 *note-passer*，這種行搶的方式是在銀行營業時間內，佯裝成來辦事的客人，然後在出納窗口前，遞出寫有脅嚇字樣的紙條，指示行員將現金裝入袋子並交給搶匪。這些 *note-passers* 通常行事低調，多半以戴帽子、掛上太陽眼鏡、或穿大衣來掩飾自己的臉或身材，搶案發生過程不超過一兩分鐘，相當快速且安靜，旁人不易發現。

　　第三種叫 *take-over*，這是最暴力的一種形態，匪徒兩或多人進入分行後，公開展現武器，大聲喝令眾人伏下，並來回走動搜刮大廳櫃檯的現金，甚至進入金庫。*Take-over robberies* 所需時間較長，但平均來講很少超過五分鐘，而且多半外頭會有車等著接應逃跑。

　　在美國，搶銀行屬聯邦罪，刑罰比一般罪行要重得許多，如果歹徒有出示武器，則罪刑更是加重，可判到二十五年牢獄。今日科技的進步，例如監視器與電腦比對檔案，更是大大地提高警方的破案率，筆者入行到現在有九年多了，風聞過的搶案大約有十件左右，據悉多數都在第一個月內被偵破。

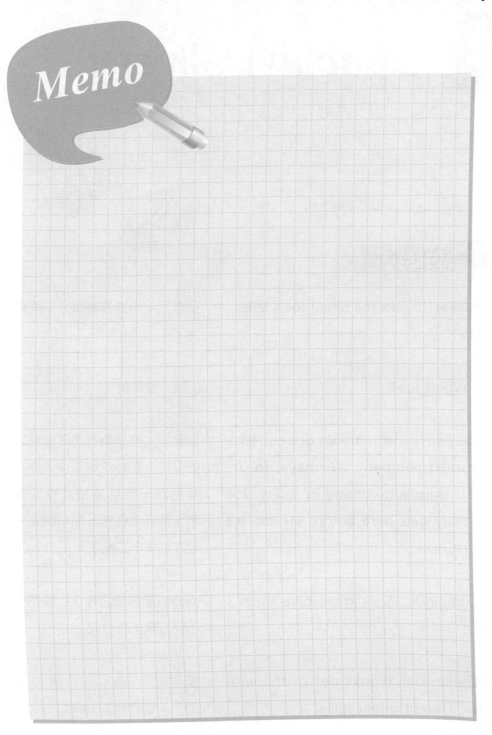

01 Chapter

02 Chapter

03 Chapter

04 Chapter

05 Chapter

06 Chapter

4.2 Special Delivery

 **對話** Dialogue

Michelle: (Checks the time.) Joe's late.

蜜雪兒：（查看時間。）喬遲到了。

Chi: Who's Joe?

季薇：誰是喬？

Michelle: He's with Brinks, our currency transport company. We have an ordered shipment coming in today. Joe normally gets here before eleven. It's almost noon.

蜜雪兒：他是為我們運送現鈔的公司：布林克的工作人員。我們有一批訂貨預計今天進來。喬通常在十一點前到達，現在都快十二點了。

Chi: Really? ... Should we give them a call?

季薇：是這樣的嗎？…我們要不要打電話給他們？

Michelle: Um. (Looks out of the window.) They're here! Finally.

蜜雪兒：嗯。（往窗外看去。）他們來了！終於。

A few minutes later, an armed **courier** walks in with a **dolly** and a **canvas** bag.

幾分鐘後，一名武裝的運貨員推著一台手推車，並背負一個帆布袋走進來。

Joe: Sorry I'm late. We changed our **route** today and we were delayed for a bit at the last two offices. So, how are you today, Michelle?

喬：抱歉我來晚了。今天我們改變路線，在前面兩間辦公室裡我們又稍微拖延了一下。所以，妳好嗎，蜜雪兒？

Michelle: Good, good. Let me get the door for you. Chi is coming with us. She is our new teller and I want to show her the ins and outs of getting our money shipment.

蜜雪兒：　好、好。我幫你開門。這回季薇會跟我們一起進金庫，她是我們新來的出納，我想讓她看看我們如何把現鈔運送進來。

Joe: Hi, Chi. How do you do?

喬：嗨，季薇，妳好嗎？

Chi: Good!

季薇：好！

Michelle: So, Chi, when Brinks arrives, the person in charge of the vault escorts the guard to the vault and stay with them throughout the whole process. Joe, how much does it say we have?

蜜雪兒：所以，季薇，當布林克抵達時，負責管理金庫的人必須一路護送警衛員到金庫，並全程與他們待在一起。喬，你的紀錄說我們有多少錢？

Joe: Uh, let me check, (opens his record) University has ... sixty-one thousand.

喬：嗯，我看看，（打開他的紀錄表）大學分行有…六萬一千元。

Michelle: (Shows the order sheet to Chi.) The amounts match. The bills are in a clear **tamper**-evident bag so I am just going to do a quick strap count: Ten, twenty—twenty thousand in hundreds; ten thousand in fifties; and ten, twenty, thirty—thirty thousand in twenties.

蜜雪兒：（給季薇瞧訂購單。）金額相符。紙鈔裝在透明的防竄改袋子裡，所以我只要很快地按捆數計算：一、二，一百元面額的有兩萬塊、五十元面額的有一萬、然後一、二十、三，二十元面額的有三萬。

Joe: And here's your coins. (Tilts the dolly then swiftly unloads boxes of coins onto the floor.) There you go!

喬：還有這是妳的硬幣。（將推車傾斜，接著巧妙地一下把成箱的硬幣卸到地板上。）都在這裡了！

Michelle: Quarters are five hundred a box; dimes, two hundred fifty; **nickels**, a hundred; and pennies, twenty five. So I ordered ... one box of quarters, (cranks her head and carefully counts the boxes) ... one box of dimes, two

蜜雪兒：兩角五分的硬幣是五百元一箱；一角的是兩百五十元一箱；五分的一百元一箱；以及一分的二十五元一箱。所以我訂了…一箱兩角五分，（扭著頭小心地計算箱數）…

boxes of nickels, and ... two boxes of pennies. Good, we've got everything. Thanks, Joe.

一箱一角、兩箱五分、還有…兩箱一分的。很好，全都齊了。多謝，喬。

Joe: No problem. Sign here please ... (Michelle signs the logbook.) Great! I'll see you two beautiful girls next week.

喬：沒問題。請在這裡簽名…（蜜雪兒在紀錄本上簽字。）太好了！我下星期再來見妳們兩位美麗的小姐。

Michelle and Chi: Take care, Joe. See ya!

蜜雪兒和季薇：保重，喬。再見囉！

單字 Vocabulary

- **courier** [`kɜɪə] n. 送貨員、信差
- **dolly** [`dɔlɪ] n.（搬運重物用的）手推車
- **canvas** [`kænvəs] n. 帆布
- **route** [raut] n. 路線、路徑
- **tamper** [`tæmpə] n. 竄改、擅自變更
- **nickel** [`nɪkl] n. 五分的鎳幣

片語 Phrases

the ins and outs（做某件事的）方法、細節

好 用句型 Useful Sentences

Sign here please. 請在這裡簽名。

你還可以這樣說

Your signature here, please.

Sign your name by the "X," please.

（向對方指出文件上標示 X 記號的位置）

May I have your autograph here, please?

May I have your John Hancock here, please?

例句

A: This is the last page of our loan application. Sign here, please.

　　這是我們貸款申請表的最後一頁，請在這裡簽名。

B: Sure.

　　好的。

略談運送現鈔

　　大概很多人會以為，一個禮拜中，銀行行員在運鈔車到達的那天會最緊張，其實不然，聰明一點的歹徒絕對不會挑這天，當銀行裡有，咳，「武裝人員」的時候來搶錢。一般來說，搶匪希望碰到的麻煩越少越好，如果在銀行進現金的時候跑來，要是正面遇上訓練有素又備有槍枝的運鈔員，豈不是吃不完兜著走了？

　　不過話說回來，現鈔進庫的時候行員還是不能就因此鬆懈警覺，除了要對一般正常的運送時間有概念以外，也要知道哪位運鈔人員是負責你的路線；通常如果固定送你分行的運鈔員即將休假或要換人，他們都會提前通知你，但是若突然來了一位不認識的新運鈔員，在要求出示公司證件外，行員還必須比照保安公司提供的人員名冊及照片以確認身份，若是這人沒有在名單上，銀行方面則必須打電話向公司求證，以確保安全；曾經有位資深的同事告訴我這樣的案例：在某家銀行預定送出現鈔的當天出現了兩位警衛人員，負責金庫的職員不假有他，將裝有大量現鈔的包裹交給那兩人，結果事後才發現他們是假冒運鈔員的匪徒！

4.3 Breaking Even

 對話 Dialogue

After banking business hours. Chi puts a bundle of bills through the counter machine. She pauses, looking puzzled.	銀行營業時候過後。季薇將一疊鈔票放入點鈔機裡。她停頓了一下,表情看來很困惑。
Kris: Is everything all right, Chi?	克莉絲:妳沒事吧,季薇?
Chi: Mm ... The computer says I am short five hundred, but I double-checked everything.	季薇:嗯…電腦說我短缺了五百元,可是我已經盤點過兩次了。
Kris: Five hundred? Would you like me to count your drawer? Sometimes a second set of eyes can help find the difference.	克莉絲:五百元?妳要不要我幫妳算妳現金櫃裡的錢?有時候另一雙眼睛可以抓出錯誤。

Chi: Please. (Steps aside to make room.)

季薇：那就拜託妳了。（往旁邊站過去。）

Kris: Let me see ... These are your straps, right? (Unwraps the bills and runs them through the cash counter.) And for your loose ... you have five hundreds, no fifties, sixteen twenties, four tens, ten fives, and twenty-two singles. Your coins ... (Finishes counting.) Do you have any **mutilated** bills?

克莉絲：我看看…這些是妳整捆的鈔票，對嗎？（把紙捆打開來並置入點鈔機。）還有妳不成捆的部份…妳有五張一百元、沒有五十元、十六張二十元、四張十元、十張五元、跟二十二張一元。妳的硬幣…（算完。）妳有任何破損缺角的紙鈔嗎？

Chi: No.

季薇：沒有。

Kris: Okay. (Presses the enter key.) Huh, exactly five hundred. That could be a box of quarters. Did you give out a box of quarters to any businesses today?

克莉絲：好。（按下輸入鍵。）哼，剛好五百元整。那有可能是一箱二角五分的硬幣。妳今天有沒有給過那個店家一整箱的二角五分？

Chi: I don't think so.

季薇：我不這麼認為。

Kris: Did you exchange bills with anybody?

克莉絲：妳曾經跟誰交換過錢嗎？

01 Chapter

02 Chapter

03 Chapter

04 Chapter

05 Chapter

06 Chapter

Chi: I did a couple times with Michelle. But we did exact exchanges right then and there and I know I got my money. And her drawer is balanced.

季薇：我跟蜜雪兒換過幾次錢。但是我們交換的都是剛剛好一樣的數量，而且有當場點清，我知道我拿到了所有應得的錢。她的現金櫃沒有短少也沒多出來。

Kris: Have you checked your trash?

克莉絲：妳翻過垃圾桶了沒？

Chi: I did.

季薇：翻過了。

Kris: Did you **reverse** anything?

克莉絲：妳有沒有曾經取消過任何交易？

Chi: Reversals? Huhhh, that rings a bell ...

季薇：取消交易？哼哼哼，這倒讓我想起來...

Kris: What is it?

克莉絲：想起什麼？

Chi: Earlier, a customer wanted to purchase two packs of traveler's cheques, but she changed her mind. Oh my God, they were two hundred and fifty each! I forgot to reverse them.

季薇：先前，有位客戶本來想買兩套旅行支票，結果改變心意。喔我的老天，那些支票是每套兩百五十元！我忘記把那項交易取消了。

Kris: There you go. We found it.

克莉絲：這就對了。我們找到妳短少的金額啦。

Chi: Thank you so much, Kris. You're a life saver!

季薇：太感謝妳了，克莉絲，妳真是我的救星！

單字 Vocabulary

- **mutilated** [`mjutə͵letɪd] **adj.** 殘缺不全的
- **reverse** [rɪ `vɜ·s ] **v.** 取消、逆轉（名詞為reversal [ rɪ `vɜ·səl]）
- **traveler's cheque** [`trævlə·s ͵tʃɛk] **n.** 旅行支票，亦可拼為 traveler's check

日常用語 Common Expressions

You're a life saver. 你真是我的救星、你幫了我一個好大的忙。

好用句型 Useful Sentences

Is everything all right? 一切都還好嗎？

你還可以這樣說

Are you okay?
Something's wrong?
What's the matter?

例句

A: You look pale. Is everything all right?
你看來臉色蒼白，一切都還好嗎？

01
Chapter

02
Chapter

03
Chapter

04
Chapter

05
Chapter

06
Chapter

B: I'm fine. For a second I thought I was being robbed. The last person I waited on passed a note through the glass.

我還好。剛才一下子我還以為我碰到搶匪了，前一個客人從玻璃下方塞一張紙條過來。

A: What does it say?

紙條上寫什麼？

B: It says, "Keep up the good work."

它寫著：「你做得很好，繼續加油。」

每天銀行關門後的勝利與失敗

出納員最怕的事情之一，就是自己的現金櫃出現短缺（*shortage*）或多出錢來（*overage*）。每個營業日即將結束時，出納都必須清算現金數額，這個動作稱為 *balancing* 或是 *proving your drawer.*

如果差額在一塊美金以下，那有可能是找錯客人零錢，或是不巧拿到了原本就有差額的整捲硬幣；差額在十元與一百元之間，可能的原因包括：拿錯面額的鈔票（譬如十元當作二十元來用）、整捲的硬幣數量算錯等；差額在一百元以上， 則可能是由於紙鈔或整箱硬幣的數量點錯、忘記輸入或更正某筆交易等。特別是這種金額在一百元以上的差異，由於通常比較難找出原因，有時會花費出納員一個小時以上的時間來修正錯誤；而若是在出納反覆盤點後仍找不出發生差額的原因時，出納主任或經理級人員就必須親自來確認你的現金櫃內容，並拉出當天所有的交易內容一一檢查。

按經驗來説，整數的差額最容易發現；如果是帶有零錢的數額，則極有可能是出納把客人的支票當作現金來存。做過銀行的人都知道，每天下午四、五點鐘拉下鐵門後，就是我們以「勝利」（一次就算齊金額，一分也不差！），或是「失敗」（算了很久或算很多次都不知道為什麼不對）總結一天工作成果的時刻。

我碰過比較誇張的例子包括：出納不小心把錢當垃圾倒掉（最後有從垃圾堆裡找出來啦）、把鈔票當支票或入款憑證送到交易中心（交易中心的人員數天後把那些錢退回分行）、甚至有人盤點自動櫃員機之後，忘了把錢放回去，一堆錢就擺在機器後面結蜘蛛網...（很久以後才被維修人員發現！）

HAL 9000 and 1

Title Note:

這個標題的靈感來自於經典科幻電影《2001：太空漫遊》（2001: A Space Odyssey）中一部名為"HAL 9000"的電腦。"HAL 9000"唸作 [ˋhaʊl ˋnaɪ ˋθaʊznḍ]。在電影中，這個具有高度人工智慧的電腦系統，不但可分析大量複雜的資訊、執行各種精密的任務，甚至能與人類互動溝通。

對話 Dialogue

Michelle: Thank you, Chi, for coming in early! Kris is going to show you how to balance the ATM since you will be our back-up **ATM custodian**. Are you ready to learn?

Chi: I am!

Michelle: Good. She's all yours, Kris. (Michelle leaves the ATM room.)

蜜雪兒：季薇，謝謝妳今天提早來上班！由於妳即將成為自動櫃員機的後備管理人，克莉絲會教妳怎麼結算機器裡的金額。妳準備好學點東西了嗎？

季薇：準備好了！

蜜雪兒：很好。那我就把她交給妳了，克莉絲。（蜜雪兒離開自動櫃員機的房間。）

Kris: Let's start by opening this bad boy up. When you are in charge of the ATM, you will use this key (shows Chi a **brass** key) to open the top. This key is labeled number twenty-three in the key box. After you make sure that no customer is outside using the ATM, you will switch it to "maintenance" mode.

克莉絲：首先，讓我們把這個小壞蛋打開。當妳負責管理自動櫃員機時，妳會使用這把鑰匙（向季薇展示一只黃銅製的鑰匙）打開機器的上層。這把鑰匙在我們鑰匙櫃裡的編號是二十三。在確認過外頭沒人正在使用這台機器以後，妳就可以把它按到「維修」模式。

Chi: (Writing down the instructions.) Got it.

季薇：（寫下操作的方式。）了解。

Kris: Then you'll print out the settlement sheets. (Presses the print option on the touchscreen monitor. Printer runs.) There will be a total of four sheets. If you forget the steps, the instructions are here. (Points to a manual laying inside the ATM.) But I think it's pretty **self-explanatory**. Just do what it says on the screen.

克莉絲：然後妳會列印出結帳單，（在觸控式螢幕上按下列印的選項。印表機開始運作。）一共會有四張單子。如果妳忘記了有哪些步驟，操作方式在這裡。（指著一本放在櫃員機內的使用手冊。）不過我認為步驟很清楚，只要照著螢幕上的指示一步一步做就好。

Chi: Uh-huh. (Writes in her notebook.)

季薇：嗯嗯。（在她的筆記本裡繼續寫著。）

01 Chapter

02 Chapter

03 Chapter

04 Chapter

05 Chapter

06 Chapter

Kris: After that, you will use this funny-looking magnetic key to open the bottom. (Shows Chi a small green tag with a round metal top.) The bottom is where we store the money and deposits received from customers.

克莉絲：再來，妳會用這個模樣有點怪的磁性鑰匙打開機器的下層。（拿給季薇看一只附有圓形金屬頂端的綠色小牌子。）機器下層就是我們儲放鈔票以及收取客戶存款的地方。

Chi: Okey-doke.

季薇：好的。

(Kris presses the magnetic key on the side of the digit dial, enters the code and turn the knob. The bottom door opens. She pulls out four **cassettes.**)

（克莉絲將磁性鑰匙緊緊壓在數碼轉輪的旁邊，輸入密碼後，轉動把手。下層的門開啟。她把四個硬盒拉出來。）

Kris: (Opens one of the cassettes.) Look, the bundled bills are pre-marked on the right-hand corner and placed in the cassette in **alternating** directions so it's easier to count. Normally we have just fifteen minutes in the morning to balance the ATM before the branch opens. So we've got to move fast. What does the settlement say we should have?

克莉絲：（打開其中一個盒子。）妳看，鈔票都一捆一捆地事先在右上角做了記號，然後一正一反地放入盒子裡以方便計算。一般來說我們早上在分行開門之前，只有十五分鐘的時間來結算自動櫃員機，所以我們的動作要快。結算單說我們應該要有多少錢？

Chi: (Reads the printed sheet.) Seventy-six thousand and four hundred.

Kris: (Opens the rest of the cassettes and counts the marked, grouped bills.) So, two, four, six, eight, TEN. Two, four, six, eight, TWENTY. Two, four, ... seventy-six. Now the loose. We'll just put them though the cash counter. (Counter runs and shows four hundred total.) Good. We're balanced. (Puts the bills back to the first cassette. Closes the lid. Pushes each cassette back into it's original **slot**.)

Kris: Will you take out that tall bin for me? It has the customer's deposits and we're going to send them to the processing center for verification. (Looks at the time on the monitor.) It's almost nine ... annnnnnnnnd (Last lock clicks into place.) we're done!

季薇：（照著印出來的表單唸。）七萬六千四百元。

克莉絲：（打開其餘的盒子並數著做過記號、分批的鈔票。）所以，二、四、六、八、一萬；二、四、六、八、兩萬；二、四……七萬六。接下來零散的紙鈔，我們就用點鈔機來算。（點鈔機運作，顯示總共四百元。）很好，結算的結果符合電腦提供的數據。（把鈔票放回第一個盒子，關閉盒蓋，將所有的盒子推回各自原來的空槽。）

克莉絲：可以請妳幫我把那個高桶子拿出來嗎？那裡面裝有客戶的存款，而我們接下來要把那些存款送到交易輸入中心去作確認。（看著螢幕上顯示的時間。）快九點了…而而而（最後一道鎖喀嚓一聲鎖上。）我們全部搞定！

單字 Vocabulary

- **ATM** [`e `ti `ɛm] **n.** 自動櫃員機（automated teller machine 的縮寫）
- **custodian** [kʌs `todɪən] **n.** 管理人、監護人
- **brass** [bræs] **adj.** 黃銅製的
- **self-explanatory** [sɛlfɪk `splænə ˌtorɪ] **adj.** 自明的、不需多加解釋的
- **cassette** [kæ `sɛt] **n.** （可抽取的）卡式盒
- **alternating** [`ɔltɚ ˌnetɪŋ] **adj.** 交替的、間隔的
- **slot** [slɑt] **n.** 狹長的槽或孔

日常用語 Common Expressions

Okey-doke. 好。

（非正式用語，為 okay 另一種戲謔的說法。也可說 okey-dokey）

好用句型 Useful Sentences

We're done! 全部搞定！

你還可以這樣說

We're all set.

We're finished here.

That wraps it up.

例句

A: Please initial here, here, and here. Great, we're done!

請在這裡、這裡、還有這裡寫你名字的縮寫。太好了，全部搞定！

B: Phew. I'm glad it's finally finished. What a long process to close a loan!

呼～我很高興它終於結束了，貸款簽約可真是一道漫長的過程啊！

自動櫃員機

　　自動櫃員機的出現，大大改變了人們到銀行辦事的時間及頻率，這些機器全年無休，每天二十四小時營業，從原本只提供基本的查詢帳戶餘額、轉帳與提款的功能，到現在不但能接受各種面額的紙鈔與支票存款（電腦已可辨識大部份個人支票上的手寫金額），許多機器甚至還提供了販售郵票的服務。

　　在享受它帶來的便利之時，一般人大概從沒想過到底是誰把錢放進機器裡，而客戶存進去的款項又怎麼變成帳戶裡的數字的呢，答案很簡單，都靠我們這些有血有肉、真正的櫃員們來維持它們一般的日常運作。每一台自動櫃員機都有一個獨特的代號，並與網路連線；如果機器出現故障，譬如說鈔票卡住出不來或收據紙用完了，不但在機器背面的電腦螢幕上會顯示錯誤訊息，遠端的電腦也會在收到故障訊息後，以電話自動語音訊息來通知銀行，然後由行員去打開櫃員機，或把夾紙拿出來，或補充印表紙。遠端主機並且會將每台機器長期的進出金額做統計，按照歷史的紀錄，每個禮拜建議分行增加或減少櫃員機裡的現金數量。

　　也正因為每家銀行都必須花人力和時間來維持自家櫃員機的正常運作，所以當你使用不同銀行提供的自動櫃員機便需付一小筆的手續費以進行交易，這筆費用是用來支付機器的維修、電力損耗、網路費、及銀行間的交換作業等成本。

01 Chapter

02 Chapter

03 Chapter

04 Chapter

05 Chapter

06 Chapter

Chapter 05

Consumer Transactions

個人戶交易

5.1 Automaton

Title Note:

單字automaton的唸法為 [ɔ `tamə͵tan]，意思是機器人，或具有像機械般舉止（不經思考便自動處理日常事務）的人。這個標題"automaton"是描述出納員在熟習銀行作業流程一段時間之後，快速並正確地處理交易的樣子。

 **對話** Dialogue

Chi: (Calls out.) Next in line please!

季薇：（喊出）麻煩下一位！

Mr. Sharp: Pardon me, but I don't have my account number with me. Can you look it up?

夏普先生：不好意思，我沒帶帳號來，妳能幫我查嗎？

Chi: Absolutely. May I borrow your **debit card** and ID?

季薇：當然可以，我可以借用一下你的金融卡和身分證嗎？

Mr. Sharp: Certainly. (Takes out his wallet and pulls out both documents.)

夏普先生：當然。（拿出他的皮夾並取出那兩份證件。）

Chi: (Examines the ID.) Mr. Sharp, how are you today?

季薇：（檢查身分證。）夏普先生，您今天好嗎？

Mr. Sharp: I'm fine, thank you for asking, how about you?

夏普先生：我很好，謝謝妳的關心，妳呢？

Chi: I'm well, thank you. (Enters the debit card number.) We're all set, now ... what can I do for you?

季薇：我也很好，謝謝。（輸入金融卡號碼。）好了，現在…請問您要做什麼？

Mr. Sharp: (Takes out a check.) I would like to deposit a thousand dollars to my savings account, and the rest to my checking, please.

夏普先生：（取出一張支票。）我想請妳把一千塊存到我的存款帳戶裡，然後剩下的存到支票帳戶。

Chi: Okay, we'll fill out two deposit slips, one thousand goes to your savings, the rest two hundred seventy-nine and fifty cents will go to your checking. (Begins to write out tickets.) Do you need any cash for yourself?

季薇：這樣的話，我們要填兩張存款單，一千塊存到您的存款帳戶，剩下的兩百七十九元五角就進到您的支票帳戶。（開始填寫單據。）您需要拿一些現金出來嗎？

Mr. Sharp: No thank you. However, I do have one more question after you're done.

夏普先生：不用，謝謝。不過，在妳做完了以後，我還有另外一個問題。

01 Chapter

02 Chapter

03 Chapter

04 Chapter

05 Chapter

06 Chapter

Chi: Definitely. (Processes the transaction.) Would you like to have the balances on both accounts?

季薇：當然。（將交易輸入電腦。）您需不需要這兩個帳戶的餘額？

Mr. Sharp: That would be great.

夏普先生：可以的話那就太好了。

Chi: (Hands receipts to customer.) I printed your **balances** on the back of the receipts. So what's your question, Mr. Sharp?

季薇：（將收據交給顧客。）我把您的存款餘額印在收據的背後。那麼您接下來的問題是什麼呢，夏普先生？

Mr. Sharp: I would like to set up **automatic transfers** once my **direct deposit** starts. What should I do?

夏普先生：我想在我的薪資開始變成直接轉帳以後，設定一部分薪資自動存到存款帳戶裡。我該怎麼做？

Chi: How often would you like your automatic transfers?

季薇：您希望電腦多久一次做自動存款的動作？

Mr. Sharp: Once a month. Right after my **payroll** hits.

夏普先生：一個月一次，薪水一進來以後就立刻存過去。

Chi: When do you get paid?

季薇：您幾號發薪水？

Mr. Sharp: The first of the month.

夏普先生：每個月一號。

Chi: How much would you like to transfer?

季薇：您想轉多少？

Mr. Sharp: One thousand.

夏普先生：一千塊

Chi: Excellent, I have all the information I need. I can set that up on the second of the month, starting next month. Would you like me to do that for you?

季薇：非常好，所有需要的資訊我都有了，我可以設定每個月的二號做自動存款，下個月開始，我這樣幫您做好嗎？

Mr. Sharp: Yes, please. Thank you for your help!

夏普先生：好的，麻煩妳。多謝妳的幫忙。

Chi: My pleasure, Mr. Sharp.

季薇：是我的榮幸，夏普先生。

單字 Vocabulary

- **debit card** [`dɛbɪt `cɑrd] **n.** 金融卡、簽帳卡（中國及馬來西亞等地區又稱「借記卡」。客戶使用這種卡到商店消費，金額會直接從其銀行帳戶中扣除。）
- **balance** [`bæləns] **n.**（收支相抵後的）帳戶餘額 **v.** 核對帳戶數字以確定收支平衡、結算
- **automatic transfer** [ˌɔtə`mætɪk `trænsfɚ] **n.** 系統自動在某一時間將預先設好額度的款項，從一個帳戶轉入另一個帳戶的過程
- **direct deposit** [də`rɛkt dɪ`pɑzɪt] **n.** 薪資轉帳、薪資自動存入銀行帳戶
- **payroll** [`pe ˌrol] **n.** 員工薪資名單；薪水總額

好 用句型 Useful Sentences

Absolutely. 當然可以。

你還可以這樣說

Certainly.

Definitely.

Of course.

Sure.

例句

A: I don't remember my account number. Can I give you my social security number to look it up?

我不記得帳號。我能不能給你我的社會安全號碼來查？

B: Absolutely.

當然可以。

客戶服務的技巧：一次解決一個問題

在今日腳步快速、分秒必爭的商業世界裡，「一心多用」，似乎變成了每個人必備的工作技巧之一；然而，這種態度若是拿到客戶服務上面，就會產生問題。

在面對客戶的時候，很重要的一點是把你全部的焦點都放在對方身上，所有之前發生的大小事件，不論如何都要暫時放下，現在要處理的是現在在你面前的這個人，而且，一個問題解決完，再解決下一個問題。

即使你知道某些捷徑、一點可能把事情加快速度的小聰明，我的建議還是讓客戶選擇他們想要的作法。每位客人都有自己熟悉的做事方式，以及能夠理解的邏輯，如果你強迫他們使用你的方法，要是最後產生的結果不佳，客戶第一個反應是怪罪這個「新方法」，而是誰建議他們走這個新的途徑呢？是你。

而多半的客戶偏好解決問題的方式，就是一件事一件事分開來作。這種方式雖然表面上看來有點浪費時間，但其實是最清楚、最不容易出錯的方法。舉例來說，在以電子郵件與客人溝通事情時，一篇電子郵件只要解決一件事就好，性質相關的問題雖然可以放在同一篇郵件裡，但每個問題一定要以數字或重點符號標示清楚；不相關的問題就用另一篇郵件來發。另一個例子是在櫃台換零錢，客人如果一百元整張鈔票要換成十元的、一百元換成五元的，最好的作法是先拿出十張十元鈔票，將客人的一百元放在桌上他能看見的（以及電子監視器能照到的）位置，把十張十元算給對方，對方表示數額對了，你將一百元放入現金櫃裡，然後再進行下一筆交換，拿出二十張五元鈔票... 依此類推。我曾有一位同事在與客戶換錢的時候分心，結果最後發現現少了錢，但是客戶已經離開銀行，祇得自己吃下這筆誤差。

5.2 Something from Nothing

對話 Dialogue

Chi: How are you, Mrs. Weis? Haven't seen you for a while!

季薇：您好嗎，威斯太太？一段時間沒看到您了！

Mrs. Weis: Good. Looks like it's time to pay my shopping bill. How are you doing, sweetie?

威斯太太：好。看起來又到了該付購物帳單的時間了。妳好嗎，甜心？

Chi: Super! Which bill are we talking about, Mrs. Weis?

季薇：超級好的！我們講的是您哪張帳單呢，威斯太太？

Mrs. Weis: Can you please check the balance on this card? (Places a credit card on the counter.)

威斯太太：妳可不可以幫我看一下我這張卡已經刷了多少錢？（將一張信用卡放在櫃台上。）

Chi: No problem. Your current balance is one thousand three hundred ninety-nine dollars and forty cents.

季薇：沒問題。您目前的金額為一千三百九十九元四角。

Mrs. Weis: What's the minimum?

威斯太太：最低應繳金額是多少？

Chi: Your minimum payment is fifty-six dollars.

季薇：您的最低應繳金額是五十六元。

Mrs. Weis: Huh, and when is it **due**?

威斯太太：哼，那什麼時候到期？

Chi: The fifth. You still have ... (checks the calendar) about a week before the due date.

季薇：五號。您還有…（查日曆）大約一個禮拜的時間才到期。

Mrs. Weis: I would like to pay three hundred on that today, dear. (Counts out the money.)

威斯太太：我想今天就付三百塊吧，親愛的。（數鈔票。）

Chi: Ok. (Processes the transaction.)

季薇：好的。（將交易輸入系統。）

Mrs. Weis: Wouldn't it be nice if we don't have to pay our bills? (Winks.)

威斯太太：如果我們都可以不用付帳單那該多好？（淘氣地眨了一下眼。）

Chi: Haha ... That does sound nice.

季薇：哈哈…那聽起來的確很美妙。

Mrs. Weis: But as great as that sounds, it's probably not a good idea.

威斯太太：不過，雖然它聽起來很棒，卻大概不是個好主意。

Chi: Oh?

季薇：哦？

Mrs. Weis: Nobody would want to work! We wouldn't have all those nice restaurants, movie theaters, or **amusement parks**.

威斯太太：這樣一來就沒有人要工作了！我們就不會有那些高品質的餐廳、電影院、或遊樂園囉。

Chi: I think you're right! (Grins.) Here is your receipt. Is that all for you today?

季薇：我想您是對的！（露齒而笑。）這是您的收據，今天就只辦這件事嗎？

Mrs. Weis: That's enough for now, sweetie. I don't see Robert, is he here?

威斯太太：目前這樣就夠了，甜心。我沒看見勞勃，他在這裡嗎？

Chi: He's at lunch.

季薇：他去吃午餐了。

Mrs. Weis: Tell him I said hi. (Shrugs.) I guess I shop too much. The holidays are just so much fun. I can't help myself. Be careful not to make the same mistake.

威斯太太：告訴他我說嗨。（聳肩）我猜我買太多了，聖誕假期真是太好玩啦，我沒辦法控制自己。妳不要跟我犯一樣的錯誤喔。

Chi: (Smiles.) I will do my best! See you next time, Mrs. Weis!

季薇：（微笑。）我會盡力！下次見了，威斯太太！

01 Chapter
02 Chapter
03 Chapter
04 Chapter
05 Chapter
06 Chapter

單字 Vocabulary

- **due** [dju] **adj.** 到期的、屆期應付的
- **amusement park** [ə`mjuzmənt `park] **n.** 兒童樂園、遊樂園

好用句型 Useful Sentences

告知來電者其要找的人暫時無法接聽電話的原因

He's at lunch. 他去吃午餐了。

你還可以這樣說

He's on break (training / in a meeting, etc.)
He's away from his desk.
He stepped out of the office.
He's not available at this moment.

例句

On the phone. 在電話上。

A: Chi Borst speaking. How may I help you?
　季薇・伯斯特。我能為您服務嗎？

B: May I speak to Robert, please?
　請問勞勃在嗎？

A: He is at lunch. Is there something I can help you with?
　他去吃午餐了。有什麼事是我能幫您的？

B: It's okay. I'll call back later.
　沒關係，我稍後再打。

Money, Money, MONEY!

不知道你有沒有想過，為什麼我們要使用「錢」？

鈔票的本身幾乎沒有任何價值，如果現在有個外星人看到一張一百元美金的鈔票，對它來說，那只不過是一張上面畫了花花綠綠圖案的紙，是我們人類，賦予錢所謂的「價值」。一張五元的紙鈔，跟一張二十元的紙鈔，兩者間價值的差別，僅僅是建立在彼此的「約定」與「信任」上面。對我們來說，真正有價值的，是錢可以換來的東西，譬如說一條能維持生命的麵包，或是能產生動力、運轉引擎、使人能到想去的地方的汽油。

既然真正有價值的不是錢，而是那些錢能換到的物品或服務，有人也許會說，何不讓我們回到過去以物易物的時代，那樣事情比較單純，例如養雞的某甲可以用一隻雞從某乙這裡換到一簍的桃子，或是某乙可以用他一簍的桃子，換到某丙鑄造的一個鋼桶等等。問題是，以物易物這個方式非常沒有效率，要是某甲想要某丙做的鋼桶，可是某丙不想要某甲的雞怎麼辦？要得到某丙的鋼桶，某甲得首先知道某丙想要桃子，然後某甲再去跟某乙用雞換桃子，最後用桃子換成某丙的鋼桶。此外，以物易物很容易造成物價的波動以及不公平的現象：要是某丙下個禮拜改變心意，一個鐵桶要三簍桃子才換得到怎麼辦？

「錢」的出現，不但能解決上述的難題，使人與人之間的交易變得容易、快速以外，它也讓人能夠跳脫物質的思考模式，進入理念與抽象的階段；我們在進行交易的時候，腦子裡不再想的是雞、桃子、鋼桶或另外一百樣不同的東西，我們想的是單一的數字；我們不用再等待雞蛋孵出小雞、小雞長成大雞，或桃樹開花結出桃子，許多時候，我們需要的只是一句承諾、或一張雙方簽字的借據，巨大的交易就能在幾秒間完成，然後接下來更多、更大、更快的交易。人類的商業、社會與文明，由於錢的發明和運用以倍數成長。我猜，錢對文明世界所帶來的這些改變，大概是過去發明錢幣的老祖宗們從未意料到的吧？

01
Chapter

02
Chapter

03
Chapter

04
Chapter

05
Chapter

06
Chapter

5.3 Waiting for Godot

Title Note:

Godot的唸法為 [gʊ ˋdo, gə ˋdo]。這齣著名的舞台劇《等待果陀》，描述兩個人在某棵樹下一直等著另一個名叫果陀的人的出現。劇中漫長的等待呼應了本篇英文對話中顧客等待銀行釋放支票款項的過程。

對話 Dialogue

Mr. Klein: I would like to deposit this check, please.

克萊先生：我想存這張支票，麻煩妳了。

Chi: Sure, Mr. Klein. (Picks up his deposit ticket and the check. Starts processing. Pauses. Turns her head from the screen back to examining the check.)

季薇：好的，克萊先生。（拿起他的存款單和那張支票，開始輸入交易內容。停頓了一下，眼睛從電腦螢幕轉開來，開始檢視支票。）

Mr. Klein: What's the matter?

克萊先生：怎麼了？

Chi: Um, Mr. Klein, the system **prompts** a large-deposit **hold**. We will have to **hold** this check.

季薇：嗯，克萊先生，由於您這筆存款額度較大，系統顯示必須扣留支票的金額，我們必須暫緩釋放這張支票的款項。

Mr. Klein: For how long?

克萊先生：要扣留多久？

Chi: Let me see … the first two hundred is available right away, forty eight hundred will be available in two business days, and the rest should be available in five business days.

季薇：我看看…您可以立即開始使用其中的兩百元，兩個工作天後您能開始用四千八百元，剩下的應該五個工作天後就都可以用了。

Mr. Klein: Is there any way you can make the funds available sooner? I need to buy some equipment for my business.

克萊先生：有沒有什麼辦法能讓我更快開始使用這筆資金？我要幫我的公司購買一些器材。

Chi: Let me check with my supervisor. I'll be right back, Mr. Klein.

季薇：讓我問問看我的上司。我馬上就回來，克萊先生。

Mr. Klein: Thank you Chi.

克萊先生：謝謝妳，季薇。

(Chi walks over to Michelle's station and shows her the check. Michelle studies it carefully while pulling up the

（季薇走到蜜雪兒的崗位並給她看那張支票。蜜雪兒一邊仔細地研讀著支票，一邊由電腦

01 Chapter

02 Chapter

03 Chapter

04 Chapter

05 Chapter

06 Chapter

customer's profile. After a while, Michelle accompanies Chi's return to Mr. Klein.)

Michelle: Hi, Mr. Klein. How are you? I haven't seen your wife since the charity dinner. How's she doing?

Mr. Klein: I'm fine, thank you. Sarah is doing well. She's at home with the kids.

Michelle: So I looked at your check, Mr. Klein. It's **drawn** from an **out-of-state** bank and thus will take us a little longer to collect the funds. We will have to place a hold on it. Meanwhile, you can still use the money you currently have in the account plus your **credit line**.

Mr. Klein: All right.

Michelle: I'm sorry about the inconvenience.

中調出客戶的檔案。過了一會兒，蜜雪兒陪同季薇走向克萊先生。）

蜜雪兒：嗨，克萊先生，您好嗎？自從上次慈善晚宴後我就沒見過您的夫人了，她好嗎？

克萊先生：我很好，謝謝。莎拉也很好，今天她待在家裡帶小孩。

蜜雪兒：所以我看過了您的支票，克萊先生，這是從本州以外的銀行開出來的支票，所以會花我們比較長的時間實際去取得款項。我們必須要扣押這張支票的金額。在這同時，您還是可以使用目前您帳戶裡的錢，以及您循環信用帳戶的額度。

克萊先生：好吧。

蜜雪兒：很抱歉造成您的不便。

Mr. Klein: That's fine. Thank you, Michelle.

克萊先生：沒關係，謝謝妳，蜜雪兒。

Chi: Thanks, Michelle. (Michelle acknowledges and leaves.) Thank you for your understanding, Mr. Klein.

季薇：謝了，蜜雪兒。（蜜雪兒點頭示意後離開。）感謝您的體諒，克萊先生。

Mr. Klein: Not a problem.

克萊先生：沒問題。

單字 Vocabulary

- **prompt** [prɑmt] **v.** 促使、驅使
- **hold** [hold] **n.** **v.** 扣押存入支票一部分或全部的金額
- **draw** [drɔ] **v.** 開出（票據、支票等）
- **out-of-state** [ˋaut ˏəv ˋstet] **adj.** 在本州以外的地區、外州的
- **credit line** [ˋkrɛdɪt ˏlaɪn] **n.** 循環信用帳戶。又稱line of credit，連結至個人或公司的支票帳戶上（也有銀行提供獨立的循環信用帳戶），當帳戶持有人有需要時，可從此一循環信用帳戶中提領現金，亦可用於預防支票帳戶裡金額不足而產生跳票的情形。使用到的金額以日息計算，客戶可隨時還款。

好用句型 Useful Sentences

I'm sorry about the inconvenience. 很抱歉造成您的不便。

你還可以這樣說

I apologize for the inconvenience.
My apology for the inconvenience.

01 Chapter

02 Chapter

03 Chapter

04 Chapter

05 Chapter

06 Chapter

139

Sorry for inconveniencing you.

Sorry for the trouble this may cause you.

例句

A: What do you mean I can't use my debit card?

你說我不能使用我的金融卡是什麼意思？

B: I'm sorry about the inconvenience, ma'am. Unfortunately, there have been a few unauthorized transactions incurred on the card. It is now being closed for your protection. You should receive a new card in about a week.

太太，很抱歉造成您的不便。不幸地，這張卡上出現了數筆未經持卡人許可的消費紀錄，為了保障您的權益，我們目前已經關閉這張卡。您在一週內應該會收到新卡。

A: Can I still use my ATM card?

那我還可以用我的提款卡嗎？

B: You certainly can, ma'am.

當然可以，太太。

銀行扣押支票存款的幾種理由

　　國人一般多以現金存錢，所以很少碰到銀行扣押存款金額的情況；但在美國，由於大部份民眾仍習慣使用支票來進行交易，而偽造支票（*fraudulent checks*）的案例又時有所聞，銀行為了防止損失，因此在面對客戶拿支票來存款時，會依照以下幾種理由，來對支票的金額進行扣押（*hold*）的動作：

　　一、新客戶（*New Customers*）：根據統計，許多假支票的案件發生在剛開戶的三十天內。不法份子利用人頭或偽造的身份文件開戶並存入假支票，一旦銀行行員信以為真、釋放款項後，便領光帳戶內所有金額逃之夭夭。因此，在新帳戶建立的第一個月內，銀行有權利扣押任何的支票存款，最長至九個工作天客戶不得從帳戶中領款出來。

　　二、高面額的支票存款（*Large Deposit*）：金額超過美金五千元即被視為高面額的支票，這類支票跳票的風險大，銀行可以將支票的金額分成兩部份扣押，第一部份是五千塊以下的部份，留在銀行裡兩個工作天以後才能讓客戶取用，第二部份是超過五千塊的部份，過了五個工作天之後銀行才開始放款。

　　三、個別案例（*Case-by-Case*）：銀行針對各種不同的情況決定扣押的時間長短，最久可達七個工作天。這些不同的情況包括：支票上有塗改的跡象、支票來源不明或可疑、客戶曾有跳票或連續透支的紀錄等。

5.4 Back-Up Plan

 對話 Dialogue

Miss White: Can I put this check in my checking and also take out a hundred using my debit card? (Takes a card out of her purse.)

懷特小姐：請問我可以使用我的金融卡，把這張支票存入我的支票帳戶，然後提一百塊出來嗎？（從她錢包裡取出一張卡。）

Chi: Yes. Go ahead, **swipe** your card. (Customer complies and enters her **PIN**.)

季薇：可以，請您刷卡。（客戶照做，並輸入密碼。）

Chi: (Reads the account information on the screen, then speaks in low volume.) Miss White, I'm sorry we'll have to deposit the whole check. Your current balance is in the negative.

季薇：（判讀螢幕上的帳戶資料，接著低聲地說。）懷特小姐，很抱歉我們必須整張支票都存進去。您目前的帳戶餘額是負數。

Miss White: REALLY? By how much?

懷特小姐：真的？負多少？

(Chi writes the balance on a **scrap paper** and hands it to Miss White.)

（季薇將帳戶金額寫在一張小紙片上後遞給懷特小姐。）

Miss White: Ohhhhhhh crap. So when would my check **clear**?

懷特小姐：噢噢噢，糟糕。所以我的支票什麼時候會清帳？

Chi: It should be available by tomorrow.

季薇：款項應該明天就可以開始使用了。

Miss White: Then I can come back and make a withdrawal, right?

懷特小姐：到時候我就可以回來這裡再領錢出來，對嗎？

Chi: Yes. May I make a suggestion, Miss White?

季薇：是的。請問我可以建議您一件事嗎，懷特小姐？

Miss White: Yes?

懷特小姐：可以呀？

Chi: I see that there has been quite a few **overdraft** charges assessed to your account. I suggest that we put in for a line of credit, that way you won't have to worry about those fees anymore.

季薇：我看到您的帳戶裡有好幾筆透支費，我建議我們幫您申請循環信用帳戶，這樣一來您就再也不必為那些費用傷腦筋了。

01 Chapter

02 Chapter

03 Chapter

04 Chapter

05 Chapter

06 Chapter

Miss White: I probably should have done it earlier. Is there an annual fee?

懷特小姐：我大概早就應該申請了。有年費嗎？

Chi: No. There is only a small five-dollar transfer fee if an overdraft occurs. Which, compared to the thirty-eight overdraft charges you have, is much, much cheaper. Do you have a couple of minutes? I can have our banker, Michael, help you apply.

季薇：沒有。只有在帳戶產生透支時會有一筆五塊錢的小額轉帳費，跟三十八塊的透支費比起來，便宜太多太多了。您有沒有幾分鐘的時間？我可以請我們的襄理麥可幫您填申請表。

Miss White: Um I ...

懷特小姐：嗯，我⋯

Michael: (Approaches the customer.) Hi, Miss White. My name is Mike. I overheard your conversation here. If you have a moment, I can explain how a line of credit could work for you.

麥可：（走到客戶身旁來。）嗨，懷特小姐，我的名字是麥可。我剛剛聽到您們之間的談話，如果您有點時間的話，我可以為您解釋循環信用帳戶如何運作。

Miss White: All right.

懷特小姐：好吧。

Chi: Thank you, Mike. Here's your receipt Miss White, will there be anything else?

季薇：謝謝你，麥可。這是您的收據，懷特小姐。還有其他的事情嗎？

Miss White: **That's all. Thank you for your help.**

懷特小姐：就這樣了。謝謝妳的幫忙。

Chi: **Thank you for banking with us, Miss White.**

季薇：謝謝您的惠顧，懷特小姐。

單字 Vocabulary

- **swipe** [swaɪp] **v.** 持證件或金融卡以帶有磁條的一端快速滑過讀卡機的動作、刷卡
- **PIN** [pɪn] **n.** 個人密碼（PIN是Personal Identification Number的簡寫）
- **scrap paper** [`skræp `pepɚ] **n.** （隨手記錄事項用的）零碎的紙片、便條紙
- **clear** [klɪr] **v.** 完成（票據等的）交換手續、結清
- **overdraft** [`ovɚ ˌdræft] **n.** 透支、超額提款

好用句型 Useful Sentences

Your current balance is in the negative.
您目前的帳戶餘額是負數。

你還可以這樣說

Your account is in the red.
Your account is currently overdrawn.
You overdrew your account.

例句

A: Can you check my card please? I tried to use it at the gas station but it was declined.

能請你幫我看一下這張卡好嗎？我拿它去加油站用，但是卡片遭拒，交易被取消了。

B: Sure. I'm sorry, sir, it appears that your current balance is in the negative.

當然。我很抱歉，先生，看起來您目前的帳戶餘額是負數。

A: What's my balance?

我的帳戶餘額是多少？

B: Negative thirty dollars, sir.

負三十塊錢，先生。

什麼？透支了？

在美國，帳戶若是發生透支的情況，對於每一筆透支，銀行都會索取三十五到四十元不等的罰款（有些銀行對五元以下的小額透支不會罰款），舉例來說，如果你帳戶裡只有十元，但是你先前寫出去一百元的支票今天被兌現了，然後你忘記帳戶裡只剩十元，到了自動櫃員機領出二十元，又到商店裡用金融卡買了總值五十元的東西，這樣一天算下來，銀行會扣你三筆罰款，假設每筆罰款是四十元，三筆就是一百二十元，要是你不知道帳戶已經透支，隔天又繼續到處消費... 等到銀行最後寄透支通知來的時候，看到罰款的總金額真的會嚇一大跳！

要保護帳戶不會透支，以下是幾種好方法：

一、時時注意自己帳戶裡的餘額。勤勞一點的人可使用記帳簿（銀行會提供免費的，叫做 *check register* 或 *register book*，可向櫃台索取），將所有的進帳與開銷記錄下來；有手機的人可以上網設定最低限額警告，如果帳戶餘額低於某個金額，手機立刻會收到自動簡訊。

二、請銀行將帳戶的透支機制設定（*overdraft settings*）改為不接受透支。這樣做以後，如果你帳戶上的餘額，少於你在外面的消費或從櫃員機提款的數目時，商店的終端機和自動櫃員機上會顯示交易取消的訊號。

三、申請一個預防透支用的循環信用帳戶（*overdraft protection line of credit*）。有良好信用紀錄的人可以考慮申請這類的帳戶，銀行在核准後會將它運到你的支票帳戶上，若是有透支的情形發生，電腦系統會自動從循環信用帳戶裡，轉出一部分金額到支票帳戶中來償付透支的部份，大大地減少了客戶跳票及透支罰款的費用。

01 Chapter
02 Chapter
03 Chapter
04 Chapter
05 Chapter
06 Chapter

Chapter 06

Business Transactions

公司戶交易

6.1 Cashing-In on Cashing-Out

對話 Dialogue

A middle-aged man walks in with a **carryall**.

一位中年男子拎著個手提袋走進來。

Kris: Ah, Benny's here.

克莉絲：啊，班尼來了。

Chi: Who's Benny?

季薇：誰是班尼？

Kris: Benny owns the **liquor** store in the **plaza**. I'll introduce you. BENNY!

克莉絲：班尼是這個廣場裡洋酒專賣店的老闆，我會介紹妳給他認識。班尼！

Benny: Hey, Kris. How are you?

班尼：嘿，克莉絲。妳好嗎？

Kris: I'm good! Benny, let me introduce you to Chi. Chi's our new teller. Chi, this is Benny and he has a surprise for you.

克莉絲：我很好！班尼，容我把你介紹給季薇。季薇是我們新來的出納。季薇，這是班尼，他等下要給妳個驚喜喔。

Chi: (Suspiciously) What surprise?

季薇：（懷疑地）什麼驚喜？

Kris: (**Snickers.**) His big bag of **goodies** of course.

克莉絲：（竊笑。）當然就是他一大袋的好康囉。

Benny: Oh, THIS little thing? (Dumps the bag's contents onto the counter.)

班尼：喔，妳是在說這個小東西呀？（把袋子的內容物倒在櫃台上。）

(Chi breathes in sharply.)

（季薇深深地吸了一口氣。）

Kris: I'll have Chi help you with your deposits today. Chi, if you have any questions just ask, okay?

克莉絲：今天我就讓季薇幫您處理您的存款。季薇，如果妳有任何疑問就儘管問，OK？

Chi: Okay. (The customer's deposits fills the entire space, leaving little room to work.) Um, Kris?

季薇：OK。（客戶的存款將櫃台上所有的空間都佔滿了，剩下極少的空間供她作業。）呃，克莉絲？

Kris: Yes?

克莉絲：怎樣？

Chi: These checks were made out to different people. Can I take them?

季薇：這些支票全是寫給不一樣的人，我能收嗎？

Kris: Yes. Benny's store cashes people's pay checks. Just make sure they are all stamped with the business's account number. (Starts singing Elton John's "Bennie and the Jets.")

克莉絲：可以。班尼的店幫人兌現薪資支票。妳只要確認那些支票全都蓋了印有班尼公司帳號的章就行了。（開始唱艾爾頓・強的「班尼和噴射機」。）

Benny: Haha... Is that my song now?

班尼：哈哈⋯那首歌現在變成是我的歌了嗎？

Kris: Of course, you're Benny and you be roll'n in money.

克莉絲：當然啦，你是班尼，而且你在錢堆裡打滾。

Benny: I don't roll in money, but I think you girls do. I bet you have a room in the back filled with piles of cash. When you take your breaks, y'all just go in and roll around in it like fall leaves.

班尼：我沒有，我認為妳們才在錢堆裡打滾。我打賭妳們後面有個房間，裡面堆滿了現金。休息時間一到，每個人就進去把那些鈔票當成秋天的落葉一樣，在錢堆裡滾來滾去。

Kris: How did you find out? I thought that was our secret! Right, Chi?

克莉絲：你怎麼知道？我以為那是我們的祕密！對不對，季薇？

Chi: Actually I prefer to sit in the gold brick **throne** we built. It's surprisingly comfortable.

季薇：其實我比較喜歡坐在我們用金磚做的那個王位上，它比想像中的還舒服。

Kris: It was good talking to yah Bennie, but I've gotta **jet**. I'll see yah later. (Begins to walk away **humming** "Bennie and the Jets.")

克莉絲：很高興有機會跟你聊天班尼，但是我最好得快點閃人，下次再見了。（一邊走，一邊嘴裡哼著「班尼與噴射機」。）

(Branch's radio suddenly starts playing "Bennie and the Jets.")

（分行內的音樂頻道突然開始播放「班尼與噴射機」。）

Bennie and Kris: (Turn towards one another in shock.) NO WAY!

班尼和克莉絲：（驚訝地轉過身來面向彼此。）不可能！

Chi: WAY!

季薇：就有可能！

單字 Vocabulary

- **carryall** [ˋkærɪ͵ɔl] **n.** （大型的）手提袋
- **plaza** [ˋplɑzə] **n.** （包含各類商店、餐廳、銀行等的）廣場、市場
- **liquor store** [ˋlɪkɚ ˋstor] **n.** 專門販售酒類的店鋪（Liquor 指「烈酒」，也就是相對於 wine（葡萄酒）和 beer（啤酒）等發酵酒，酒精濃度較高的蒸餾酒。美國各州的法令不一，有些州限定 liquor stores 只能販售烈酒與葡萄酒，不能賣啤酒，有些州除了烈酒與葡萄酒外，啤酒、汽水、果汁、甚至糖果與樂透彩券也能在這些店裡出售。）

- **snicker** [`snɪkɚ] v. 吃吃地笑、竊笑
- **goody** [`gʊdɪ] n. 非常吸引人的東西（常指小禮物、糖果等）
- **throne** [θron] n. 王位、寶座
- **jet** [dʒɛt] v. 快速地移動
- **hum** [hʌm] v. 哼唱、用鼻音或低聲哼歌

片語 Phrases

rolling in money 擁有大量的財富、極有錢

職場須知 Business Know-how

Procedural Etiquette for a General Introduction
介紹兩人互相認識的方式

Introducer: (Person A), let me introduce you to (Person B).
介紹人：（A的名字），容我把你介紹給（B的名字）。
(Introducer provides a brief description of B and briefly allows A to respond with a general pleasantry.)
（提供一段對B的簡短敘述，暫停，讓A有機會跟B打招呼）
(Introducer provides person A's brief description and then allows B to respond with a general pleasantry.)
（接著提供一段對A的簡短敘述，暫停，讓B有機會跟A打招呼）

實境對話

Robert: Mike, let me introduce you to Pierre. He's going to be our new financial advisor.
勞勃：麥可，容我把你介紹給皮耶。皮耶即將成為我們新的財經顧問。

Mike: Pleasure to meet you.

麥可：很榮幸認識你。

Robert: Pierre, this is Mike. Mike is my relationship manager and he is one of the top salesmen in the district.

勞勃：皮耶，這是麥可。麥可是我的客服經理，他是這個分區中最出色的經理人之一。

Pierre: Wow, that's amazing. I look forward to working with you.

皮耶：哇，太好了，我期待接下來跟你合作。

01 Chapter

02 Chapter

03 Chapter

04 Chapter

05 Chapter

06 Chapter

銀行以外的選擇

在美國你不一定需要到銀行去兌現、開立支票，甚至換取外幣，許多民間的私人機構也提供與銀行類似的服務，這類的商店統稱為 *money service business*，或簡稱 *MSB*。這些商店有的幫顧客兌現他們的薪資支票（註一），有的販賣小額個人本票、旅行支票或禮物卡（註二），也有的做國內外匯款（註三）。

這些商店就像其他商店一樣，也需要把多餘的現金存入銀行，並把從客人那裡取得的支票，存進戶頭裡讓銀行向原發票銀行請款，才能拿到錢。而當 *MSB* 商店來到銀行要求開戶時，由於其業務內容每天涉及大量的現金交易，可能協助犯罪份子洗錢的疑慮較高，通常要經過銀行內部防制洗錢部門嚴格的審查，以及區域經理的核准後，才能正式開戶。在開戶後，若是單個營業日內的現金交易量超過一萬元美金，那天接受存款或提款的出納員還要填寫報告；如果隔天又超過一萬元，再寫一次，依此類推。因此銀行對這種特殊形式的商業客戶，有時還真是存在著一種又愛又怕的情結！

註一：在美國若是你沒有一個自己的銀行帳戶，兌現支票可不是免費的！這些店家會收取手續費來為你兌現支票。

註二：禮物卡，又譯作「禮金卡」，英文為gift card。購買禮物卡的客人將現金交給商家，由店員在電腦上輸入卡號和金額，一經啟動後顧客即可拿著卡片到其他商店消費。有的禮物卡可讓客人決定金額多寡，有的則是固定額度；有些可重複加入金額，有些在預購的額度用完後即失效；有的卡片必須在特定的商店使用，有的則沒有限制；總而言之，卡片用法須視種類而定。

註三：目前Wester Union（西聯匯款）和MoneyGram是在美國最大的兩家匯款公司，這些機構經常在藥房、酒類專賣店、雜貨店與超市裡設點，顧客可在許多商店招牌或窗戶上看到Wester Union或MoneyGram的標示。

01 Chapter

02 Chapter

03 Chapter

04 Chapter

05 Chapter

06 Chapter

Mystery Man

對話 Dialogue

A tall man approaches Chi's window.

一位身材高挑的男子走到季薇的窗口前。

Man: Excuse me, can you help me? I need to check on the balance of this account. (Shows Chi a bank statement.) It's for the district fire department.

男子：不好意思，可以請妳幫忙一下嗎？我需要知道這個帳戶裡目前的餘額。（向季薇出示一份銀行對帳單。）它屬於這邊分區的消防隊。

Chi: May I see your ID please?

季薇：請問我可以看一下你的身分證件嗎？

Man: Sure. (Hands over his driver's license.)

男子：當然。（把他的駕照遞過來。）

Chi: (Computer displays the account details. Chi clicks on the "related cus-

季薇：（電腦顯示出帳戶的詳細內容。季薇按下「相關客

tomers" button.) I ... I am sorry, sir, but you do not appear to be an **authorized signer** on the account?

Man: I'm not. But I need to know how much there is in the account now so we can know how much to leave to the new **crew**. We're in the process of switching team members, and none of the **treasurers** are available for me to get the account information from. Can't you make an exception here?

Chi: (Glances at the **insignia** on the tall man's shirt.) Let me talk to my manager and see what we can do.

Man: Thank you, (looks at the name plate on the counter) Chi.

Chi walks to Robert's office and explains the customer's situation. While Robert is looking up the business' contact information, the man approaches the two.

戶」的按鈕。）我…很抱歉，先生您好像不是這個帳戶上授權的簽名人？

男子：我不是。但我需要知道現在這個帳戶裡有多少錢，這樣我們才曉得要留多少給下一批新的成員。我們正在更換隊員的過程中間，然而我無法連絡到任何財務以取得帳戶的資料。妳就不能開個特例嗎？

季薇：（瞥了一下高個子男人衣服上的標誌。）讓我跟經理講，看我們能做什麼。

男子：謝謝，（看著櫃台上的名牌）季薇。

季薇走到勞勃的辦公室裡，向他解釋那位客戶的情形。正當勞勃在查公司的連絡資料時，男子走近兩人。

01 Chapter

02 Chapter

03 Chapter

04 Chapter

05 Chapter

06 Chapter

Man: Hi, I am from the district fire department. Is there any way we can get that account balance today? I'm in a bit of a rush.

男子：嗨，我是從分區消防隊來的。有沒有什麼辦法可以讓我們今天就能知道帳戶餘額的？我有點趕時間。

Robert: I'm sorry sir, but we can not **disclose** private account information to non-signers. We are legally responsible for protecting our customer's assets. However, what I can do is call Brent Spiner, the signer on the account, and provide HIM with that information. Would you like me to do that?

勞勃：先生，很抱歉，我們不能將帳戶資料透露給沒有簽名權限的人員。依法我們有責保護客戶的資產。不過，我能夠打電話給布蘭特‧史賓納，也就是這個帳戶授權的簽名者，然後給他帳戶的存款數字，您要我這麼做嗎？

Man: Nuh, Brent is not around, I've tried. Can't we make an exception? I'm wearing our department's uniform and I showed you my ID!

男子：沒用的，布蘭特不在，我試過了。難道就不能開個特例嗎？我穿著我們部門的制服，還給你們看過我的身分證！

Robert: I do not doubt you are who you say you are, sir. I want to help you, but our policy prohibits me from giving out detailed financial information about any account unless you are a signer on that account. My apologies.

勞勃：先生，我不是懷疑你的身份。我也想幫你，但是銀行的政策禁止我將任何帳戶的細節洩露給他人一除非你是帳戶上具有簽名權力的人。我很抱歉。

6.2 **Mystery Man**

01
Chapter

02
Chapter

03
Chapter

04
Chapter

05
Chapter

06
Chapter

(Man leaves.)

（男子離去。）

Chi: (**Draws out** name.) Roooooberrrt?

季薇：（拉長語調地說勞勃的名字）勞勞勞勃勃勃？

Robert: I know! That was a bit odd. I think we'd better give a **heads-up** to their signers just in case something else is going on.

勞勃：我知道！那是有點怪怪的。我想我們最好通知他們的授權簽名者，以防萬一。

單字 Vocabulary

- **authorize** [ˋɔθə ˌraɪz] **v.** 授權、許可
- **signer** [saɪnɚ] **n.** （有權在支票上）簽名的人
- **crew** [kru] **n.** 一組團隊的成員、全體員工
- **treasurer** [ˋtrɛʒərɚ] **n.** 財務總管、會計
- **insignia** [ɪn ˋsɪgnɪə] **n.** 徽章、標誌
- **disclose** [dɪs ˋkloz] **v.** 透露、洩露
- **draw out** [ˋdrɔ ˋaʊt] **v.** 拉長（地講）、延長（演説等）
- **heads-up** [ˌhɛdz ˋʌp, ˌhɛdz ˋʌp] **n.** 預警、事先的警告

好用句型 Useful Sentences

I'm in a bit of a rush. 我有點趕時間。

你還可以這樣說

I'm in a hurry.

I'm a little busy at the moment.

Let's be quick. I don't have a lot of time.

例句

A: Ah, Mr. Donegan, I have good news for you. You're pre-qualified for a Platinum credit card! If you'd like, I can put in the application for you.

啊，唐尼根先生，我要告訴你個好消息，您符合申請白金卡的資格！如果您想要的話，我可以幫您申請。

B: Not right now. I'm in a bit of a rush. Let's do it next time.

現在不行，我有點趕時間。下次再申請吧。

A: Not a problem. Let me know when you're ready.

沒問題。您準備好的時候再告訴我。

01 Chapter

02 Chapter

03 Chapter

04 Chapter

05 Chapter

06 Chapter

公司帳戶上具有簽名權力的人員

公司不像人，可以自己跑到銀行來辦事或簽署支票，它需要人來運作、來推動各種事務。在公司規模還小的時候，當然可以靠老闆（*the owner*）一個人做存款、開支票買東西等的事項，但是當老闆忙不過來的時候，他／她會指定其他的人，來代表公司處理業務；在這些業務中如果有牽涉到金融交易，站在銀行的角度來看，我們稱這些代表人為*signers*。

Signer 這個單字望文生義，簡單說來是「簽名的人」，在什麼東西上簽名呢？一般來說就是像支票、領款單這類銀行文件。*Signers* 的角色十分重要，他們能直接連絡銀行以取得帳戶資料、在公司的帳戶間轉帳、存錢、領錢，而當銀行對某項交易有問題時，也會聯繫這些 *signers* 來釐清疑惑。

在公司一開始建立銀行帳戶的時候，*singers* 不但必須在銀行的 *signature card*（類似國內的開戶印鑑卡）上簽名，也需要在 *business resolution*（註）上簽名，這兩份文件會留在原開戶的分行裡存檔，是銀行藉以確認誰是帳戶上有權簽名的人，以及比對簽名樣式的憑據。

註：Resolution在這裡是「決議」、「決定」的意思，business resolution 也就是公司開會決議的紀錄。銀行開戶文件中用到的 business resolution，內容包括誰是公司的老闆/持有人、財務（treasurer）、具有簽名權力的人員（signer）、以及支票上需要一個人還是兩個人的簽名才算有效等的條款。

6.3 Open for Business

對話 Dialogue

Chi: Hi, Steve, I have your change order ready!

季薇：嗨，史提夫，我把你預約的零錢準備好了！

Steve: You do? Awesome. (Walks towards Chi's window.) How is it going?

史提夫：妳準備好啦？太好了。（走向季薇的窗口。）今天生意如何？

Chi: It's all right, kind of **slow** for a Monday. How about you? Is it busy at Starbucks?

季薇：還好，就禮拜一來說算是滿清淡的。你呢？星巴克那邊忙嗎？

Steve: Not really, its still early. It'll pick up later during the rush.

史提夫：不怎麼忙，現在還早，晚點尖峰時間的時候生意就會多起來。

Chi: (Brings out the change.) Any plans for the summer?

季薇：（把零錢拿出來。）這個夏天有什麼計畫嗎？

Steve: Actually, I'm thinking about starting a business.

史提夫：老實說，我正在考慮開一家公司。

Chi: You serious? That's exciting. What kind of business?

季薇：你講真的？那真令人興奮。是什麼樣的公司啊？

Steve: Investigating **paranormal** activity.

史提夫：調查超自然現象。

Chi: PARANORMAL?

季薇：超自然？

Steve: Yeah, a couple friends and I have been doing it for quite some time. We have people send in requests to have their "haunted" properties looked at. We would go in and set up equipments to try to capture and record any abnormal activities. We analyze the data gathered and send them out to other professionals for **cross** examination. I really enjoy what we do and I want to take this hobby of mine to the next level.

史提夫：是啊，我與幾位朋友從事這類的調查已有一陣子了。人們會要求我們去勘察他們的「鬼屋」，然後我們就到房子裡面架設器材，試圖拍攝與紀錄任何不正常的活動。接下來我們會分析蒐集到的數據，並送到其他專家那裡作交叉檢驗。我真的很喜歡我們做的這些事，而我想把這項個人嗜好提升到另一個境界。

Chi: I thought you were taking criminal justice?

季薇：我以為你在進修犯罪司法學？

Steve: I am, but I'm also taking business management classes. And you know what? Last week, we recorded a deep voice—in an empty house—that said, "Go away!"

史提夫：我是啊，不過我也同時在唸商業管理的課程。還有我告訴妳喔，上星期，我們錄到一個低沈的聲音一在一間空洞洞的房子內一說：「滾遠點！」

Chi: (**Gasps.**) Whoa!

季薇：（屏息。）哇！

Steve: I know, <u>isn't that something?</u> We haven't had much success with image recording though. Most of the time it's just **fireflies** and rats.

史提夫：我知道，超酷的對吧？不過我們在影像紀錄這方面還沒有什麼成功的例子，大多時候只是螢火蟲跟老鼠。

Chi: You know what? Right now we happen to have a promotion for new business accounts. If you really want to set up the business, you should open the account now to take advantage of that promotion.

季薇：嘿你曉得嗎？我們現在剛好有個促銷新公司帳戶的活動。如果你真的想要開公司，你應該把握這個機會，現在就開個帳戶。

Steve: What kind of promotion is it?

史提夫：是什麼樣的促銷活動啊？

Chi: (Pulls out the flyer.) The campaign says that once the business account is

季薇：（取出宣傳單。）活動內容是，在開立公司帳戶之

set up, as soon as the account owner uses our on-line bill pay twice, the bank will deposit two hundred dollars into the account.

後，一旦帳戶持有人使用了兩次網上付帳單的功能，銀行就會存兩百元到這個帳戶裡。

Steve: Really? I'm really interested. How long is the promotion? I'll have to talk to my friends about it.

史提夫：真的嗎？我很感興趣。這個促銷活動會持續多久？我要跟我的朋友商量看看。

Chi: It goes on till the end of this month.

季薇：一直到這個月底為止。

Steve: I'll be back before that. (Gathering the stacked coins.) See you later!

史提夫：月底前我會再過來。（將成堆的錢幣收起來。）晚點見！

Chi: See you!

季薇：再見！

單字 *Vocabulary*

- **slow** [slo] **adj.** 生意清淡的、沒有很多交易或活動的
- **paranormal** [ˋpærəˏnɔrml̩] **adj.** 超自然的、目前科學無法解釋的（字首 para 有「在... 旁邊的」及「超越」的意思，para+normal 直接翻譯成「在正常的旁邊」或「超越正常的」，故引申意義為「超自然的」。）
- **cross** [krɔs] **adj.** 交叉的、交互的
- **gasp** [gæsp] **v.** （因恐懼、驚訝引起的）屏息、倒抽一口氣
- **firefly** [ˋfaɪrˏflaɪ] **n.** 螢火蟲

167

日 常用語 Common Expressions

Isn't that something?

超酷的對吧？很誇張吧？（形容某件非比尋常或令人印象深刻的事物。）

好 用句型 Useful Sentences

Any plans for the summer? 這個夏天有什麼計畫嗎？

（句中"for the summer"可換成其他不同的時段，如later, this afternoon, for the evening, for the rest of the day … 等）

你還可以這樣說

What are you doing afterwards?

Doing anything fun this weekend?

You got plans after your shift?

例句

A: Any fun plans after work, Michelle?

下班後有什麼好玩的計畫嗎，蜜雪兒？

B: I am going to the shop and get a piñata! Tomorrow's my daughter's birthday.

我要去店裡買一個皮納塔！明天是我女兒生日。

（作者按：「皮納塔」，唸作[pɪn `jɑdɑ]，是一種以碎彩紙做的玩具，內部裝滿糖果，在生日宴會上被懸掛於半空中，由眼睛被蒙起來的小壽星，按照眾人指示以棒子揮打，一旦打中了，裡面的糖果就會從破洞中掉出來。）

開立公司銀行帳戶的幾個要件

一般説來，會到銀行來開戶的公司行號大部份都是新成立的公司（也有很小的一部份是已成立一段時間的商家，因為不滿意現在銀行的服務所以換到不同的銀行），而這些新鮮人老闆，對於如何設立一個公司帳戶的細節不會很清楚，這時如果身為銀行行員的你，能給他們一些基本的指示，對雙方未來的合作會有很大的幫助。大致上，銀行開立公司戶需要以下幾份資料：

一、公司的型態。在美國，做生意或成立組織團體有幾種常見的型態：*sole proprietor*（又稱 *DBA*，為 *Doing Business As* 的縮寫，即老闆一人獨資並承擔所有風險的公司）、*partnership*（合夥，由兩人或兩人以上分攤成本、勞力、盈虧和風險）、*limited liability corporation*（縮寫為 *LLC*，意思是「有限股份公司」）、*limited company*（常簡寫為 *Ltd.*，取自第一個字 *limited* 的簡寫，意思是「有限公司」）、*corporation*（常簡寫為 *corp.*，唸成[kɔrp]，意思是「企業」或「股份公司」，是這幾個型態中結構最複雜的一種）以及 *nonprofit*（非營利組織）。來開戶的老闆必須告訴銀行人員，自己公司的型態是屬於哪一種。

二、公司的名稱。公司準備成立之前，新老闆們都必須到公司所在地的州秘書長（*Secretary of State*）網站上登記一個公司名稱。請老闆在登記後將州立登記證明（*state registration*）的那頁列印出來，提供給銀行以確認公司的名字。

三、公司的「生日」。公司的生日也就是公司的成立日期，這項資料通常可以在公司/組織條款（*articles of incorporation* 或 *articles of organization*）上找到。

　　四、公司的報稅號碼。每一個在美國合法居留的人士都有一個社會安全號碼（*social security number*），這個號碼是用來辨識個人及報稅用的；同樣地，每一個公司行號也會有一個報稅用的號碼，它叫做雇主辨識號碼（*employer identification number*，簡稱 *EIN*），新公司的老闆必須到國稅局（*Internal Revenue Service*，簡稱 *IRS*）的網站上去申請這個號碼，然後提供給銀行開戶。

01
Chapter

02
Chapter

03
Chapter

04
Chapter

05
Chapter

06
Chapter

6.4 The Long Way Around

 對話 Dialogue

Mr. Rodriguez: I would like to deposit this check and take out three hundred cash, please. (Places a pre-filled deposit ticket and a check on the counter.)

羅德里奎茲先生：我想把這張支票存進去，然後取三百元現金出來，麻煩妳。（將一張預先填好的存款單跟一張支票放在櫃台上。）

Chi: (Looks at the deposit slip.) Mr. Rodriguez, you're depositing to your business checking account, right?

季薇：（看著那張存款單）羅德里奎茲先生，您是想存到您的公司支票帳戶，對嗎？

Mr. Rodriguez: Yes.

羅德里奎茲先生：是的。

Chi: You will have to fill out two separate tickets. One's for the deposit and the other for the withdrawal.

季薇：那您必須填寫兩張分開的單據；一張存款，一張領款。

Mr. Rodriguez: Sure. Whatever works.

羅德里奎茲先生：好，只要能搞定怎麼做都行。

Chi: (Fills out the slips and hand out the withdrawal ticket to the client.) Please sign at the X. (Customer complies. Chi processes the transactions and counts out the money.) Was that all for you, Mr. Rodriguez?

季薇：（填好單子後，將領款單遞出給客人。）請在打叉的地方簽名。（客人照做。季薇輸入交易內容，並算錢給客戶。）還有其他要辦的事嗎，羅德里奎茲先生？

Mr. Rodriguez: Done. Thanks, Chi.

羅德里奎茲先生：沒有了，謝謝妳，季薇。

Chi: No problem. See you next time! (Customer leaves.)

季薇：沒問題。下回再見喔！（客人離去。）

Chi: Michelle, I don't understand why we don't do cash-back deposits for businesses. Why do we need a separate withdrawal ticket?

季薇：蜜雪兒，我不懂，為什麼我們不讓公司行號在存款的同時順便取現金出來。為什麼我們必須另外填寫一張領款單？

Michelle: It is required in order to create a paper **trail**.

蜜雪兒：這是必要的，如此在文件上才有跡可循。

Chi: Paper trail?

季薇：文件上有跡可循？

01 Chapter

02 Chapter

03 Chapter

04 Chapter

05 Chapter

06 Chapter

Michelle: Yes. The bank cannot give cash back on a deposit or cash checks payable to a business because of the possibility of **embezzlement** or tax **evasion**. By separating deposits and withdrawals, we create a paper trail that shows how the funds are being used and distributed.

Kris: (Interrupts.) Plus the checks are made to the business, not the individual. The "company" is not here to cash their checks!

Michelle: Exactly. A company may have multiple signers who can go to a bank and make deposits on behalf of their employer. However if cash-back deposits were allowed, it would be difficult for the company to determine which signer took out the funds. By creating a separate withdrawal ticket with the signer's signature, the bank avoids the **liability** of aiding possible embezzlement and **fraud**.

蜜雪兒：對呀，銀行不允許公司法人在存款時取回一部分現金，或兌現受款人為公司的支票，因為這麼做有協助客戶挪用公款或逃稅的可能。將存款和提款分開來，我們就能在文件上清楚地顯示出資金是如何被使用，以及如何分配的。

克莉絲：（插嘴）再加上那些支票的受款人寫的是公司，不是個人。「公司」又不在這裡幫自己兌現支票！

蜜雪兒：沒錯。一家公司可能有多位具有簽字權力的員工代表老闆來到銀行存錢。然而，要是我們允許他們取回一部分的存款，公司那邊將會有困難確認到底是哪一個人把錢拿出來的，因此銀行會要求客戶另外填一張領款單並簽上提款者的名字，以避免負上協助客戶盜用公款或詐欺的法律責任。

Chi: That makes sense. **Thanks.**

季薇：這樣說的確有道理。謝了。

Michelle: **Any time!**

蜜雪兒：任何時候都歡迎來問！

單字 *Vocabulary*

- **trail** [trel] **n.** 足跡、走過的路線
- **embezzlement** [ɪm `bɛzḷmənt] **n.** 盜用、私自挪用
- **evasion** [ɪ `veʒən] **n.** 逃避、規避
- **liability** [laɪə `bɪlətɪ] **n.**（法律上的）責任
- **fraud** [frɔd] **n.** 詐欺、欺騙行為

好用句型 *Useful Sentences*

That makes sense. 這樣說的確有道理。

你還可以這樣說

That explains it.

That's understandable.

I get it.

例句

A: Why can't we cash a Best Bank check that's made out to "Cash" for someone who doesn't have an account with us?

為什麼我們不能為沒有在我們銀行開戶的人，兌現受款人欄位裡寫「現金」的支票呢？

01 Chapter

02 Chapter

03 Chapter

04 Chapter

05 Chapter

06 Chapter

B: Once the check is cashed, the money is gone. Since we don't have an account with that person we can't get the money back if it is fraud. The risk is too high and therefore we only cash checks for people who are clients or directly named.

一旦支票被兌現，錢就追不回來了。如果之後發現是牽涉詐欺的犯罪行為，由於那人在我們銀行沒有帳戶，銀行無法索回損失的金錢。這種作法的風險太高了，因此我們只幫有帳戶的客人，或是其姓名直接被寫在受款人欄位內的人兌現支票。

A: That makes sense. I'll be careful not to do that.

這樣說的確有道理。我得小心別那麼做。

第三方支票

　　在「公司戶交易」的第一篇對話裡我曾提到班尼的洋酒量販店會收取客人的薪資支票，然後將其存入公司的銀行帳戶。問題來了，這些薪資支票原本都是寫給不同的人，班尼的公司怎麼能把它們當作自己的錢收下呢？這裡我們就要來談談一種稱為「背書轉讓」的程序：

　　假設現在有一張支票是由發票人A寫給受款人B，但是由於某種原因，B希望把這張支票上的金額送給C；這時B和C可以怎麼做呢？答案是B可以在支票背面的簽名欄位中寫下這一行字樣："*Pay to the order of*"，緊接在 *of* 之後，或下一行裡寫C的全名，然後在下下一行裡B簽自己的名。之後C就可以拿這張支票到銀行，在B的簽名下面簽自己的名字，交給櫃員兌現或存入自己的帳戶，完成整道背書轉讓的程序。

　　由於這種情況牽涉到三方：發票人A、第一位受款人B、和後來追加的第二位受款人C，受款人C就是所謂的第三方（*the third party*），因此這一類的支票被統稱為"*third-party check*"。

　　然而，近來由於侵占與盜竊的案例頻頻發生，很多銀行為了避免法律上的糾紛，已經開始不接受third-party checks了，所以若是你收到了這樣的一張支票，或是你想把自己的支票轉讓給別人，在你做任何動作之前，最好先與銀行確認他們是否願意收這類支票："*My co-worker endorsed the check over to me. Can I cash it here?*"（我同事把這張支票背書轉讓給我，我能在這裡兌現嗎？）或者"*I would like to sign my check over to my wife. What do I need to do?*"（我想把我的支票轉讓給我太太，我該怎麼做？）

Chapter 07

Monetary Instruments

支付工具

7.1 As Good as Cash

對話 Dialogue

Chi: Hi, Mr. Donegan, I haven't seen you in a while!

季薇：嗨，唐尼根先生，我好久沒見到您了！

Mr. Donegan: Yeah, I have been quite busy for the past few weeks.

唐尼根先生：是啊，過去的幾個禮拜以來我都很忙。

Chi: I hope it was a "good busy."

季薇：我希望您的忙碌是那種有建設性的忙碌噢。

Mr. Donegan: (Smiles.) Yes, it was. Thank you.

唐尼根先生：（微笑。）是，是那種有建設性的忙碌，謝謝。

Chi: So what can I do for you today?

季薇：所以今天您想辦什麼事呢？

Mr. Donegan: I would like to get a bank check for three thousand dollars, please.

唐尼根先生：我想買一張三千元的銀行本票。

Chi: Of course. And who is the payee gonna be?

季薇：好的，那受款人要寫誰？

Mr. Donegan: The payee is "Berkeley **Remodeling** Inc." Here's their card. (Shows Chi the business title.)

唐尼根先生：受款人寫「柏克萊房屋改建工程公司」。這是他們的名片。（給季薇看公司的名稱。）

Chi: Thanks. Normally there's a seven-dollar fee for a cashier's check, but because you have a **premier** account, Mr. Donegan, the bank will **waive** the fee for you. Your total is three thousand dollars, and how would you like to pay for the check?

季薇：謝謝。通常銀行本票一張的費用是七塊錢，但由於您持有我們的尊榮帳戶，唐尼根先生，銀行不收您這部份的費用。您的總額是三千元，您想要怎麼付款呢？

Mr. Donegan: You can debit my checking account.

唐尼根先生：妳就從我的支票帳戶裡面扣吧。

Chi: Sure. (Starts processing the transaction.) So, let me guess. You're **remodeling** your home?

季薇：好。（開始輸入交易內容。）所以，讓我猜猜看，您在重新裝修您的家？

07 Chapter

08 Chapter

09 Chapter

10 Chapter

11 Chapter

12 Chapter

13 Chapter

Mr. Donegan: Yes, my wife and I are re-modeling both of our bathrooms and the kitchen. This is the first payment.

唐尼根先生：是的，我太太跟我準備把我們的兩間浴室跟廚房都作改建。這是第一筆費用。

Chi: Ooooo, how exciting!

季薇：唔唔唔唔，好令人興奮喔！

Mr. Donegan: Quite. Marge has always wanted a new kitchen. I figured we've waited long enough. We're both retired and if we don't do it now, we will never get to enjoy the money we've saved over the years. The thing is, we may have to stay in a hotel nearby once the construction starts.

唐尼根先生：非常令人興奮。瑪姬一直想要有個新廚房，我想我們等得也夠久啦。我們倆都退休了，如果不現在做的話，我們就沒有機會去享受這麼多年來努力存下來的錢了。唯一一點是，一旦工程開始，我們也許必須搬到臨近的旅館去住。

Chi: I imagine it's going to be a beautiful kitchen when it's done!

季薇：我想等整個做好以後，一定會是個很漂亮的廚房！

Mr. Donegan: (Nodding.) I think so, too.

唐尼根先生：（點頭。）我也這麼認為。

Chi: Here's your bank check for three thousand, Mr. Donegan. The top part is

季薇：這是您的三千元銀行本票，唐尼根先生，上面這一部

for your records. Would you like to have an envelope?

份是給您存底用的。您需要一個信封嗎？

Mr. Donegan: Yes, please.

唐尼根先生：是的，麻煩妳。

Chi: (Hands out the check with a blank envelope.) All set. I'm so happy for you and your wife. Congratulations!

季薇：（將一個空白信封跟支票同時遞出。）都弄好了。我好為您與夫人高興，恭喜喔！

Mr. Donegan: Thank you, Chi. See you next time!

唐尼根先生：謝謝妳，季薇。下回見！

單字 Vocabulary

- **remodel** [rɪ`madḷ] **v.** 改建、改造（房屋等）
- **premier** [prɪ`mɪr] **adj.** 首席的 、最重要或最好的
- **waive** [wev] **v.** 放棄（權利、費用等）、免除

好用句型 Useful Sentences

How would you like to pay for that? 您想要怎麼付款呢？

你還可以這樣說

How would you like to pay?
What payment option do you prefer?
Cash or credit?

例句

A: Check, please.

麻煩結帳。

（作者按：現代英文中把「帳單（bill）」叫成「支票（check）」的原因，乃源自舊時當客人準備結帳時，告知侍者他／她希望以個人支票付款的緣故。）

B: How would you like to pay, sir?

您想要怎麼付款呢，先生？

A: Credit's fine.

就用信用卡。

B: I'll be right back with your receipt.

我一會兒就給您收據。

A: Thank you.

謝謝。

07
Chapter

08
Chapter

09
Chapter

10
Chapter

11
Chapter

12
Chapter

13
Chapter

四種主要支付工具

一般說來，所有美國的銀行都會販售這四種主要的支付工具（*monetary instrument*）：銀行本票、個人本票、旅行支票及國際匯票。容我來為您一一解釋它們的用途和區別：

銀行本票：稱為 *official bank check* 或 *bank check* 或 *cashier's check*。銀行本票是支票的一種，客戶須付每張七至十元的費用來購買這種票券；很多人也許會好奇，為什麼美國人不用自己的個人支票，而還要特地花錢來買銀行本票？原因是客戶只能以兩種方式換取銀行本票：一是用現金，二是用自己存在銀行帳戶內的錢，所以銀行本票基本上就相當是等於現金；再加上支票附有銀行行員的簽名，表示銀行擔保一定會償付票面上的金額，不像個人支票，跳票的風險比較高。牽涉到比較高額的交易時，像買房子或汽車等，大多數賣方都會要求買方以銀行本票來付款。

個人本票： 英文是 *personal money order* 或 *money order*。跟銀行本票一樣，客戶只能用等值的現金或銀行存款來轉換成個人本票，所以相較於私人支票來說，個人本票有銀行的擔保，跳票的風險幾乎沒有（除非是造假）。個人本票與銀行本票的分別在於，第一，個人本票的面額最高只到美金一千元，銀行本票則沒有面額的限制；第二，購買個人本票的手續費較低，通常是四到五元一張，而銀行本票的手續費則介於七至十元間。通常在繳稅、繳罰款甚至是繳房租時，政府機關或房東會要求收取個人本票。

旅行支票：*Traveler's check* 的"*check*"這個字也可拼成"*cheque*"。旅行支票的好處是出國時比身上帶大量現金要安全許多，若是不小心遺失，客人可打電話到幾乎全世界都有據點的美國運通或 *VISA* 服務中心申報，

並於二十四小時內收到補發的支票。然而，由於造假的案例時有多聞，目前越來越多的銀行只幫有帳戶的客人兌現旅行支票，對短期至國外當地旅行的人士形成很大的不便，又加上信用卡的普及及外幣匯兌的便利性提高，旅行支票的熱門程度近年來已大幅降低。

國際匯票：英文為 *foreign draft* 或 *international draft*。這是一種由銀行的國際部門開出的票券，票上的金額單位依照客戶指示的外國貨幣而印製。這種國際支付工具，由於客戶在付錢後，分行必須將表格送至內部作業，再由負責的部門寄到分行，由分行通知客戶去領取，所耗時間較長，且費用昂貴（每次手續費在三十五至四十元美金間），因此在其他各種更快速、更便宜的跨國匯款方式（如國際電匯及旅行支票等）出現以後，漸漸不如以往流行。

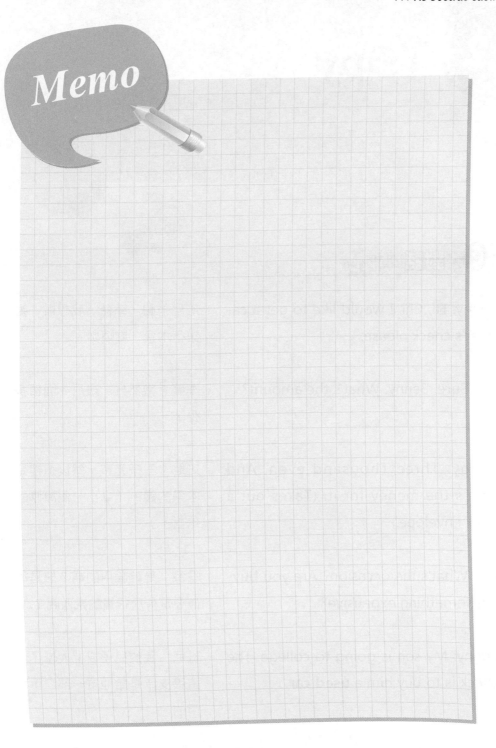

07
Chapter

08
Chapter

09
Chapter

10
Chapter

11
Chapter

12
Chapter

13
Chapter

7.2 I Spy

Benny: Hi, Chi. I would like to get a cashier's check please.

班尼：嗨，季薇，我想辦一張銀行本票，麻煩妳。

Chi: Sure, Benny. What's the amount?

季薇：當然好，班尼。面額多少？

Benny: Three Thousand even. And here's the money for it. (Takes out a thick envelope.)

班尼：三千元整。然後這裡是本票的錢。（拿出一個厚厚的信封。）

Chi: What's the occasion? Are you buying something expensive?

季薇：是幹嘛用的啊？您是準備要買什麼很貴的東西嗎？

Benny: My son is going to college. The check is to buy him a **used car**.

班尼：我的兒子要上大學了。這張支票是給他買一部二手車用的。

Chi: Wow, that's wonderful!

季薇：哇，太好了！

Benny: Yeah, he is a good kid. He got a soccer scholarship and he plans on studying computer programming.

班尼：是啊，他是個好孩子。他剛拿到足球獎學金，而且他在計畫唸電腦程式設計。

Chi: That sounds great. Paul talks about computers all the time.

季薇：那聽來很棒，保羅常常談到電腦喔。

Benny: Really? Whats he do?
　　（作者按："Whats he do?"為"What does he do?"的非正式說法。）

班尼：真的嗎？他是做什麼的？

Chi: He's a physics teacher.

季薇：他是個物理教師。

Benny: It's amazing isn't it? Everything about the future is tech this tech that. It's all a bit overwhelming for me to **take in**, but I **digress** ... may I ask you to make the check out to "**Fremont Honda**"?

班尼：那真是個令人驚奇的領域，不是嗎？所有有關未來的事物淨是科技這個科技那個的，對我來說有點難以一下子全部理解，不過我離題了…我能請妳把支票的受款人寫「本田汽車佛利蒙中心」嗎？

Chi: Of course! (Verifies the cash amount. Processes the transaction.) Will that be all for you today?

季薇：當然！（確認現金總額。輸入交易內容。）您今天就只辦這件事嗎？

07 Chapter

08 Chapter

09 Chapter

10 Chapter

11 Chapter

12 Chapter

13 Chapter

Benny: Yes, thank you.

班尼：是的，謝謝。

Chi: (Hits the enter key. Pauses.) Um, could I please borrow your ID, Benny?

季薇：（按下輸入鍵，停頓了一下。）嗯，我能不能借用一下您的身分證，班尼？

Benny: Okay. (Takes out his driver's license.) Here you go.

班尼：好的。（取出他的駕照。）喏拿去。

Chi: I'm gonna fill out a short report, Benny. This is your current address, right? (Points at the address line on the license.)

季薇：我要填一個簡短的報告，班尼，這是您目前的住址，對嗎？（指著駕照上的地址欄。）

Benny: Yes, it is.

班尼：是。

Chi: (Enters customer's date of birth and address information into computer.) Sorry, this will only take a sec.

季薇：（在電腦上輸入客戶的生日和住址。）抱歉，這只會花一點點的時間。

Benny: Why do you need to file a report?

班尼：為什麼要填報告啊？

Chi: Because of the amount of the check and the fact it was purchased with cash. O...kay, Benny, it's done!

季薇：因為這張支票的面額、還有它是用現金購買的關係。好…了，班尼，報告填好啦！

Benny: That's not too bad. I thought it was going to take longer.

班尼：噢，還好嘛，我還以為要更久。

Chi: Nah, I told you it was gonna be short and sweet! (Grins.) So, are you going to go pick up the car now?

季薇：沒的事，我就跟您說了，填這個報告是三兩下就可以解決的事！（露齒微笑。）所以，您現在就要去買車了嗎？

Benny: No. I have to meet up with my son in **Union City** first.

班尼：還沒，我得先跟我兒子在聯合市碰面。

Chi: Please send him my regards. Congratulations and good luck with school! I will see you next time, Benny

季薇：請向他傳達我的祝福：恭喜，還有祝入學順利！再見囉，班尼。

單字 Vocabulary

- **used car** [`juzt `kɑr] n. 二手車（美國人很少說 "second-hand car"）
- **take in** [ˌtek `ɪn] v. 吸收、理解並接受
- **digress** [daɪ `grɛs] v. 偏離主題、離題
- **Fremont** [`frimɑnt] n. 佛利蒙市。位於北加州舊金山灣區（Bay Area），屬於所謂「矽谷」（Silicon Valley）的一部分。
- **Union City** [`junjən `sɪtɪ] n. 聯合市。佛利蒙市北側相鄰的城市。

 **Phrases**

short and sweet

（形容某道程序，例如一段演講、會議等）簡短又令人愉悅。

好 用句型 *Useful Sentences*

This will only take a second. 這只會花一點點的時間。

你還可以這樣說

Just a moment please.

It'll only take a moment.

This won't take long.

I'll be done before you know it.

例句

A: Mr. Sharp, the bank would like to offer you an upgrade of your personal line of credit! The new rate is going to be just five point nine nine percent. Plus no annual fee!

夏普先生，本銀行想提供您一個私人信用循環帳戶的升級機會！新利率只有百分之五點九九，而且沒有年費！

B: Really?

真的？

A: Yes. With your permission, I can submit the new line for you. This will only take a second.

是的。只要有您的首肯，我就能為您送審申請表。這只會花一點點的時間。

B: Sounds good. I'll wait.

聽來很不錯，我可以等。

07 Chapter

08 Chapter

09 Chapter

10 Chapter

11 Chapter

12 Chapter

13 Chapter

支付工具與洗錢

　　根據1970年起生效的銀行祕密法（*Bank Secrecy Act*，銀行界一般簡稱為 *BSA*），顧客若是於同一個營業日內，在銀行以現金購買總值三千元以上，一萬元以下的銀行本票、個人本票及旅行支票這類的支付工具，行員必須將交易內容與客戶的基本資料記下、填寫報告以供政府查驗（註），這種報告叫做 *Monetary Instrument Check Log* 或 *Monetary Instrument Log*，簡稱為 *MICL* 或 *MIL*。注意這裡「現金」的定義是客人從銀行外面帶進來的現鈔和硬幣；如果客戶使用的是個人支票或提款單來購買支付工具，銀行則不需填寫 *MICL*。

　　這是為什麼呢？因為現金不像那些已經存在帳戶內的金錢，一進一出都有紀錄；循著文件的路線，我們比較容易追查到資金的來源及去向。而政府追蹤金錢出入的目的之一，即是在於防制犯罪份子洗錢。洗錢，英文為 *money laundry*，望文生義就是把不乾淨的錢，洗一洗變成乾淨的錢；不乾淨的錢，指的是從不法行為中產生的利益；而犯罪份子怎麼洗錢呢？其中一種常見的手法，是教唆許多人到銀行開戶，用各種方式把非法的資金存入這些戶頭裡，然後做成各種票據、或以電匯的方式傳送到另一個目的地。這麼做的目的，是因為運輸大量現金容易引起人們的注意，分成小筆小筆的金額，並以不同的方法進入並通過金融機構轉換成不同的形式，可以把這些錢的來源跟去向變得難以追查。

　　註：你或許會問，那超過一萬元的話，政府難道就不查了嗎？答案是任何只要超過美金一萬元的「現金交易」，不論你是領出一萬元零一分的現金、存入一萬元零一分的現金、甚至是領出五千元現金同一天內又存入五千零一分的現金（牽涉的金額總和超過一萬元），銀行都要填一份稱為Currency Transaction Report，簡稱為CTR的報告。這種報告與MICL一樣都是屬於銀行祕密法的一部份。

7.3 Secured Alternative

 **對話** Dialogue

Miss White: Hey, Chi, can I get a, um, what's that called, an order check? Or something of that nature.

懷特小姐：嘿，季薇，我能不能買一張，嗯，那個叫什麼來著，本票？或是類似那樣子的東西。

Chi: You mean a "personal money order"?

季薇：妳是指「個人本票」嗎？

Miss White: YES! THAT! Sorry, this is my first time buying a personal money order.

懷特小姐：對對！就是那個！不好意思，這是我第一次購買個人本票。

Chi: It's okay. There's first time for everything. I wouldn't know what a money order is if I didn't work here! How much do you want me to put on it?

季薇：沒關係，凡事皆有第一次。我要不是因為在這邊上班，也不會知道什麼是本票！妳想要多少錢的個人本票？

Miss White: Nine hundred and fifty. Here, (takes out a blank check) I brought my own check. Who should I make it out to?

懷特小姐：九百五十元。這裡，（拿出一張空白支票）我帶了我自己的支票來。受款人要寫誰？

Chi: You can make it out to the bank or yourself. Either way is fine. Personal money orders cost five bucks a piece, so you'll need to add that to your total.

季薇：妳可以寫我們銀行或寫妳自己，兩種方式哪一種都行。個人本票一張的費用是五塊錢，所以妳必須把費用加到總金額上去。

Miss White: WHHAAAAT? Five dollars? That's so expensive! (Frowns.)

懷特小姐：什什什麼麼？五塊錢？那麼貴！（皺眉。）

Chi: Can the person you're paying take your check instead?

季薇：收款的對方能不能改收妳的個人支票哇？

Miss White: No. (Sighs.) My last rent check didn't **go through** so my **landlord** requested that I mail him a money order. He doesn't take cash, either. (Fills out the check and passes it to Chi.)

懷特小姐：不能。（歎氣。）我上一次付房租用的支票跳票了，因此房東要求我寄給他一張個人本票。他也不收現金。（把支票填好遞給季薇。）

Chi: I am sorry to hear that.

季薇：聽到妳說的這種情形我很難過。

Miss White: It's not your fault. I'll just suck it up and pay the five bucks.

懷特小姐：不是妳的錯啦。啊我就乖乖認命付這五塊錢吧。

Chi: So what happened to the line of credit? Did Mike help you with the application?

季薇：那個循環信用帳戶後來怎樣了？麥可有幫妳申請嗎？

Miss White: He did, but my credit history was not long enough so it was declined. Mike got me a student credit card instead. He said I could build my credit this way and maybe later on try again.

懷特小姐：他有啊，可是我的個人信用歷史不夠長，所以被退件了。麥可改幫我申請到一張學生信用卡。他說我可以這種方式建立信用紀錄，也許晚點再試。

Chi: That's a good idea. (Finishes the transaction and hands over a printed check.)

季薇：好點子。（結束交易內容並拿出一張印好的支票。）

Miss White: Is that it? Do I need to fill out the payee myself?

懷特小姐：這樣子就好了？我要自己填入受款人的名字嗎？

Chi: Yes. Also, you will need to sigh your name. (Points to the signature line on the front.)

季薇：是的。還有，妳還要簽上妳的姓名。（指著支票正面的簽名欄。）

Miss White: Thanks, Chi. (Writes the apartment's name on the check and puts it in a stamped envelope.) You've been very helpful. I'll see you around.

懷特小姐：謝啦，季薇。（在支票上填寫公寓的名稱，並把它放入一個貼了郵票的信封。）妳的服務真好，下次見喔。

Chi: Take care, Miss White. See you next time!

季薇：保重，懷特小姐，下回見！

單字 Vocabulary

- **go through** [ˋgo ˋθru] **v.** 通過、被認可接受
- **landlord** [ˋlæn(d)ˌlord] **n.** 房東、地主

片語 Phrases

suck it up 接受令人不舒服的事實。

（作者按：這句用語原來是在教人遇到挫折時深吸一口氣，挺起胸膛去面對問題。"It"指的是胸腔，suck it up 即 suck up your chest。）

of that nature 具有那種性質的（東西）、類似那樣子的

日常用語 Common Expressions

There's first time for everything. 凡事都有第一次。

職 場須知 Business Know-how

The Importance of Follow-Up 追蹤客戶後續狀況的重要性

Follow-up says that you care. It says that you remember what your customer has said to you previously, and that you want to earn and retain their business. Asking follow-up questions opens a conversation and can save a sale that may have been lost due to miscommunication or lack of communication. Plus, you may discover more sales opportunities and valuable feedback in the process. So don't be afraid to ask the customer. Find out what they are thinking, what they are doing, and figure out what you can do to help move things along.

追蹤客戶後續情形的作為顯示出你關心，它表示你記得顧客對你說過的事，以及你希望贏得並保持繼續跟他們做生意的機會。詢問客戶的後續狀況不但能展開新的對話，並可能挽回一筆因溝通不良或缺少溝通而錯失的生意。另外，你還可能在過程中發現更多的銷售機會與顧客的寶貴意見，所以不要怕去問你的客人，找出他們在想什麼、在做什麼，還有你能提供什麼樣的協助，好讓事情進展地更順利。

實境對話

A: Benny, last time we talked about your 401(k). Have you spoken with Pierre about rolling it over?

班尼，上次我們談到了您的401(k)退休金帳戶，您後來有沒有跟皮耶討論把那裡面的錢整筆轉出到個人退休帳戶的事啊？

B: I just had an appointment with him this past Friday.

上個禮拜五我才跟他碰面談過。

A: How did it go?

談的怎樣？

B: It went well. My wife is opening an account with him, too.

十分順利。我太太也準備要跟他開戶呢。

07
Chapter

08
Chapter

09
Chapter

10
Chapter

11
Chapter

12
Chapter

13
Chapter

是 "Cleared"，還是 "Available"？

一次有位韓國的留學生拿了四張淺藍色、印著 *"International Money Order"* 字樣的支票到我們分行來兌現。由於從來沒有見過這種樣子的個人本票，我於是將她的支票交給經理作更進一步的鑑斷，經理表示她也沒看過這樣的所謂國際個人本票（註），因此我們就跟這個女孩說，我們沒辦法立刻兌現這些支票，而如果她堅持的話，我們可以把支票存到她帳戶裡，等到銀行確定收到款項之後，她再回來提款。女學生同意。

三個禮拜之後，就當我差不多快忘光這件事的時候，某天這個女生又出現在我們的大廳裡，然而這回她人一現身，就立即被請到經理辦公室裡私下談話。事後，經理告訴我，這四張國際本票經證實是偽造的假支票，而女學生表示，她在 *eBay* 上出售了數個名牌皮包，買方告訴她她可以拿這些支票到銀行換錢。

很多人以為，只要支票上面印有 *Cashier's Checks* 或 *Money Order* 這些字樣，銀行就得毫無異議地立刻付款，或者，如果行員願意幫你把這些支票存進戶頭，而幾天後帳戶餘額顯示金額可以使用，就代表這些本票沒問題，這些想法其實是錯誤的。現在歹徒只要有一台印表機，搭配一組支票印製軟體，就可以印出惟妙惟肖的銀行或個人本票；再加上大多數人不清楚什麼時候一張支票是 *"cleared"*，跟什麼時候支票的金額是 *"available"*，不法份子就利用這個盲點來詐騙受害者。

當我們說某張支票 *has been cleared*，意思是收到這張支票的銀行，已經跟原來發出支票的銀行結清、取得款項了；只有當走到這一步，我們才能確定支票是真的（美國人這時說 *"The check is good."*）。然而按照美國法律，銀行在接受了支票後，必須於一到五個工作天內就能讓客戶取

款，問題是，*check clearing* 這個過程花費的時間，從數天到一整個月都有可能，也就是說，很多時候銀行在尚未真正向發票銀行拿錢之前，就必須依法先容許客人提款出來。許多人一見到帳戶明細上顯示*"The funds are available,"* 就放心地把貨物寄給買方，或按照對方的指示匯回多餘的款項，結果等到銀行跟原發票銀行要不到錢，把偽造的本票退回來之後，才發現自己上了當。

女學生這個故事給我們的教訓是，不要輕易接受陌生人的支票（即便是標明了銀行或個人本票）、注意支票上寫的發票銀行地點，如果不是當地的支票，或是從國外銀行發出來的也都不能收、對於票面上填寫的金額比實際成交金額還多的支票要特別小心，歹徒可能在藉此誘引貪心的賣家。

註：個人本票通常的來源為：國內銀行、郵局、和匯款公司如 Western Union 與 MoneyGram 這三類機構，大部份行員在經手支票幾個月後，就會熟悉這些機構所販賣的個人本票獨特的色彩和設計。

07
Chapter

08
Chapter

09
Chapter

10
Chapter

11
Chapter

12
Chapter

13
Chapter

7.4 Going Abroad

對話 Dialogue

Mrs. Robinson: (Approaches the counter.) Excuse me, do you sell traveler's cheques here?

羅賓森太太：（走到櫃台前。）不好意思，妳們這裡有在賣旅行支票嗎？

Chi: (Turns around.) Oh, hi, Mrs. Robinson. Sorry I was putting some coins away. Yes, we do.

季薇：（轉身。）噢，嗨，羅賓森太太。抱歉我正在把硬幣擺到櫃子裡。是的，我們有賣。

Mrs. Robinson: How much are they?

羅賓森太太：它們多少錢？

Chi: For single-signer cheques, the fee is two percent of the cheques' value; for double-signer cheques, two point five percent.

季薇：一人簽名的旅行支票，費用是支票總額的百分之二；兩人簽名的旅行支票，百分之二點五。

Mrs. Robinson: Let me get five hundred's worth. Single signer.

羅賓森太太：我要總值五百元、一人簽名的旅行支票。

Chi: Pardon me for a moment, the cheques are in the vault, I'll be right back.

季薇：恕我離開一下，支票在金庫裡，我馬上就回來。

Mrs. Robinson: Very well.

羅賓森太太：好。

A minute later, Chi returns with a white box with the "American Express" logo on top. She takes out several packages.

一分鐘後，季薇手上捧著一個白色的盒子回來，盒子上印有「美國運通」的標誌。她取出數個包裹。

Chi: Mrs. Robinson, we have a few different **denominations**. Do you have a preference?

季薇：羅賓森太太，我們有幾種不同的面額，您有特別的偏好嗎？

Mrs. Robinson: What are my options?

羅賓森太太：我有哪些選擇？

Chi: They come in twenties, fifties, and hundreds.

季薇：支票的面額有二十元、五十元、以及一百元的。

Mrs. Robinson: I'll take the fifties. Give me two of those. (Points at the two-hundred-fifty packs.)

羅賓森太太：我就拿五十元的，給我那個兩份。（指著兩百五十元的包裹。）

Chi: Definitely. Your total is five hundred and ten, Mrs. Robinson. (Starts to process.)

季薇：好的。您的總金額是五百一十元，羅賓森太太。（開始輸入交易。）

Mrs. Robinson: Okay. (Counts out the money.)

羅賓森太太：好。（數錢。）

Chi: (Breaks the **seal** of the packages and takes out a form.) Please fill out the requested information ...

季薇：（撕開包裹的封條並取出一張表格。）請填寫所需的資料…

Mrs. Robinson: (Cell phone rings.) Hold on. (Answers the phone.) Marisa Robinson. Oh, yes ... Uh-huh. Um. No? Okay, I guess not. All right, I'll see you when I get home. Bye. (Put the phone down.) Sorry, Chi, my husband just called and he says to **hold off** on the purchase. Can we cancel it?

羅賓森太太：（手機響起。）等一下。（接聽電話。）瑪麗莎‧羅賓森。噢，是…嗯哼。嗯，不要？好吧，我猜那就不要囉。好啦，我等下就回家。掰。（把手機放下。）抱歉，季薇，我先生剛打電話來，他說先暫緩買旅行支票的事。我們能不能取消？

Chi: Not a problem.

季薇：沒問題。

Mrs. Robinson: We can use our debit card overseas, right?

羅賓森太太：我們可以在海外使用金融卡，對嗎？

Chi: Definitely. I recommend that you call the number on the back of your card and inform the bank when and where you are going, that way your card won't get **locked out**.

季薇：當然可以。我建議您打您卡片背面上的號碼，告知銀行方面您旅行的時間和地點，以避免鎖卡。

Mrs. Robinson: Thanks, I'll do that. I've got to go now. I still may come back for those cheques though. I'll let you know!

羅賓森太太：謝謝，我會。我得走了。不過我仍然有可能回來買那些支票，我會再通知妳！

單字 Vocabulary

- **denomination** [dɪ ˌnɑmə `neʃən] n. （貨幣等的）單位、面額
- **seal** [sil] n. 封條、封紙
- **hold off** [`hold `ɔf] v. 暫停、拖延
- **lock out** [`lɑk `aʊt] v. 將（某人或物）鎖於門外

好用句型 Useful Sentences

What are my options? 我有哪些選擇？

你還可以這樣說

What choices do I have?

What selections are available?

例句

(Business meeting at a restaurant.)（在餐廳內進行商務會談。）

A: Mm, I guess today I'll have the house salad!

嗯，我猜我今天就點主廚沙拉吧！

B: What kind of dressing?

要什麼樣的沙拉醬呢？

A: What are my options?

我有哪些選擇？

B: We have ranch, Italian, blue cheese and raspberry vinaigrette.

我們有鄉村、義大利、藍紋乳酪跟覆盆子醬。

A: Blue cheese, please.

藍乳酪醬，麻煩你。

07
Chapter

08
Chapter

09
Chapter

10
Chapter

11
Chapter

12
Chapter

13
Chapter

旅行支票的用法

　　旅行支票有三種，第一種是最普遍的一人簽名式支票，第二種是兩人簽名式，第三種是禮物支票。今天就讓我來介紹它們的用法吧：

　　一人簽名式：客人在購買時，必須立刻在櫃員的面前，把自己的名字簽在支票的上方；注意這時還不要填日期，日期等到準備好要兌現的時候再填。等到要兌現時，將你的支票帶到銀行，當著櫃台出納員的面前，在支票中間那一行受款人欄，也就是 *pay to the order of* 字樣旁的空格裡，以印刷體寫上自己的名字，然後在最底下的簽名處，按照原先在支票上方簽名的方式，再簽一次名。這麼做的原因，是好讓幫你兌現支票的行員能藉由比對兩次的簽名樣式，來確認你是這張旅行支票的持有人。

　　兩人簽名式：只要付比一人簽名式支票多一點點的費用，購買旅行支票的客人就能與跟自己同行的伴侶分享這些支票。使用的方式是，購買人在銀行櫃員面前，當場在支票的最上方簽名（有兩個預留空位的簽名欄），買好以後再交給第二位支票的使用人，於另一個簽名欄中簽名（第二位使用者不須在購票時當場簽名）。準備兌現支票的時候，兩位使用者任何之一皆可單獨至銀行或特約兌換處，在中間受款人欄寫上自己的印刷體姓名，填入日期，然後在最下方簽名，完成兌現的程序。

　　禮物支票：英文是 *gift check*。購買人不用在支票上簽名，只需在中間受款人處以印刷體寫上接受這張禮物支票的人全名。接受禮物支票的人在收到支票後，叼先在上方空白處簽名，然後帶著它到銀行，再一次當著櫃員的面在支票下方簽名。

　　最後要提醒你的一點是，購買旅行支票之後，存根那一張要跟支票分開，另外收好帶在身上。存根上印有支票的序號以及全球客服中心的電話，萬一遺失了支票，你可以根據支票的序號來申請補發。

Chapter 08

Training for Career Advancement

為升職做準備

8.1 Great Expectations

對話 Dialogue

At the dinner table.	在餐桌上。
Chi: You remember Mike, right?	季薇：你記得麥可，對吧？
Paul: That guy at the bank?	保羅：在銀行做事的那個男生？
Chi: Yeah. Today, he told me that he had spoken with Robert about leaving!	季薇：是啊。今天他告訴我，他已經跟勞勃提出離職的事了！
Paul: And?	保羅：還有呢？
Chi: He said he wanted to go back to school full-time.	季薇：他說他想回學校做全職學生。

Paul: You should go to Robert and tell him you want Mike's job.

保羅：妳應該去跟勞勃講妳想要麥可的工作。

Chi: Me telling Robert WHAT? Are you crazy? I can't do that!

季薇：我跟勞勃講啥？你瘋了嗎？我不能那麼做！

Paul: Why not?

保羅：為什麼不能？

Chi: Um, I don't know, it doesn't seem right. Mike is not gone yet and I'm already asking for his position!

季薇：嗯，我不知道，這樣感覺很怪吧，麥可人還沒走，我就已經在爭取他的職位了！

Paul: Do you like banking or not?

保羅：妳到底喜不喜歡在銀行做事啊？

Chi: Of course I do. (Whispers.) I love it.

季薇：當然哪。（低聲說）這是我熱愛的工作。

Paul: Then go talk to Robert, before they find someone else.

保羅：那妳就在他們找到別人之前，去跟勞勃談。

Chi: But I don't have any training.

季薇：可是我一點訓練背景也沒有。

Paul: They will train you. And I know they like you. You are their brightest

保羅：他們會訓練妳。還有我知道他們喜歡妳，妳是他們最

07 Chapter

08 Chapter

09 Chapter

10 Chapter

11 Chapter

12 Chapter

13 Chapter

and most hard-working employee. If they fail to see that, it's their loss.

聰明、最努力工作的員工,如果他們沒辦法看到這點,是他們的損失。

Chi: What ... what should I say?

季薇:那…我要講什麼?

Paul: Just tell Robert that you want Mike's job and ask him what you need to do.

保羅:就跟勞勃講妳想要麥可的職位,然後問他妳需要做什麼。

Chi: Just like that?

季薇:就那樣子?

Paul: Yes. Just like that and nothing else. Pay attention to what he says then go back to work. Tell me you will talk to him tomorrow.

保羅:對,就那樣,其餘什麼都不用說。仔細聽他接下來說的話然後回到妳的工作崗位上繼續做事。告訴我妳明天就會去跟他談。

Chi: TOMORROW?

季薇:明天?

Paul: YES, tomorrow. Let's **get to** it! Chop, chop, there's no time like the present.

保羅:沒錯,明天。廢話不多說趕快開始做!快,快,沒有比現在更好的時候了。

Chi: But ... what about ...

季薇:但…要是…

Paul: DO YOU LOVE BANKING OR NOT?

保羅：銀行到底是不是妳熱愛的事業啊？

Chi: YES.

季薇：是。

Paul: Then shut up. I don't want to hear another word. Leaders move when the time is ripe and that time is tomorrow.

保羅：那就閉嘴，我不想再聽到任何藉口。領導者見到時機成熟的時候就立刻行動，而這個時機正是明天。

Chi: Right. Let's do this!

季薇：好，我就給它撂下去！

單字 Vocabulary

• **get to** [ˋɡɛt ˋtu] **v.** 著手、開始做

日常用語 Common Expressions

Chop, chop! 快，快！
There's no time like the present. 沒有比現在更好的時候了。
（用來鼓勵人不要拖延、立刻就著手進行某件事。）

好用句型 Useful Sentences

How to Ask for Training 主動要求受訓的機會

What do I need to do to train for Mike's old job?
How do I apply for the relationship manager position?
I would like to request additional training in order to become a

manager. What do I do?

例句

A: I heard Mike's leaving. If I want to became the new RM, what do I need to do?

我聽說麥可要離職。如果我想成為新的客服經理，我要怎麼做？

B: I'm glad to hear that you want to advance in your career. Currently there are some courses available online and I want you to take those first. Being a relationship manager is not easy, but we will get you there!

我很高興聽到妳有向上爬升的意願。目前網路上有些課程開放供人選讀，我要妳先去唸一下那些課程。做客服經理不是件容易的事，但我們會協助妳！

A: Thank you, Robert. I really look forward to it.

謝謝你，勞勃，我真的很期待接下來的訓練。

07
Chapter

08
Chapter

09
Chapter

10
Chapter

11
Chapter

12
Chapter

13
Chapter

愛在心裡口難開？

季薇從剛進銀行時被主任唸說聲音太小，到後來被分行經理誇獎我對自動櫃員機是一學就上手，擢升我為後備主任出納，這中間只不過短短五個月的時間。我們亞州人學習速度快、對於上司及同事的教訓都肯虛心接受、又比別人願意努力工作，是國際間眾所皆知的「好員工」。但是一片望過去，在美國企業（*Corporate America*）中擔任領導階級的東方人卻是少之又少，究竟原因何在呢？答案之一，在於我們不敢問。

而不敢問的原因之一，是我們不知道怎麼問。

其實，這個我們覺得最難的問題，對美國人來說是最簡單的問題。他們從小就被訓練成，如果想要什麼東西，就直接向大人要；如果直接要要不到，他們就問：那我要怎麼做，才能得到我想要的那個東西？亞州人的教育則不同，我們從小被教要乖、要聽話，如果你守規矩、很有耐心地等，總有一天你想要的事情會發生... 錯！在這個世界上，臺灣也好，美國也好，你如果想要什麼，都要由你自己去爭取、去問、去做，事情才會發生。少之又少的老闆會主動來問你要不要升遷或加薪。跟一般人所想不同的是，在成人的商業世界裡，具有主控權的那個人其實是你，你想不想要升遷，你想不想要加薪，如果你想要，那你願不願意採取行動，你願不願意走進老闆的辦公室說：*I want to apply for this position. What do I need to do?*

8.2 The Padawan

Title Note:

Padawan發音為[`pædə ˌwɑn]，意思是「學生」。這個名詞源自於電影《星際大戰》，指跟隨絕地武士學習的絕地學徒。

 **對話** Dialogue

Mike: Hey, Chi, you have a moment?

麥可：嘿，季薇，妳有空嗎？

Chi: Yeah.

季薇：有啊。

Mike: Over here please. (Waves Chi over to desk.)

麥可：麻煩妳過來這裡。（搖手示意季薇到他的辦公桌旁。）

Chi: Sure. (With her drawers and computer screen locked, she walks across the lobby to Mike's desk.)

季薇：好。（把抽屜和電腦螢幕都鎖起來後，她走到大廳另一邊麥可的辦公桌旁。）

Mike: I heard you're interested in this position. (Fingers tab on the plate that says, "Relationship Manager" placed on his desk.)

麥可：我聽說妳對這個職位很感興趣。（手指頭敲著他桌上那個印著「客服經理」的名牌。）

Chi: (Shyly) Yes.

季薇：（靦腆地）是。

Mike: You know what I think?

麥可：妳知道我心裡怎麼覺得嗎？

Chi: (Nervously) What?

季薇：（緊張）怎樣？

Mike: I think ... I think IT'S GREAT!

麥可：我覺得…我覺得這真是太棒了！

Chi: Really?

季薇：真的？

Mike: I want to be your **mentor.** I'll show you everything I know. There was one time a manager from another district called me on the phone regarding a question about our safe deposit system. He said that our district manager asked him to contact me, saying "I'm not sure about the answer to your question but I'm sure Mike would

麥可：我想做妳的啟蒙導師，我會把我所有的知識都傳授給妳。有一次，某位經理從不同的分區打電話給我，詢問有關保管箱系統的問題，他說是我們的區域經理要他來連絡我的；我們區域經理跟他說：「我不確定你的問題答案是什麼，但是我確定麥可會知

know." I take pride in my knowledge in banking and I think that I am the right man for the job.

道。」我對我的銀行背景知識感到相當自傲，我認為我是妳啟蒙導師的正確人選。

Chi: What about your school?

季薇：那你學校怎麼辦？

Mike: It won't be a problem, I'm taking night classes. Chi, I want YOU to take over this position when I leave. I've talked to Robert and Michelle, from now on, I will spend one hour with you every Tuesday and show you how to open accounts and **navigate** through different internal systems.

麥可：那不成問題，我在唸夜間課程。季薇，當我離開公司的時候，我要妳接手這個職位。我已經跟勞勃還有蜜雪兒談過了，從現在開始，每星期二我都會花一個鐘頭的時間，教妳怎麼開戶，並如何於不同的內部作業系統間通行。

Chi: REALLY?

季薇：真的？

Mike: Yes!

麥可：是啊！

Chi: I ... I don't know what to say.

季薇：我…我不知道該說什麼。

Mike: A simple thank you will do.

麥可：說謝謝就好啦。

Chi: Wow Mike, thank you.

季薇：哇，麥可，謝謝你。

Mike: You're welcome. Your lessons start next week. Read this until then. (Slides a manual over to Chi.)

麥可：不客氣。妳的課程下禮拜開始。在那之前妳先讀這個。（將一本手冊滑過桌面到季薇面前。）

Chi: I can't wait!

季薇：我等不及了！

單字 Vocabulary

- **mentor** [`mɛntɚ] **n.** 指導者、良師
- **navigate** [`nævə͵get] **v.** 操控（交通工具等）以順利通過、航行

日常用語 Common Expressions

I can't wait! 我等不及了！

（表示自己對於即將發生的某件事感到興奮，並迫不及待想要參與。）

好用句型 Useful Sentences

You have a moment? 你有空嗎？

你還可以這樣說

Can I borrow you for a minute?

Can I talk to you for a sec?

Can I see you in my office/ in the break room/ outside?

例句

A: Kris, you have a moment?

克莉絲，妳有空嗎？

B: I'm actually with a customer right now... Give me a second, okay?

事實上我目前有位客戶... 等我一會兒，好嗎？

A: Not a problem. I'll come back later.

沒問題，我等下再過來。

如何在職場中找到你的啟蒙者？

數年前，一位分行經理介紹我看馬修・凱利的《在清潔公司，發現夢想經理人》（*The Dream Manager, by Matthew Kelly*），在書中作者藉由一間清潔公司試圖降低員工離職率的故事，向讀者揭曉了企業留住並激勵人才的祕密：幫助員工達成個人的夢想。

夢想的力量十分巨大，如果員工覺得他們每天都又向朝自己的夢想邁進了一步，人們的鬥志會變得高昂起來，工作的效率會更好，公司發出的紅利增加，使得員工們更想待在原本的公司內。

你、我都有自己的夢想，但當我們任職的公司，不像這本書裡的清潔公司一樣配有「夢想經理」時，我們是不是也能幫自己找到一位夢想經理，帶領我們持續地往目標邁進，並以綜觀大局的角度，提醒我們應該注意的事項，一直到夢想實現的那天呢？

這個「夢想經理」，換句話說，就是商業界中所謂的「啟蒙導師（*mentor*）」。接下來你會問：那我要如何找到一位啟蒙導師？第一步，跟你的老闆坐下來談，告訴他/她你的目標，並誠懇地聽取老闆對你的評估及計畫。你的態度要虛心、表現出積極的活力，但不可咄咄逼人；這時，有些老闆會建議他/她認為能夠幫助你的人士，有些老闆甚至會自告奮勇做你的啟蒙者；如果你是那個萬中選一的幸運兒，能獲得老闆的教導，恭喜你！（有什麼比老闆的親身背書更有力的證明？）而得到其他公司同事作為指導者的人，也恭喜你，這些同事通常在這個行業裡待過一段時間，知識豐富、人際關係廣，相較於老闆本人來得容易親近（你不用怕在他們面前說錯話！），而且畢竟同樣是過來人，也會比較有耐心來教你；沒有立即獲得老闆指派啟蒙者的人，也不用灰心，你的老闆是屬於那

種需要多一點時間來醞釀想法的人，給他們幾天的時間，他們會直接或間接地讓你知道他們的計畫（像我故事中的勞勃！），如果過了一個禮拜都還沒有什麼動靜，你也可以主動出擊，找個適當的時機，問問老闆能不能幫你建議啟蒙導師的人選。

總之，你一定要讓老闆知道你的想法和目標，他/她才能公開並全力地支持你。能夠在公司中獲得一位啟蒙導師是件非常好的事情，這位指導者的聲望會在許多領域裡幫助你，讓你在起跑點就贏過了一大票人；而或許未來的某天，你也會成為別人的啟蒙者，幫助另一個「你」，達成他們的夢想。

——獻給Renée Nicholson，我最棒的啟蒙導師

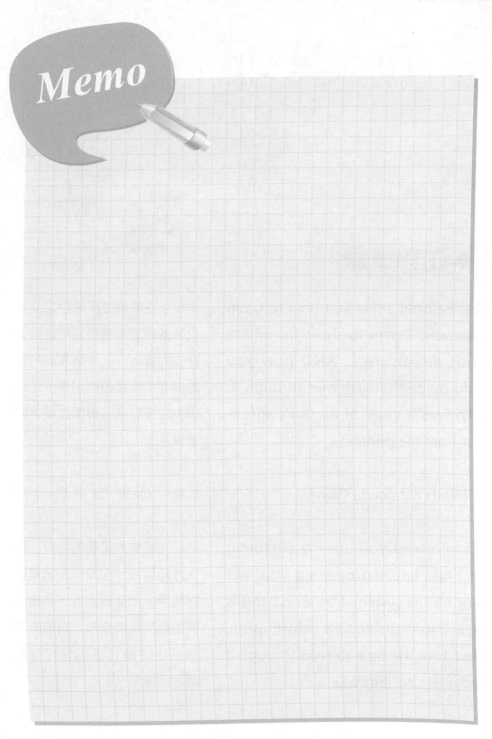

07
Chapter

08
Chapter

09
Chapter

10
Chapter

11
Chapter

12
Chapter

13
Chapter

8.3 Time's Up

Mike: Before I show you how to open an account, I want to show you what's in our disclosure ... AND how you would guide the customer through it. (**Retrieves** a copy of account agreement from the printer.)

麥可：在教妳怎麼開戶之前，我想讓妳看看我們帳戶說明書裡的內容…還有妳應該如何幫助顧客閱讀這份說明書。（從印表機裡取回一份開立帳戶同意書。）

Chi: (Nods her head.) Okay!

季薇：（點頭。）好！

Mike: Pretend you are my customer and I just finished opening your account on the system. Mrs. Borst, this is our account disclosure information. Please take the time to read through it at your leisure. (Smiles.)

麥可：假裝妳是我的客戶，而我才剛剛幫妳在銀行系統裡開好帳戶。伯斯特太太，這是我們的帳戶說明資料，請您有空時抽出時間從頭到尾好好閱讀。（微笑。）

Chi: (Stares at the twenty-some pages of account agreement.) Ha ... I don't think people are gunna take the time to read that.

季薇：（瞪著二十幾頁的帳戶同意書。）哈…我不認為人們會真的花時間去讀這些。

Mike: You're right. Most people don't. So your role is very important. You will read the disclosure to them. (Takes out a **highlighter** from his drawer.) When you explain the terms and conditions to the customer, you will **highlight** the key parts that you know are important to their specific case.

麥可：妳說得對，大部份人不會，所以妳的角色就很重要了，妳會唸這份資料給他們聽。（從抽屜裡取出一支螢光筆。）在妳跟客戶解釋這些條款的時候，可以一邊用螢光筆劃出對那位客人來說特別重要的部份。

Chi: May I have this copy?

季薇：我能不能保留這份複本？

Mike: Sure. Keep it at your station and review it from time to time. It's a great resource for answering customer's questions. Most people are concerned about fees, so start there first. For example: "Mrs. Borst, I would like to remind you that the bank charges a twenty-five dollar early **closeout** fee, should you close the account within

麥可：當然可以。把這份同意書擺在妳的工作枱旁，三不五時拿出來翻閱；對於解答客戶的疑問而言，它是一個很棒的資源。多數的人關心費用這一項，所以妳可以從那裡開始解釋，例如：「伯斯特太太，我要提醒您，若是您在六個月內關閉帳戶，銀行會收取一筆二

the first six months." You're also going to want to spend a little more time on overdrafts. Show them why an overdraft occurs and what they can do to avoid penalties. The more time you spend educating your customers about overdrafts now, the less likely they will come back later with an overdrawn account. Solve their problems before they start.

Chi: Agreed.

Mike: Make sure your customer understand the difference between a "calendar day" and a "business day." Inform them that weekends and holidays are not business days. When they make a deposit on Saturday, they should know that the bank's system has already been switched to Monday. The deposit will be considered as a "Monday" deposit and therefore will not be available for withdrawal until Tuesday. However,

十五元的提早結清帳戶費。」妳也應該在透支這項上多花點時間解釋，告訴他們透支發生的原因，以及如何避免罰款。妳現在花越多時間教育客戶有關透支的知識，未來他們帳戶發生透支的機率就越低。預防勝於治療。

季薇：同意。

麥可：確定妳的客戶瞭解「日曆日」和「營業日」間的不同。告知他們週末和國定假日不是營業日，當他們在星期六來存款時，應該曉得銀行的系統已經調到星期一了，存款將被視為「星期一」的存款，因此要等到星期二才能提領。然而，如果星期一是假日，那麼這筆存款就被視為是下一個營業日的存款，也就是星期二，

if Monday is a holiday, then the deposit is considered to have been made on the next business day, which is Tuesday, so the funds won't be available until ...

因此客戶要等到什麼時候才能使用這筆資金…

Chi: Wednesday?

季薇：星期三？

Mike: Correct. Remind them that ATMs have a **cutoff** time. Deposits made after six pm are considered next day's business. (Highlights all the sections mentioned and hands the disclosure over to Chi.) Next time I open an account I'll have you sit by my side, so you can hear what I say to the customer and when. Sound good?

麥可：正確。提醒他們自動櫃員機每天有截止收件的時間。晚間六點以後放進去的存款將視為隔天的存款。（把所有提到的部份都用螢光筆劃起來，並將說明書交給季薇。）下次我開戶的時候，我會讓妳坐在我旁邊，這樣妳就可以聽到我怎麼跟客人解釋。這建議聽來如何？

Chi: Sounds good!

季薇：聽來很棒！

07 Chapter

08 Chapter

09 Chapter

10 Chapter

11 Chapter

12 Chapter

13 Chapter

單字 Vocabulary

- **retrieve** [rɪ `triv] **v.** 將... 取回、收回
- **highlighter** [`haɪˌlaɪtɚ] **n.** 螢光筆
- **highlight** **v.** 以螢光筆劃出、強調
- **closeout** [`klozˌaʊt] **n.** 結清（帳戶、出清貨物等）、關閉
- **cutoff** [`kʌtˌɔf] **n.** 截止、截止點

片語 Phrases

take the time (to do something)
花足夠的時間來做某事、抽出時間好好地做...
at someone's leisure 當某人有空閒之際、方便時

好用句型 Useful Sentences

使用should的條件子句

The bank charges a twenty-five dollar early closeout fee, should you close the account within the first six months.

如果你在六個月內關閉帳戶，銀行會收取一筆二十五元的提早結清帳戶費。

你還可以這樣說

Ten dollars will be debited from the balance, should you request for a replacement card.

Your account will be assessed a service charge, should you ask for a paper statement.

Should you exceed your credit limit, the bank imposes a one-time, thirty-eight dollar fee for that statement cycle.

例句

A: I had some issues with the other bank. They charged me thirty-eight dollars for each overdraft. It adds up quickly! How much do you charge here?

我在另一家銀行有發生過些問題，他們在帳戶每次透支時收我三十八元，那些費用短期間內即累積成嚇人的金額！你們這裡收費多少？

B: Our fee is thirty-five dollars for each occurrence. There will be an additional twenty-nine dollar charge, should you remain overdrawn for two consecutive weeks.

我們的費用是每次三十五元。如果你連續透支兩個禮拜，則再加收二十五元。

07 Chapter
08 Chapter
09 Chapter
10 Chapter
11 Chapter
12 Chapter
13 Chapter

當收據顯示出下一個營業日的日期

　　許多人在拿到收據後，只要看到列印的金額無誤，收據上頭其他的資料就很少去注意了；但是如果你碰巧在週日、週六的白天，甚至星期五晚上，使用自動櫃員機存支票或到銀行櫃台辦事（現在很多銀行在週末、例假日以及平常日晚上超過六點鐘後也照常營業），你會發現收據或開戶文件上顯示的，不是當天，而是下週一的日期。

　　為什麼會出現這種情況呢？這是因為在這些日子或時段裡，各間分行特意將它們的作業系統轉換到下一個營業日的時間。你接下來會問，為什麼銀行要這麼做？答案是，由於美國處理票據和現金交換的聯邦準備系統（*the Federal Reserve System*）在週末和法定假日不上班，所以基本上，在這段時間內，分行雖然有開門、看來像是在營業的狀態，但是它們在收到客戶存入的支票以後，其實是無法把資料傳到聯邦準備系統的，因此，選擇在這個時候開門的銀行，就先把所有交易資料儲存起來，打上下一個營業日的日期（通常是星期一，若遇到假日則順延到星期二，以此類推），等到聯邦銀行又開始營業時，再統一將資料傳輸過去。

　　因此，從顧客的角度看，他們把支票在星期六或日就已經存到銀行戶頭裡了，卻要等到星期二才能領現金出來，感覺銀行把他們的錢扣留得非常久；然而從銀行的角度來看，它們為了平常方便在週一到週五也在上班、沒法到銀行辦事的客人，所以開放分行在週末假日裡營業，其實這時收到的支票都沒辦法立即透過聯邦準備系統向原發票銀行請款，因此必須要算成下一個工作天的交易。

07 Chapter

08 Chapter

09 Chapter

10 Chapter

11 Chapter

12 Chapter

13 Chapter

8.4 One Too Many

對話 Dialogue

Mike is explaining the **savings** account disclosure to a young man at his desk. Chi sits next to Mike watching **attentively**.

麥可正在他的辦公桌,向一個年輕人解釋存款帳戶的説明書,季薇則坐在麥可旁邊專注地看著。

Mike: ... and I would like to point out, there is a limit on the frequency of withdrawals you can make on the savings account. You are allowed six per month. The only exceptions are withdrawals made in person either at the teller window or an ATM.

麥可:…還有我想要指出,從存款帳戶領錢出來有次數的限制。每個月你只能領六次。唯一的例外是除非你親自到出納窗口來領錢,或使用自動櫃員機。

Young man: How about if I transfer money between my accounts on-line?

年輕人:那要是我到網路上在我的帳戶之間轉帳呢?

Mike: The six-withdrawals-per-month rule applies to transactions over the telephone, on-line, and automatic payments. If for some reason, you exceed the limit, every additional withdrawal will be **assessed** a five-dollar fee.

麥可：這條每月只能領六次的規則應用於電話、網路與自動轉帳付款。如果由於某種原因，你超過了限制的次數，超過之後每次的提款會加收五元費用。

Young man: I see.

年輕人：這樣子啊。

Mike: Any other questions?

麥可：還有其他的問題嗎？

Young man: Nah, I think that's it. Thanks, Mike.

年輕人：沒有，我想就這些了。謝啦，麥可。

Mike: Not a problem. Let me know if there's anything I can do to help. I'll see you around. (The young man leaves.)

麥可：沒問題，讓我知道還有沒有其他我能幫忙的地方。咱們下次再見囉。（年輕人離去。）

Chi: I didn't realize there was a limit on the number of withdrawals for a savings account!

季薇：我不知道原來存款帳戶有提款次數的限制！

Mike: You're not alone, not many people figure that out until it's too late.

麥可：不是只有妳一個，並不是很多人曉得這項限制，結果發現時已經太晚。

07 Chapter
08 Chapter
09 Chapter
10 Chapter
11 Chapter
12 Chapter
13 Chapter

Chi: Uh, Mike. There is something I want to tell you.

季薇：嗯，麥可，有件事我想跟你説。

Mike: What?

麥可：什麼事？

Chi: I want to thank you for letting me **sit in** with you. I want you to know that I really appreciate it. Thank you for taking the time to show me the ropes.

季薇：我要謝謝你讓我在你旁邊見習，我想讓你知道我真的是非常感激，謝謝你花這些時間來教我。

Mike: No, Thank YOU, Chi. Thank you for letting me do this.

麥可：不，謝謝妳，季薇。謝謝妳讓我教妳。

Chi: Huh?

季薇：吭？

Mike: I enjoy showing you stuff. Through teaching, I learn from you too. It gives me the opportunity to self-examine how well I thought I understood something and it gives me a purpose beyond just getting a **paycheck**. I feel like I'm looking at my job through a fresh perspective and that excites me.

麥可：我喜歡教妳。經由教妳做這些事情，我也同時從妳身上學到東西。教導妳，讓我有機會來檢視我自己到底有多瞭解某件事，而且給了我一種比領薪水還重要的目的。我覺得我現在是從全新的觀點來看待我的工作，那讓我感到充滿活力。

Chi: I'm glad to hear that. (Mike **beams** at Chi.)

季薇：　我很高興聽到你這麼說。（麥可神采奕奕地對季薇微笑。）

Mike: Next, I think you should learn about "Best **Counselor**," our account opening system. It's really easy, you won't have any problem using it. (Sees a customer walk in.) Stay here, I'm going to go see what she wants.

麥可：接下來，我想妳應該開始學習「最佳顧問」：我們的開戶系統。它真的很簡單，妳操作絕對不會有問題。（見到一位客人走進來。）妳待在這裡，我去問問她要辦什麼事。

單字 Vocabulary

- **savings** [`sevɪŋz] **n.** （注意是複數形名詞）存款、儲蓄金

（作者按：這個字常跟另一個字 "saving" 混淆，字尾沒有s的saving是形容詞，意思是「節省的」，美國人在春季把時鐘調快一小時，在秋季調慢一小時的作法，即稱為 daylight saving time，中文翻譯為「日光節約時間」，不要講成 daylight saving "s" time 了！）

- **attentively** [ə `tɛntɪvlɪ] **adj.** 專注地、留意地
- **assess** [ə `sɛs] **v.** 課徵（罰款、稅金等）
- **sit in** [`sɪt `ɪn] **v.** 參觀、見習
- **paycheck** [`pe `tʃɛk] **n.** 薪資支票、薪水
- **beam** [bim] **v.** （高興地）微笑
- **counselor** [`kaʊnslə] **n.** 顧問、輔導員

片語 Phrases

show someone the ropes 為某位新手解釋如何做一件工作

好用句型 Useful Sentences

I really appreciate it. 真是感激不盡。

你還可以這樣說

I would like you to know that I am grateful for what you did for me.

Words can't describe how thankful I am.

I can't thank you enough.

例句

A: Thank you for taking all this time looking up those transactions for me. I really appreciate it.

謝謝你花這麼多的時間來幫我查詢那些交易紀錄，真是感激不盡。

B: I can e-mail you your monthly statements, if you like, Mr. Klein.

如果您需要的話，我還可以把每月明細表用電子郵件的方式寄給您，克萊先生。

A: Will you do that for me? That would be very helpful! Thank you.

可以麻煩你嗎？這樣會對我很有幫助！謝謝你。

為什麼不能超過六次？

要解釋為什麼銀行限制你每個月從存款帳戶用錢的次數，我們得先解釋這個觀念：存款準備要求（*reserve requirements*）。

銀行最基本的操作模式，就是把顧客的存款集中起來，貸款給公司、個人與其他金融機構以賺取利息；然而，如果某家銀行把它所有的存款都借出去，要是一時間出現大量的客人跑到銀行領錢，而貸款產生的利息又不夠客戶需要的現金數量，這時銀行的運作就會產生問題。為了避免這種情況發生，美國的聯邦準備理事會（*Federal Reserve Board*）就規定，銀行不能動用其支票帳戶的存款總額的百分之十，也就是說，客人支票戶頭裡每十塊錢，銀行最多只能借出去九塊，一塊錢剩下來不能碰，這就是所謂的存款準備要求。

相對於支票帳戶，客戶放在存款帳戶裡的錢就沒有那麼大的波動（註），因此，聯準會說銀行可以將存款帳戶中所有的數額都借出去，但是加上一條規定，顧客每個月最多只能從存款帳戶取出六次錢，藉此來限制銀行存款帳戶裡金額的變化。

銀行把存款帳戶跟支票帳戶分開來，並且在存款帳戶上提供利息，目的就是要吸引顧客把錢多擺到存款帳戶裡，並盡量少去動用。如果遇到客人把存款帳戶當成支票帳戶用，進出次數太過頻繁，銀行不但會對超過六次的額外領款在月底時罰錢外，還可能更進一步主動通知客人關閉帳戶，所以可別忽視了這個存款帳戶每月只能轉出六次錢的規定！

註：美國人的支票帳戶是作一般日常消費用的，舉凡取現金、寫支票、用金融卡或自動轉帳付費，都是用支票帳戶來辦，故戶頭餘額經常上下浮動。

Chapter **09**

Opening Accounts

開戶

9.1 Trust, but Verify

Title Note:

這是美國已故前總統雷根相當著名的一句話。"Trust, but verify." 是從俄國的諺語 "Доверяй, но проверяй" 翻譯過來的，中文的意思為「要信任，但也要查證。」冷戰期間，在致力於消除雙方軍事對峙的會議上，雷根曾多次使用這句話來描述美國與蘇聯之間的關係。

對話 Dialogue

Mike returns to the desk with a tired-looking woman.

麥可與一位神情疲憊的女士回到辦公桌旁。

Mike: Please have a seat. This is Chi. Chi's my **protégé**, so she will be observing how we open an account from beginning to end. I hope you don't mind.

麥可：請坐。這是季薇，季薇是我的學生，所以她將在這裡觀察我們如何從頭到尾把一個帳戶設立起來。希望您不會介意。

Linda: Not at all.

琳達：一點也不。

Chi: Nice meeting you. (Smiles.)

季薇：很高興認識您（微笑。）

Linda: (Smiles and nods.) You, too.

琳達：（微笑並點頭。）我也很高興認識妳。

Mike: I see you have your social security card like I asked.

麥可：我看到您照著我的指示帶來了您的社會安全卡。

Linda: Sure do. Here you go. (Removes small blue card from a plastic cover.)

琳達：當然，在這裡，喏給你。（從塑膠套裡取出一小張藍色卡片。）

Mike: Good. So as we discussed previously, we are setting up a basic checking account for you today.

麥可：好。就像我們先前討論過的，今天我們要幫您開一個基本型支票帳戶。

Linda: Correct.

琳達：對。

Mike: Very well. May I also have your drivers license or ID? (Linda gives Mike her license. Mike enters her information into the system. Pauses briefly.) Oh dear. I'm sorry, Linda, but unfortunately I won't be able to open an account for you today. There appears to be a **red flag** in the system.

麥可：很好。可以也給我您的駕照或身份證嗎？（琳達把駕照拿給麥可，麥可將她的資料輸入系統。停頓了一下。）喔，我非常抱歉，琳達，很不幸地我今天沒辦法幫您開戶，因為系統顯示出警告的訊號。

07 Chapter

08 Chapter

09 Chapter

10 Chapter

11 Chapter

12 Chapter

13 Chapter

Linda: (A **somber** expression visible on her face.) That must be from the time when they closed my account at Bank of America.

琳達：（臉上露出消沈的表情。）那一定是從美國銀行關閉我的帳戶開始的。

Mike: (Retrieves a piece of paper from the printer.) On the notification there is a ChexSystem's address. You can write to them and request a copy of your report if you think there has been an error. I'm terribly sorry, Linda.

麥可：（自印表機取回一張紙。）這個通知書上面有ChexSystems的地址，如果您認為他們的紀錄有誤的話，您可以寫信要求他們送您一份報告。我真的是十分遺憾，琳達。

Linda: It's all right. I expected as much.

琳達：沒關係，我有預感結果會這樣。

Mike: Linda?

麥可：琳達？

Linda: Yes?

琳達：怎樣？

Mike: Some of the **credit unions** don't use ChexSystems. You can get a fresh start there, ok?

麥可：有些信用合作社不使用ChexSystems，您在那裡可以有個嶄新的開始。

Linda: I'll give them a try. Thanks Mike. (Leaves.)

琳達：我會試試看，謝了，麥可。（離去。）

Chi: What's ChexSystem?

季薇：什麼是ChexSystems啊？

Mike: It is a **third-party company** that collects information on closed checking and savings accounts. Banks use it to determine the potential reliability of applicants.

麥可：它是一間獨立的第三方公司，專門收集已關閉的支票與存款帳戶的相關資料。銀行使用它來判斷新客戶潛在的可靠程度。

Chi: A black list? Is that legal?

季薇：黑名單？那是合法的嗎？

Mike: It is not a black list, it is a temporary assessment on your ability to manage your account. Without it the bank could be taking on too much risk, leaving us vulnerable and possibly **liable**. It's like starting a relationship. You're going to want to know more about them first before taking it further.

麥可：它不是一份黑名單，它是一種對你管理個人帳戶能力的短期評估。若是沒有了它，銀行可能會承擔過多的風險，不但容易被投機份子利用，還可能牽扯上法律的責任。就好像展開一份新的關係，在深入交往之前，你會想先多了解對方。

Chi: I understand. I hope she manages to get herself back on track.

季薇：我了解。我希望她能又重新回到常軌。

Mike: With a little bit of hard work, I'm sure she will.

麥可：只要能下點苦功，我相信她一定可以。

單字 Vocabulary

- **protégé** [`protə ˌʒe] **n.** （源自法語）學生、愛徒
- **red flag** [`rɛd `flæg] **n.** 暗示事情可能不如表面上看來那麼好的徵象、警告訊號
- **somber** [`sɑmbɚ] **adj.** 憂鬱的、暗沈的
- **credit union** [`krɛdɪt `junjən] **n.** 信用合作社

（作者按：信用合作社跟銀行（banks）的不同之處包括：它們是非營利機構，客戶必須符合特定資格才能開戶，例如是某個公司的員工、居住或工作於某個地區、或有親屬是目前的客戶等。優點是其提供的存款利息較高、貸款利率與各項收費較低。缺點是分行少及自動櫃員機不普及。）

- **third-party company** **n.** 第三方公司：在某項契約或交易中，非屬主要交易的兩方公司，但提供外圍服務或產品的公司。常見的例子包括提供法律諮詢的顧問公司，以及承保買賣物品的保險公司（即並非買方或賣方）等。
- **liable** [`laɪəbḷ] **adj.** （法律上）有責任的

片語 Phrases

get oneself back on track
生活恢復正常，又再度能按照原來的時間表進行

好用句型 Useful Sentences

You, too. 你也是。

可用 "You, too."回應的句子例如：（注意以下這些句子不能用 "Me, too." 來回答）

It's nice talking to you.
I will be seeing you.
Good luck to you.
I really like what you are wearing.

（作者按：當對方在稱讚你，而你也認為對方值得受到相同的讚美（或任何相對應的行為。注意對方的句子中一定要有 "you" 這個受詞）時，你就可以用 "You, too." 來回答。譬如本篇對話中當季薇對琳達說 "Nice meeting you."，琳達的回應就是 "You, too." 即等於 "Nice meeting you, too." 的簡略講法。這種以 "You, too." 來作回應的用法，連在你聽到親愛的另一半對你說 "I love you." 時也可以派上用場喔！）

07
Chapter

08
Chapter

09
Chapter

10
Chapter

11
Chapter

12
Chapter

13
Chapter

銀行拒絕往來戶

　　想像哪一天你突然沒有了銀行帳戶：一切開銷都得使用現金、 身上的錢都花光時，也沒有辦法用提款卡領款；還有，所有你賺來的錢都必須擺在家裡... 嘿，你有沒有發現，原來銀行帳戶還真的滿重要的喔？

　　在美國有數百萬的人沒有銀行帳戶，造成這種情況的原因之一，是這些人被銀行列為拒絕往來戶，而銀行之所以拒絕跟他們打交道，則是由於這些客戶先前在銀行曾有過戶頭，但是因為嚴重透支或出現連續退票，產生大筆的罰款；這些客戶可能因為還不出來，或不願意償還罰款，人一走了之而迫使銀行將帳戶關閉；這時戶頭中所有客戶欠繳罰款的情形，銀行都會報告到 *ChexSystem*；一旦客人的社會安全號碼被紀錄到*ChexSystem*的資料庫裡，當這些人再到其他銀行準備開戶，行員輸入相同的社會安全號碼，電腦螢幕上即立刻顯示警告訊息，行員一見到這種訊息 就會停止開戶的程序。

　　ChexSystem，唸作[ˋtʃɛk ˏsɪstəm]。與這家公司資料庫連線的銀行，大約佔美國銀行總數的百分之八十，幾乎所有主要的大型銀行都使用*ChexSystem*來過濾新客戶。個人的社會安全號碼一旦被通報，這份紀錄就會留檔七年，在這七年的期間，他／她到任何 *ChexSystem* 的關係銀行或信用合作社都無法開戶。所有曾經歷過這種情形的人，都會告訴你那是多麼不愉快、多麼走投無路的經驗。

　　那麼要如何避免自己被報告到 *ChexSystem* 裡呢？第一，當然是小心保護帳戶不產生透支；但是如果一不留意，戶頭裡發生了許多透支的罰款，而你又一時無法全數償付時，最好的作法是與銀行協商，大多數的銀行都會提供償還計畫（*repayment plans*），讓客人分期還款，同時保留原有的帳戶，避免產生不良的紀錄。

07
Chapter

08
Chapter

09
Chapter

10
Chapter

11
Chapter

12
Chapter

13
Chapter

9.2 Anticipated Growth

 對話 Dialogue

Chi: I have a couple questions about CDs.

季薇：我對定存有幾個問題。

Mike: Go ahead.

麥可：直說。

Chi: The interest rates are low, so why would people still put their money in a CD?

季薇：現在利率這麼低，為什麼人們還會願意把錢放在定存裡？

Mike: CD rates follow inflation predictions closely. A one-year, one-percent CD, is expected to **counter** a market inflation of one percent by year's end. Locking your money in a CD **offsets** actual inflation and protects the principal. CDs are insured by FDIC and therefore offset investor risk.

麥可：定存利率緊跟著銀行對通貨膨脹的預測走。人們期望一份一年期、利率百分之一的定存單，應該要能對抗一年下來百分之一的市場通膨率。把錢鎖在定存裡，不但能抵消實際的通膨，並能保障本金。定存受到FDIC的保障，因此削減了投資的風險。

Chi: Huh, FDIC?

Mike: FDIC stands for Federal Deposit Insurance Corporation. It's an independent agency of the federal government. The FDIC does not receive funding from the Fed; it operates on the **premiums** paid by its member banks and investment's income from U.S. Treasury securities. They also verify insured banks are in compliance with federal laws. It's an entity that operates alongside federal policy and yet is separate from the government itself. Regardless of this **technicality**, FDIC's main function is to insure consumers' bank deposits up to two hundred and fifty thousand dollars per ownership.

季薇：吭，FDIC？

麥可：FDIC代表的是聯邦存款保險公司，它是聯邦政府中的一個獨立機構。FDIC運作的資金來源不是聯邦政府的預算，而是會員銀行繳納的保險費，以及投資美國國庫債券的收入。它確認參加保險的銀行都有遵守聯邦法律，它是一個按照聯邦政策運行，然而與政府分開的個體。撇開這項技術性的細節不談，FDIC主要的功能是承保消費者的銀行存款，每人最高保至二十五萬元。

（作者按：FDIC承保的金額，按照每個人或公司，於每家銀行、每種帳戶形態及帳戶的總持有人數而不同，有時還可能高於（或低於）二十五萬元！有興趣的讀者可洽詢銀行行員，或至網址fdic.gov下載PDF格式的說明書作進一步的了解。）

07 Chapter

08 Chapter

09 Chapter

10 Chapter

11 Chapter

12 Chapter

13 Chapter

Chi: Wow, two hundred and fifty thousand dollars. That's a lot of money.

季薇：哇，二十五萬元，那是很多的錢耶。

Mike: It used be half that. The amount was increased a few years back in order to further promote confidence in America's financial system.

麥可：以前只有一半。幾年前，政府為了提升大眾對美國金融系統的信心而將額度提高。

Chi: What about various CD rates? How does the bank determine interest rates? Why is there sometimes a CD with a longer term at lower rates? Or **jumbo CDs** that require a higher locked-in amount at a similar rate?

季薇：那麼像各種不同的定存利率呢？銀行是怎麼決定利率的？為什麼有時候期間較長的定存反而提供較低的利息？或是要求客戶鎖定高額存款的超大型定存單，利率卻差不多？

Mike: It's all about **timing**. Bank's reserves are determined by flow rates that vary over time. If the bank's analysts believes that the bank will need a little extra cash, say, in seven months, it will **entice** customers to purchase CDs with a rate that's comparatively high on a seven-month CD, **whereby** the bank is practically "buying" money from the market.

麥可：那都要看時間點。銀行的存款準備量隨著現金流動率而變動。當銀行的分析人員相信銀行，舉例來說，在七個月後，會需要多一點額外的現金，它就會用相對高的七月期定存率來引誘客戶購買，實際上銀行是藉此從市場上「買」錢進來。

Chi: So, that explains why a one-year jumbo CD doesn't have a higher rate than a one-year regular CD! The bank doesn't need the money at the one-year mark.

季薇：所以，那就解釋了為什麼一年期的超大型定存單，利率不比一年期的普通定存來得高！銀行一年之後不需要那筆錢。

Mike: You got it. Another factor in setting CD rates, is the bank's **outlook** of the future. If it thinks that the overall interest rates will go up, in order to stay competitive, it will increase its CD rate or vice versa.

麥可：答對了。另一個決定定存利率的因素，是銀行對未來的看法。如果它認為整體的利率會上揚，為了保持競爭力，它就會提高定存利率，反之亦然。

Chi: Good lesson! Now, let's open some CDs!

季薇：上了一堂好課！現在就讓我們來開一些定存戶吧！

單字 Vocabulary

- **counter** [ˋkaʊtɚ] **v.** 反擊、對抗
- **offset** [ɔfˋsɛt] **v.** 抵消、 與... 相抵
- **premium** [ˋprimɪəm] **n.** 保險費
- **technicality** [ͺtɛknɪˋkœlotɪ] **n.** 技術性的部份
- **jumbo CD** [ˋdʒʌmbo ˋsi ˋdi] **n.** 超過十萬元美金（$100,000）的特大型定存單
- **timing** [ˋtaɪmɪŋ] **n.** 時間的配合與安排
- **entice** [ɪnˋtaɪs] **v.** （以低價或優惠獎品）招攬、引誘
- **whereby** [(h)wɛrˋbaɪ] **conj.** 由是（by which）、藉以
- **outlook** [ˋaʊtͺlʊk] **n.** 展望、看法

好 用句型 Useful Sentences

當單字 "get" 的意思為「懂」、「了解」時

以下句型 1、2 和 3 裡的 "get" 用現在簡單式、過去式或過去分詞都可以。不同的 get 時態，雖然意思稍有一點差異— 例如 I get it.（我懂）相對於 I got it.（我已經懂了）——在美式英文中這點差異卻不是那麼重要，交互使用的情形常見。句型 4 和 5 由於這兩句是在描述一種能夠體會、理解對方個性或人生態度的情況，用過去式或過去分詞都不合邏輯，因此只能用現在簡單式。

1. 問句：「你懂了嗎？」

Do you get it?

You got it?

Have you got it?

（作者按：注意當 get 的意思為「懂／了解」時，不要用它的另一種過去分詞形式 "gotten"，也就是說，這一句不可講成 "Have you 'gotten' it?"。）

2. 直述句：「我懂了。」

I get it.

I got it.

I've got it.

3. 直述句：「你了解了。」

You get it.

You got it.

You've got it.

4. 直述句：「你了解我／你最懂得我。」

You get me.

5. 直述句：「我了解你／我懂你。」

I get you.

開立定存應注意的事項

定存，美國人常簡稱為 *CD*，全名為 *Certificate of Deposit*。開立定存帳戶的英文很簡單，就是 *open a CD* 或是 *set up a CD*，你也可以像中文裡面講的「買」定存單一樣，講*purchase a CD*。CD的優點是抗通膨、保值和安全，尤其當現在年年物價上漲幾乎是不可避免的趨勢，為了確保資產不跟著貶值，任何時候手邊有一筆短期間不會用到的錢，你都應該考慮放到CD裡。

CD 要怎麼開呢？第一步當然你會希望拿到最多的利息，除了比較各家銀行提供的利率外，我也建議你與你目前使用的銀行詢問，看看他們有沒有提供既有客戶特別的定存率（有時他們不會對外廣告這種優惠利率）。在你決定了銀行之後，下一步就是帶著你的支票本到分行去，與行員確認金額後，寫張支票交給他去完成開戶手續。務必記得將 *CD* 的到期日（*maturity date*)紀錄到個人行事曆裡，因為 *CD* 一旦到期後，多數的銀行只容許客人在之後十天內變更定存的約期或解約。這個十天的期限，英文稱 *grace period*，意思是緩衝期或寬限期間；注意這個十天是「月曆日」，而不是銀行的營業日，也就是說銀行沒開門的星期六、星期天和國定假日都包含在這十天以內。如果你錯過了這十天，第十一天起，銀行的系統就會自動把這份存單延長（*automatic renewal, automatic rollover*），舉例來說，一份原來是一年期、二〇一四年十二月三十一日到期的定存，由於客戶沒有在十天內告知銀行他／她要如何處置這筆定存，在二〇一五年的一月十一日，這個定存就變成另一個新的一年期的定存單，新的到期日是二〇一六年的一月十一日。

　　讓銀行自動延長定存期限對客戶來說是非常不利的，因為各種長、短期定存的利率隨時都在變，用上面的例子來說，假設原來那份定存有百分之二‧五的利率，但是在二〇一五年的一月十一日緩衝期結束的那天，銀行的一年期定存利率只有百分之〇‧五，較高的利率是在其他期限的定存單上，這時客戶就損失了獲得最佳利率的機會。

9.2 Anticipated Growth

07
Chapter

08
Chapter

09
Chapter

10
Chapter

11
Chapter

12
Chapter

13
Chapter

9.3 Nest Egg

對話 Dialogue

A couple walk in.

一對男女走進。

Chi: Hey, Steve. Haven't seen you a while!

季薇：嘿，史提夫，好一陣子沒見你了！

Steve: I know, it's been crazy! (Smiles.) Are you working on this side now?

史提夫：對啊，最近我的生活亂瘋狂的！（微笑。）妳現在換到這邊來做事啦？

Chi: I am training to be an officer. I am kind of going back and forth between the teller line and the **platform**.

季薇：我正在受訓成為經理人員，現在我有時候在出納櫃台做、有時候在大廳裡做。

Steve: Can you open accounts?

史提夫：妳能開戶嗎？

Chi: Absolutely.

季薇：當然可以。

Steve: I want to apply for a joint account with my new wife, Alice.

史提夫：我想要跟我的新婚妻子愛麗絲申請一個聯名帳戶。

Alice: Hi.

愛麗絲：嗨。

Chi: Hi, Alice. Wow, when'd you two get **hitched**?

季薇：嗨，愛麗絲。哇，你們兩個什麼時候結婚的啊？

Steve: Just last week. We managed to collect three thousand dollars in wedding gifts and we'd like to use that to start a **nest egg**. (Takes out a stack of checks from his pocket.)

史提夫：上個禮拜。我們一共收到了三千元的結婚禮金，而我們希望用這筆錢開始存錢。（從他的口袋裡取出一疊支票。）

Chi: You sure you just want a checking account today? Starbucks is in our "Best@Work" program, which means you can get a **money market account** with no monthly fee, as long as your direct deposit goes into the checking. Interest rates of money market accounts is five times higher than a regular savings account!

季薇：你確定你今天只想開一個支票帳戶嗎？星巴克公司有參與我們的「最佳工作夥伴」活動，也就是說，只要薪資直接轉帳存入你的支票帳戶，你就能得到一個零月費的貨幣市場帳戶。貨幣市場帳戶的利率是一般存款帳戶的五倍！

Steve: (Looks over to Alice.) What do you think?

史提夫：（看著愛麗絲。）妳覺得怎樣？

Alice: We should open the money market.

愛麗絲：我們應該開個貨幣市場帳戶。

Steve: Okay, we'll do it.

史提夫：好，我們就開吧。

Chi: Awesome! May I have two forms of ID each, your phone numbers, and your social security numbers? (Looks at drivers license.) Is this your current address?

季薇：太好了！我需要你們分別提供兩種形式的身份證明、你們的電話號碼、以及社會安全號碼。（看著駕照。）這是你們現在的住址嗎？

Steve: No. We moved into a new apartment last month. (Takes out a document.) Here is the **lease**.

史提夫：不是，我們上個月搬進一間新公寓了。（拿出一份文件。）這是租屋契約。

Chi: Is this your mailing address, too? (Studying the lease.)

季薇：這也是你們的通訊地址嗎？（研究著契約書。）

Steve: Yes.

史提夫：是的。

Chi: (Reading the message on her screen.) The bank would also like to offer you a credit line for overdraft pro-

季薇：（判讀螢幕上顯示的訊息。）銀行想提供你們一個保護透支用的信用循環帳戶，沒

tection. There is no annual fee and it protects you from acquiring an inconvenient bank fee due to any **extenuating circumstances**.

有年費，並能避免由於任何不可抗力的因素而產生的費用。

Steve: We should, right? (Nodding at Alice.) Sure, Chi.

史提夫：我們是應該申請，對吧？（對著愛麗絲點頭。）好啊，季薇。

Chi: I use this service myself, it's a lifesaver!

季薇：我自己也使用這項服務，它在你有困難時會救你一命！

單字 Vocabulary

- **platform** [`plæt͵fɔrm] **n.** 銀行大廳中業務為客戶開戶、辦貸款等事項的區域。Platform原來有「提供人員工作或活動的加高平台」的意思，延伸到銀行經營裡，即指「大廳內開戶或申辦貸款的地方」，與作一般存錢和領錢的出納櫃台分開。另外，美國人也稱呼那些在 platform 中工作的人士為 platform officers 或 platform associates。

- **nest egg** [`nɛst `ɛg] **n.** 積蓄、儲備金。

 （作者按：此名詞源自養雞場的飼主為了刺激母雞下蛋，會在巢裡預先放顆蛋，這個蛋就叫做 nest egg；由於 nest egg的作用就像儲蓄一樣，會激勵人越存越多（蛋越生越多），後來演變成為積蓄的意思。）

- **money market account** **n.** 貨幣市場帳戶。貨幣市場帳戶是存款帳戶的一種，其利率根據貨幣市場中的利率而上下浮動，一般來說利息比較高；貨幣市場帳戶的另一個特徵是客戶可使用支票來進行提款或付款，因此摻雜了

一點支票帳戶的性質。然而，由於它被歸類為存款帳戶（savings account），所以也受限於每月只能領款六次的規定。

（作者按：貨幣市場是還款期限為一年以下的貸款與其他短期金融商品的交易市場，與作長期投資的資本市場（capital market）有別；貨幣市場和資本市場兩者都是整體金融市場的一部份。）

- **lease** [lis] **n.** 房屋租賃契約、租約
- **extenuating circumstances** [ɪk `stɛnjʊ ˌetɪŋ `sɝkəm ˌstænsɪs] **adj.** （因不可抗力之因素，如疾病、死亡或其他情有可原的理由而造成的）特殊情形

片語 Phrases

get hitched （俚語）結婚。

日常用語 Common Expressions

It's a lifesaver! 它在你有困難的時候會救你一命！

（作者按：另外，當有人跟你說："You're my life saver!"時，他的意思是：「你真是我的救星（你幫了我好大的忙）！」

職場須知 Business Know-how

Basic Sales Technique: Uncovering Customer Needs and Matching It with the Appropriate Product

基本銷售技巧：發掘出客戶的需求，並提供適當的產品

Ask questions. Get your customers to talk and then LISTEN. Sell your products to complement people's lives. Explain your products in an easy-to-understand manner. Practice your speech so it flows

07 Chapter

08 Chapter

09 Chapter

10 Chapter

11 Chapter

12 Chapter

13 Chapter

naturally. Do not rush the sale. Offer a small set of poignant options and let the customer choose what they feel will best serve them. Your goal is to become a trusted advisor so that when your clients need to buy new services they come back to you.

發問，使你的客戶開口講話，然後仔細聆聽。用你的商品去補足人們生活中缺乏的部份。以簡單易懂的方式解釋你的商品。練習你的説詞，讓它聽起來自然而流暢。不要催促客戶做出購買的決定。提供一小組帶有強烈訴求的產品，讓客人去挑他們認為對自己最有利的選項。你的目標是成為客戶信賴的顧問，如此一來當他們有新的需要時，他們會回來找你。

實境對話

A: Oh my God, Mrs. Klein! This is your new baby? He is sooooo adorable!

我的天哪，克萊太太！這是妳新生的寶寶？他好～可愛喔！

B: Thank you, Michelle. Say Hi to Michelle. (Baby cooing.)

謝謝妳，蜜雪兒。跟蜜雪兒説嗨。（寶寶發出咕喃聲。）

A: (Smiles.) Hi, baby.

（微笑。）嗨，寶寶。

B: I have a question for you, Michelle.

我想問妳一個問題，蜜雪兒。

A: Yes?

好啊？

B: We received a few checks from our friends and family written to our son. Can I cash them?

我們從朋友和家人那邊收到了幾張寫給我們兒子的支票，我可以兌現它們嗎？

A: Um, yeah, we can cash those checks for you since he's a minor. But technically those checks should be deposited into an account with your baby's name. Have you thought about opening an account for him? We have a savings account for kids that has no minimum balance required and you can deposit his birthday checks, Christmas checks, etc. into the account. He will have access to the funds when he turns eighteen!

嗯，可以，因為他還未成年，所以我們能夠幫妳兌現那些支票。不過，技術上來講，那些支票應該要存到有妳寶寶名字的戶頭裡面。妳有沒有考慮過為他開個戶呢？我們這裡有提供無最低餘額限制的兒童存款帳戶，妳可以將他的生日及聖誕禮金等存到這個戶頭裡。當他十八歲的時候，他就能夠開始使用這筆基金！

B: Really? Do you have a brochure, Michelle? I would like to think about it.

真的嗎？妳有沒有說明書，蜜雪兒？我要認真考慮考慮。

A: Sure, here you go, Mrs. Klein.

當然，在這裡，克萊太太。

07 Chapter

08 Chapter

09 Chapter

10 Chapter

11 Chapter

12 Chapter

13 Chapter

當帳戶上有一個以上的人名（上）

在美國，個人銀行帳戶上出現一個以上的人名是很普遍的的情形，而這些情形包括以下四種類型：

一、聯名帳戶（*joint accounts*）：夫妻、或者父母與其子女共同持有聯名帳戶是十分常見的。每一位帳戶持有人都對這個戶頭、以及戶頭裡的存款擁有相同的處置權，也就是說，任何一人都能從帳戶中提款出來，甚至連把所有款項領光並關閉帳戶，也可獨自完成，不須其他帳戶持有人同時在場。唯一的例外是帳戶持有人不能將另外一位帳戶持有人從戶頭上除名，如果客戶需要將其中一位持有人移除，被除名的人必須主動向銀行提出要求，然而由於這種情形會使帳戶的控管變得複雜起來（譬如已被除名的人可能會用先前印有自己名字的支票去付款等），目前越來越多銀行在碰到客戶想變更聯名帳戶持有人時，會要求客人將原有帳戶整個關掉，重新開一個新的帳號。

二、兒童帳戶（*minor's accounts*、*custodial accounts for minors* 或 *accounts for kids*）：許多家長為了鼓勵孩子養成存錢的習慣會為他們設立兒童帳戶。在這種帳戶上面，家長的名字列為監護人（*custodian*，發音為[kʌs `todɪən]），小孩的名字則列為未成年人（*minor*）。通常小孩子只能存錢、不能領錢，如果真的必須從帳戶中拿錢的話，必須家長親自到銀行，以監護人的身份填寫提款單來領。兒童帳戶一旦到了小孩十八歲的生日當天會自動轉成普通的存款帳戶，這時家長必須到分行，將帳戶上的 *custodian* 及 *minor* 這兩個字樣去掉，讓成年後的孩子不需家長的陪同就能獨立處理自己的存款。（下篇待續）

9.4 Be Prepared

 對話 Dialogue

Chi: Welcome to Best Bank Mr. (pauses) and Mrs. Donegan! You two usually come in on alternating days. Are you having a special occasion?

季薇：歡迎光臨倍斯特銀行，唐尼根先生（停頓了一下）還有唐尼根太太！您倆通常在不同的日子裡過來，是有什麼特別的事嗎？

(Mrs. Donegan looks over at Mr. Donegan with a forced smile.)

（唐尼根太太朝唐尼根先生的方向看去，勉強地微笑著。）

Mr. Donegan: We, uh, we would like to make some changes to our accounts.

唐尼根先生：我們，嗯，我們想在我們的帳戶上做些變更。

Chi: Have a seat, please. Is everything all right?

季薇：請坐。一切都還好吧？

Mr. Donegan: (Sits down. His wife puts her hand on his shoulder.) Chi, I have

唐尼根先生：（坐下。他的妻子將手放在他的肩膀上。）季

been diagnosed with brain cancer. I'm dying.

Chi: (Breathes in sharply.) Let's not get ahead of ourselves, Mr. Donegan. I hardly think of you as a man who is going to simply lie down and die. There is much to do and dying is not one of them.

Mr. Donegan: You're right, but we want to be as prepared as we can be should I fail to meet the challenge.

Chi: I understand. In the meantime, what can I do for you?

Mr. Donegan: Marge and I want to **designate** our sons as **beneficiaries** to our accounts. What do we need to do?

Chi: I'll need their names, date of birth, social security numbers and addresses.

薇,我被診斷出患有腦癌,我快要死了。

季薇:(深深倒吸一口氣。)咱們先不要太快下結論吧,唐尼根先生。我不認為您是那種願意乖乖躺下等死的人。要做的事情太多了,死不包括在其中。

唐尼根先生:妳說的對,不過萬一我沒辦法通過這場挑戰,我們希望能做好一切的準備。

季薇:我瞭解。在這同時,我能如何為您效勞?

唐尼根先生:瑪姬跟我想指定我們的兒子為帳戶受益人,我們要怎麼做?

季薇:我需要他們的姓名、生日、社會安全號碼以及住址。

07 Chapter

08 Chapter

09 Chapter

10 Chapter

11 Chapter

12 Chapter

13 Chapter

Mrs. Donegan: I have their information here. (Takes out a piece of paper from a **manila folder**.)

唐尼根太太：我這裡有他們的資料。（從文件夾裡取出一張紙。）

Chi: Thank you. (Starts entering the information into the system.)

季薇：謝謝。（開始將資料輸入電腦系統。）

Mr. Donegan: Everything's good in the bank? Didn't you get a promotion recently?

唐尼根先生：銀行這裡一切都還好吧？妳不是最近升官了嗎？

Chi: Actually Mike has been training me to take the relationship manager position. He has taught me so much, but I don't have it yet.

季薇：事實上麥可一直在訓練我取得客服經理的職位，他教了我好多東西，不過我還沒被擢升。

Mrs. Donegan: Well, keep up the good work, you'll get there!

唐尼根太太：維持現在的好成績，繼續加油，妳一定會升上去的！

Chi: (Printer spits out a form.) This is our beneficiary **designation** form. Please make sure everything on it is correct before you sign and date it at the bottom.

季薇：（印表機吐出一張表格。）這是我們的受益人指定書。麻煩您確認上面寫的都正確，然後在底下簽名並寫上日期。

Mr. Donegan: Looks fine. (Mrs. Donegan nods in agreement. The two sign the form.) Anything else we need to sign?

唐尼根先生：看來都對。（唐尼根太太點頭附和，兩人在表格上簽名。）還有其他我們需要簽的嗎？

Chi: Nope! That's it.

季薇：沒了！就這樣。

Mr. Donegan: We better get going. (Stands up.) Good luck with your training, Chi. You're a bright young lady; I know they'll promote you soon.

唐尼根先生：我們最好告辭了。（起身。）祝妳訓練一切順利，季薇。像妳這麼年輕又聰明的小姐，我知道他們很快就會升妳職。

Chi: (Stands up and walks around her desk.) Thank you, Mr. Donegan. (Holds out her arms and gives Mr. Donegan a gentle hug. Then she hugs Marge.) Give my best to your family. I look forward to seeing you next week. Ok?

季薇：（起身並走到辦公桌的另一邊。）謝謝您，唐尼根先生。（伸出她的雙臂並給予唐尼根先生一個擁抱，接著她擁抱瑪姬。）請為我向您的家人問候。我希望下個禮拜再看到您，好嗎？

Mr. Donegan: Ok, (softly) I'll be here.

唐尼根先生：好的，（輕聲地回應）我下禮拜會再來。

07 Chapter
08 Chapter
09 Chapter
10 Chapter
11 Chapter
12 Chapter
13 Chapter

單字 *Vocabulary*

- **designate** [ˋdɛzɪgˏnet] **v.** 指定（某人為⋯）、指名；名詞為 designation [ˏdɛzɪgˋneʃən]
- **beneficiary** [bɛnəˋfɪʃɛrɪ, – fɪʃɪ ˏɛrɪ] **n.** （遺產、保險金的）受益人
- **manila folder** [məˋnɪlə ˋfoldɚ] **n.** （一種以厚硬紙對折而成、外表呈淺黃或皮膚色的）文件夾。Manila 指的是馬尼拉麻（Manila hemp），原始的文件夾／袋就是使用這種韌性強、不易撕裂的馬尼拉麻所製成，其名稱沿用至今。

日常用語 *Common Expressions*

Keep up the good work. 維持現在的好成績，繼續加油喔！
（用以讚許對方目前優異的表現，並鼓勵其繼續努力。）

職場須知 *Business Know-how*

How to Hug？如何跟美國人擁抱？

Hugging shows that you care about a person and that you support that person through good times and bad. People hug at work for various reasons. However, due to the fact that we are showing our affection in a professional setting, we need to know how to hug "appropriately." Here are the steps:

擁抱不但顯示出你對某人的關懷，並表達你對那人，不論在順境或逆境中，都始終如一的支持。在工作環境裡人們因各種理由互相擁抱；然而，由於擁抱是在專業的場所內顯露情感上的一面，我們必須知道如何「適當地」擁抱。以下幾個步驟供你參考：

1. Smile and extend your arms to show that you are ready to give your friend a hug.

   微笑，伸出你的雙臂，表示你準備好要給你的朋友一個擁抱。

2. Approach him or her and tilt your head towards the left. (So you can use your dominate right arm to grip their upper shoulder.)

   朝他／她接近，並把你的頭向左邊傾。（這樣你就能順勢用右臂環扣對方的上肩。）

（作者按：由於大部份人是右撇子，所以習慣上多舉起主宰的右臂來抱對方。）

3. Gently wrap your arms around him or her. Keep your hips slightly out.

   輕輕地以雙臂環抱他／她。腰臀部不要靠著對方。

4. Hold a three-count, and then let go.

   停頓心裡數三下後，放開對方。

07 Chapter

08 Chapter

09 Chapter

10 Chapter

11 Chapter

12 Chapter

13 Chapter

當帳戶上有一個以上的人名（下）

三、 附有代理人的帳戶（*Accounts with a Power of Attorney*）：當帳戶持有人由於年老體衰或生病行動不便，有困難處理財務時，他／她可以指定某一個人作為自己的代理人到銀行存提款、付貸款、和簽發支票。*Power of Attorney* 指的是「代理人的權力」，單字 *power* 的意思是權力，而單字 *attorney*[ə `tɜnɪ] 就是法定代理人；一份委託書（*power of attorney document*、*power of attorney paper*、或直接就簡稱 *power of attorney*）上面會清楚地列出代理人有哪些權力，也就是他能夠代表帳戶持有人做哪些事。帳戶持有人在經由律師的協助完成委託書後，即可與代理人一同至銀行，出示委託書開立新的帳戶，開好的帳戶上會顯示兩個人名，第一個是帳戶持有人，第二個是代理人的名字並加註power of attorney的字樣。值得注意的一點是，「代理人」英文的正式說法是attorney-in-fact或agent，不過很多人也習慣直接借用*power of attorney*來稱呼這些財務代理人，譬如你可以說：*"I am my mother's power of attorney."*（我是我母親的代理人。）或問某人：*"Are you the power of attorney on this account?"*（您是這個帳戶的法定代理人嗎？）

四、附有受益人的帳戶（*Payable-on-Death Accounts*、*In-Trust-For Accounts*）： 視各州的法律而定，有些州叫這些指定受益人的帳戶為*payable-on-death account* 或簡稱 *POD account*，有些州則稱之為 *in-trust-for account*或 *ITF account*，不管怎麼叫，這些帳戶都提供了同一種功能： 當帳戶持有人在世的時候，受益人沒有權利取用帳戶內的資金（銀行也不得告知受益人有這項約定的存在）；而在原帳戶持有人死亡之後，戶頭裡的金錢即皆歸受益人所有。 如果你在某個帳戶上看到人名的寫法是：

Mary Smith

POD John Smith

或

Mary Smith in trust for

John Smith

就代表這個帳戶的持有人是 *Mary Smith*，而受益人為 *John Smith*。

　　在我們提到的這四類具有多個人名的帳戶中，除了兒童帳戶在一開始的時候就必須設定為兒童帳戶以外，其他三種都可以從簡單的個人帳戶開始，後面再慢慢做變更；舉例來說，假設你有一個私人帳戶，如果哪天你結婚了，想把配偶加到你的帳戶上，這時原來的個人帳戶就變成聯名帳戶；而如果你想指定某位家人幫你處理銀行的事務，這時你就可以在你的個人帳戶上加一個代理人；最後，如果你希望在你去世後，帳戶裡的錢通通留給孩子，那麼你就可以請銀行幫你把小孩指定為受益人。

Chapter 10

Credit Products

信用商品

10.1 Dream Car

At the training center.

訓練中心裡。

Colleen: Welcome our new bankers! During today's course, I'm going to walk you through the steps of a car loan application using Best Counselor. There is a very useful button on Best Counselor called "What-if." Using this function, you can calculate customer's monthly payment and the total interest the customer will pay before starting a new application.

柯琳：新鮮銀行經理人，歡迎！今天這堂課，我將會教你們如何使用最佳顧問，一步步地申請汽車貸款。在最佳顧問上面有個非常好用的按鍵，叫做「試算」，利用這項功能，你們可以在正式申請一筆新的貸款前，計算客戶的每月應繳金額，以及客戶總共會付多少利息。

Let's get right to it: In front of each of you there's a **worksheet**. Let's look at the first scenario: Your customer wants to purchase a pre-owned 2008 Honda

就讓我們立刻開始：在你們每個人的面前有一張練習問題表，我們來看第一個情況：你的客戶想要買一部兩千零八年

Civic. He would like to know if he applies for a five thousand dollar loan and pays it back within three years, what his monthly bill is gonna look like.

Everybody, click on your "What-if" button for me. **Plug in** the loan amount five thousand dollars. The customer wants to pay off the loan in three years, so that's thirty six months. Type in thirty six as the term. Now, can anyone tell me how to get the interest rate?

Trainee#1: The rate for auto loans is located in the section of "**installment** loan" under "Rate Tool."

Colleen: Excellent. I encourage you all to print out a rate sheet every Monday morning and keep it at your desk for quick referencing. I pre-printed the rate sheet, you will find it under your worksheet. (Trainees turn over the page and take out a piece of paper.) Now that the loan amount and the term have been specified, you can now click on

的二手本田思域。他想知道如果他申請一筆五千元的貸款，於三年內還清，他每個月的帳單是多少。

每個人都請按下你的「試算」鍵。填進五千元的貸款金額。這個客戶希望在三年內還清貸款，也就是三十六個月，鍵入貸款期間三十六。現在，有沒有人可以告訴我怎麼取得利率的資料？

受訓員工一：汽車貸款的利率在「利率工具」下方的「分期貸款」裡。

柯琳：非常好。我鼓勵你們每個人在每週一早上把利率表列印出來，放在辦公桌裡以供快速查詢。我已經預先把利率表列印好，放在練習問題表的下面。（受訓員工翻頁，取出一張紙。）現在貸款金額跟期間都確定了，你們可以按下「計算」鍵來看估計的結果。（受

the "Calculate" button to see the esti-mate. (Trainees comply.) You should see that the interest rate and the **origi-nating fee** have been pre-filled. The calculator shows you the monthly pay-ment amount, the interest, and the to-tal payment amount.

Explain the result to your customer. You can change the loan amount and/or the term according to the customer's preference. Once you reach an agree-ment, it's time to put in an application!

Exit the "What-if." Start from customer's profile, then click on "Products" until you reach "Auto Loan." The system will fill in customer's basic information for you. Next step, tell the **underwriter** about the car. What's the year, **make** and model?

Trainees: (Together) A 2008 Honda Civ-ic.

訓員工照做。）你們應該會看到利率和開辦費都已經自動填好，這個計算軟體顯示出每月應繳金額、利息、以及總共繳付的金額。

向你們的客人解釋計算結果。你們可以按照客戶的喜好改變貸款金額與／或期間，一旦達成共識，你們就可以開始正式填寫申請表了！

跳出「試算」。從客戶的個人頁開始，點選「商品」直到你們找到「汽車貸款」為止。系統會自動幫你填入客戶的基本資料。下一步，向授信人員描述這部車。車子的年份、廠牌跟車款為何？

受訓員工：（同聲）兩千零八年的本田思域。

Colleen: Good. Enter the information in those columns. Then we will finish up the application with the vehicle's **VIN, milage**, customer's employment history, annual income and housing expenses. You will find these data in the **appendix**. I am going to give you a few minutes to fill out the form. After you all are finished please print it out and give it to me.

柯琳：很好，把資料輸入那些欄位中。接下來，要把申請表完成，我們需要加入車子的車輛識別號碼、哩程數、客戶的工作紀錄、年收入和房貸/租屋費用，你們可以在附錄裡找到這些資料。我現在要給你們幾分鐘填表，所有人填好之後請列印出來交給我。

單字 Vocabulary

- **worksheet** [ˋwɝkˏʃɪt] n. 附有問題以提供學生練習的表單、作業單
- **plug in** [ˋplʌg ˋɪn] v. 放入、填入
- **installment** [ɪn ˋstɔlmənt] n. 在一段約定的時間內將某筆債務分成數筆較小的金額攤還、分期付款
- **originating fee** [ə ˋrɪdʒəˏnetɪŋ ˋfi] n. 開辦費
- **underwriter** [ˋʌndəˏraɪtə] n. 金融機構內評估客戶信用狀況並核准貸款或保險單的人員、徵授信人員。

（作者按："Underwrite" 這個動詞來自於十七世紀末，在英國倫敦的金融家們，在對船隻出航旅程的保險文件中，於願意承擔風險的條款部份下方簽名（under + write）的習慣。）

- **make** [mek] n. 廠牌、品牌
- **VIN** [vɪn] n. 車輛識別號碼。VIN 是 Vehicle Identification Number的簡寫，以十七個英文字母與數字組成（不含字母 I、O 或 Q，以免與數字 1 和 0 混淆）；在美國每一部汽車都有一組獨特的 VIN，就好像每個人都有

屬於自己的身份證字號一樣,這組號碼可以在駕駛座儀表板前方靠近擋風玻璃處,或駕駛座側門開啟的地方找到。

- **milage** [ˋmaɪlɪdʒ] **n.** (已行駛的)哩程數
- **appendix** [əˋpɛndɪks] **n.** 附錄

好 用句型 Useful Sentences

Let's get right to it! 讓我們立刻開始吧!

你還可以這樣說

Let's have at it!

Let's get this rolling!

例句

At the branch meeting.

在分行會議中。

Robert: Let's get right to it. To start the next quarter strong, we really need to focus on business lending. I know that y'all have been mailing out flyers, so thank you for that. Now, I want you to start asking business customers who come to your window or desk to see if they have plans for expansion. Our "Best Equipment Financing" program can cover equipment that is purchased sixty days prior. We have a very competitive rate among our peers.

勞勃:讓我們直接切入主題。下一季,為了要有個好的開始,我們必須把全力集中在商業貸款上。我知道你們一直都有在寄傳單,感謝大家的幫忙。現在,我要你們開始詢問到你窗口或辦公桌洽公的商業客戶,看他們有沒有擴增的計畫。我們的「最佳設備貸款」方案能針對六十天前購買的設施作貸款,其利率在同業間是相當有競爭力的。

Mike: And don't forget the business credit card! Business owners can earn three percent cash back on gas and office supplies.

麥可：還有，別忘了商務信用卡！公司老闆們可以在汽油和辦公室耗材的支出上獲得百分之三的現金回饋。

Robert: Exactly. They need to spend money on those items anyway, why not get some cash back for their purchases? Our goal is to put in a business credit card application every two weeks, and one equipment financing per month. Think we can do it?

勞勃：說得一點也沒錯。他們本來就必須花錢買這些東西，何不從這些開銷中獲得一些現金回饋？我們的目標是每兩週拿到一份商務信用卡的申請表，每個月一件設備貸款，認為我們做得到嗎？

Everyone: Yes!

每個人：做得到！

Robert: Excellent. Meeting adjourned!

勞勃：非常好。散會！

07 Chapter

08 Chapter

09 Chapter

10 Chapter

11 Chapter

12 Chapter

13 Chapter

如何貸款購買一部車？

　　美國幅員遼闊，通常一般人工作、購物和出遊都是以汽車代步，臺灣街頭上四處可見的機車在這裡是非常希罕的物品；另外，如果你不是住在具有地下鐵的主要都市裡，大眾交通工具像公車或鐵路等，也不像國內那樣，熱門地點內經常每十至十五分鐘就有一班，住在郊區的人們為了搭乘巴士，等上一個鐘頭或更久是常有的情況，其路線選擇也相當少；所以在美國，可以說如果沒有車，就好像沒有腳一樣，到哪裡都不方便。

　　那麼要怎樣買一部車呢？首先，去看車。選好想要的車以後，你可以直接與銷售員表示購買的意願。通常這些銷售中心都有合作的貸款公司，現場處理貸款的人員會將你的個人資料放進電腦，以取得貸款的初步條件如利率、每月應繳金額、與期間長短等。如果你對他們提供的利率不甚滿意，你可以記下那台車的年份（*year*）、製造廠商（*make*）和車款（*model*），如果想買的是二手車，除了以上的資料外，再加上其車輛識別碼（*VIN*）、跑過的哩程數（*milage*）與特殊的加值配備（註），拿這些資料到銀行去做比價。

　　在申請好貸款之後，接下來要做的，說簡單也不簡單，說難也不難，那就是：每月準時付款。我強烈建議你在帳戶上設定自動扣款，以免忘記或遲繳。擁有一份汽車貸款，並每月準時交錢，對你的信用評分（*credit scores*）會有非常正面的幫助。有關信用評分這部份，我會在後面的文章中再做詳細的解釋。

　　交完最後一個月的貸款後，貸款公司/銀行會寄給你一張釋放債權的聲明（*lien release*；lien發音為[lin]，意思是「債權」、「抵押權」），以及汽車的所有權狀（*title*），證明你是全權擁有這部車子的人。

註：額外的裝備如電動天窗（electric sunroofs）、加熱車椅（heated seats）、定速巡航系統（cruise control），甚至車用衛星導航（GPS navigation system)，都可被視作為汽車加值的配備。

07
Chapter

08
Chapter

09
Chapter

10
Chapter

11
Chapter

12
Chapter

13
Chapter

Hidden Resources

對話 Dialogue

Mike: How was Banker School? Who's your instructor?

麥可：銀行人學校課上得如何？你們的講師是誰？

Chi: Our instructor was Colleen. She was amazing. So **informative** and knowledgable about various loan products. I learned a ton!

季薇：我們的講師是柯琳。她好厲害，對各種融資商品的資訊都不吝分享並博學廣識。我學到好多！

Mike: Colleen was my instructor, too. Got to love that gal! Tell me what you've learned about home **equity** lines of credit— in my opinion, one of our best products.

麥可：柯琳也是我的講師，你非愛那個女孩不可！告訴我妳對循環性房屋權益貸款的認知為何？循環性房屋權益貸款在我看來是我們最棒的商品之一。

Chi: Um, home equity? Okay, let me see if I understand it correctly. Home equity

季薇：嗯，房屋權益？好，讓我試著解釋看看，看我的理解

line of credit allow people to use the equity in their homes to borrow money from the bank and pay it back whenever they can, providing a great deal of convenience and flexibility. And because it is **secured** by a real property, the rates are generally lower than those on the loans that don't have **collaterals,** such as personal loans.

對不對。循環性房屋權益貸款讓人能利用他們對房子持有的權益部份向銀行借錢，並於他們有能力還款時還款，提供客戶相當大的便利與彈性。另外，由於它以房產作擔保，其利率一般來說比其他沒有抵押品的貸款—譬如個人貸款—的利率都來得低。

Mike: Define home equity.

麥可：為房屋權益下定義。

Chi: Home equity is the difference between the **appraised** value of the house and the current **mortgage** balance.

季薇：房屋權益就是房屋的估價與目前貸款餘額之間的差異。

Mike: (Smiles.) So, a three-hundred-thousand-dollar house, with a mortgage balance of two hundred thousand dollars, the equity is ...

麥可：（微笑。）所以，一間三十萬元的房子，貸款餘額是二十萬元，房屋的權益部份就是…

Chi & Mike: (Simultaneously) One hundred thousand.

季薇和麥可：（同時講出）十萬元。

07 Chapter

08 Chapter

09 Chapter

10 Chapter

11 Chapter

12 Chapter

13 Chapter

Chi: But the bank can only loan out eighty percent of that amount, which is eighty thousand.

季薇：不過銀行只能借出去這個金額百分之八十的部份，也就是八萬元。

Mike: Good! I see you've paid attention.

麥可：很好！我看妳真的有專心在上課。

Chi: (Shyly.) I try. However, having equity in your home does not necessarily guarantee the approval of the line. Colleen says the underwriters also look at people's payment history, credit scores, as well as other factors like their debt-to-income, and combined **loan-to-value** ratios to determine if they turn down the application or increase the rate to compensate for potential risks.

季薇：（靦腆地）我盡量啦。然而，擁有房子的部分權益，並不一定保證申請就一定會通過。柯琳説，銀行的授信人員還要視客戶的繳款紀錄、信用評分，以及其他因素像是他們的負債所得比率，與貸款總額對屋價的比率等，來決定他們是否該退件，或者提高利率以彌補銀行可能承擔的風險。

Mike: Correct. Did Colleen also mention that right now we are waiving the originating fee and that we offer **HELOC** clients the option to re-lock in their balance at a lower rate if the rate drops?

麥可：正確。柯琳有沒有提到，我們現在免收開辦費，並且讓循環性房屋權益貸款的客戶能夠趁利率下降的時候，把借出的部份重新設定在更低的利率上？

Chi: Yeah, she did! I think the promotion is pretty cool.

Mike: Can't agree more. As a matter of fact, I have a **closing** tomorrow. The customer gets a rate that's lower than her current mortgage rate, so she is going to use the line to pay off the mortgage.

Chi: Wow, that's gonna save her a lot of interest!

季薇：對呀，她有提到！我認為這個促銷活動非常酷。

麥可：再同意也不過。說到這裡，我明天正好有客戶要來簽約，這個客人拿到的利率比她目前房貸的利率還要低，所以她準備要用這個循環性貸款來還清她的房貸。

季薇：哇，那會省下她很多利息錢耶！

單字 *Vocabulary*

- **informative** [ɪn `fɔrmətɪv] **adj.** 資訊豐富的、提供知識的
- **equity** [`ɛkwətɪ] **n.** 以房屋的市價在減去貸款額度後之剩餘價值、屋主對其房產持有的權益部份
- **secure** [sɪ `kjʊr] **v.** 擔保
- **collateral** [kə `lætərəl] **n.** 抵押品、擔保品
- **appraise** [ə `prez] **v.** 估價
- **mortgage** [`mɔrgɪdʒ] **n.** （注意t不發音）以不動產為抵押品的貸款、房屋貸款
- **combined loan-to-value ratio** [kəm `baɪnd `lon tə `vælju `reʃo] **n.** 貸款總額對屋價的比率。貸款總額對屋價的比率是銀行常用來評估風險的指標之一，百分比越高，表示銀行承擔的風險越高。這個比率計算的方式為，將房屋目前的貸款餘額加上客戶欲申請的新貸款額度，除以房屋的估價。舉例

來說，一間估價為三十萬美金的房子，目前貸款餘額十五萬，客戶想申請三萬元的循環性貸款，那麼其貸款總額對屋價的比率為：(150,000+30,000)/300,000=0.6，以百分數來表示，即**60%**。

- **HELOC** [`hi͵lak] **n.** 循環性房屋權益貸款。HELOC 即 Home Equity Lines of Credit 的簡稱。

- **closing** [`klozɪŋ] **n.** 借貸或買賣雙方簽署契約以完成交易的過程、對保手續

職場須知 Business Know-how

Practice Sessions with Coworkers 與同事複習產品內容

Your coworkers are one of your best resources when it comes to product knowledge and presentation, especially when they have experiences selling a particular product. They know what features or benefits would draw a customer's attention and pique his or her interest.

講到有關產品的知識與介紹，你的同事是你最棒的資源之一，特別是當他們有賣過某項特定產品的經驗時。他們知道哪些特徵和好處可以吸引客戶的注意力，並引發他/她的興趣。

實境對話

A: Robert, I have a question about our equipment finance.

勞勃，我對我們的設備貸款有個問題。

B: What is it?

你的問題是什麼？

A: You mentioned that the program can cover purchases made sixty days prior to the loan application. My question is, if the business customer can buy the equipment himself and has already done so, why would he want to finance it afterwards?

你曾説這個方案可以針對申請表送出六十天前購買的設備作貸款。我的問題是，如果一個商業客戶可以自己買器材，而且也已經買了，為什麼他會想要之後再貸款呢？

B: There can be a number of reasons. For one, companies need to keep a certain amount of cash on their book. The scenario could be that after they make the purchase, they realize that they have to increase their cash balance due to other unexpected expenses. Another scenario is to refinance.

這可能有幾種原因，第一，公司企業必須在它們的財務表上保持一定的現金量，情況也許是在它們購買了設備以後，發現由於其他預期之外的支出，使得它們必須提高現金額度。另外一種情況是重新做貸款。

A: Oh that's right! You did say our rate is lower than our competitors'. So by refinancing with us, the customer can use the new loan to pay off the other loan and save money on interest. I get it now. Thanks, Robert.

噢，對喔！你的確有講我們的利率比競爭同業低。所以如果客戶跟我們重新做貸款，他就能用新的貸款付清另一個貸款以節省利息錢。這樣我就懂了，謝謝，勞勃。

什麼是非循環性和循環性房屋權益貸款？

讓我用一個簡單的例子來解釋「房屋權益」的概念：假設你跟銀行貸款十萬美金，買下一間市價十萬美金的房子，在繳貸款繳了一段期間之後，銀行的貸款餘額剩下六萬元，而你已經繳的四萬元（假設頭期款和利息都忽略不計），從許多金融機構的角度來看，相當於你對這間房子擁有四萬元的權益，因此，在你有額外借款需求的時候，這些金融機構可以讓你用這四萬元的「房屋權益」來做抵押，跟它們申請新的貸款，或者申請循環信用帳戶。以房屋權益作擔保的定期貸款，我們稱作「 非循環性房屋權益貸款（*home equity loan*）」，而以房屋權益作擔保的循環信用帳戶，就是「循環性房屋權益貸款（*home equity line of credit*）」。（註一）

非循環性房屋權益貸款和循環性房屋權益貸款的不同，在於非循環性房屋權益貸款是以一整筆的金額付給客戶，利率固定，客人按照契約於一定期間內，以同樣的金額分次攤還；而循環性房屋權益貸款則類似使用一張信用卡，額度申請下來以後，客戶如果有需要用錢才去從帳戶裡面提，還款之後額度可以被重新循環使用，在申請核准後的五至二十年間，客戶能夠隨意地提款與還款（這段期間稱為 *draw period*），其利率可能變動（註二），而且按照客戶不同期間內所使用的不同額度，每個月的最低還款金額也會有所變化。

你或許會想：這種以房屋權益作抵押的融資聽起來好像是投機份子才會做的事情，為什麼我還特別把這項金融商品挑出來介紹？其實房屋權益貸款，跟正常的房屋貸款一樣，都是用房子的全部或部份的價值當作抵押品；許多人更進一步分析：當人們買下一棟房子，通常屋主無法真正獲得或享受到房屋帶來的價值，除非把房子賣掉以換得金錢；但由於房屋權益貸款這類商品的出現，提供了屋主在出售房子以外，另一個能夠利用到房產價值的選項，因此絕對不能忽略它們的重要性。

　　註一：在臺灣每家銀行可能有不同的稱呼，舉例來說，臺灣銀行（Bank of Taiwan）的home equity loan稱為「治家成長貸款（非循環性）」或「治家成長貸款（定期）」；而home equity line of credit則叫做「治家成長貸款（循環性）」或「治家成長貸款（活期）」。

　　註二：大多數銀行循環額度的利率，乃是根據華爾街日報發表的基本放款利率（prime rate，或譯「優惠利率」），再按照客戶的個別情況，加上零至數個百分點而成。

10.3 Special Privileges

對話 Dialogue

At Chi's desk.

背景為季薇的辦公桌。

Mrs. Robinson: Can the bank waive the two overdraft fees? We were out of the country when the automatic mortgage payment posted. James and I have been long-time customers at your bank and we have never had an overdraft before.

羅賓森太太：可不可以請銀行不要收這兩筆透支費用啊？當房子的貸款自動從帳戶裡扣除時我們正好人在國外。詹姆士跟我是你們銀行很久的客戶了，我們從來沒有透支過。

Chi: I understand, Mrs. Robinson. Things like this happen. Let me talk to Robert and I'll see what we can do for you.

季薇：我了解，羅賓森太太，這種情況的確會發生。讓我跟勞勃談，看我們能為您做什麼。

Mr. Robinson: We appreciate it, Chi.

羅賓森先生：我們非常感激妳，季薇。

Chi relays the customer's request to the branch manager. After a brief discussion, she returns.

Chi: Mr. and Mrs. Robinson, we can waive the two charges. (Customers look relieved.) But I would like to suggest that we link a preferred line of credit to your checking account in order to avoid any overdraft fees in the future.

Mr. Robinson: What's a "preferred line of credit"? Does that mean we get to use the money for free?

Chi: Haha... Not quite, but <u>you're not far off</u>, Mr. Robinson. The reason why it's called "preferred" is because, compared to a regular line of credit, this product has a higher credit limit and a lower rate.

Mr. Robinson: Not because we are your "preferred customers," too?

季薇將客戶的要求轉達給分行經理，經過一番短暫的討論後，她回到座位上。

季薇：羅賓森先生跟羅賓森太太，我們可以取消這兩筆費用。（客戶露出鬆了口氣的樣子。）不過我想建議我們把一個優惠循環信用帳戶連到您的支票帳戶上，以避免未來任何的透支費。

羅賓森先生：什麼是「優惠循環信用帳戶」啊？意思是我們能免費使用這筆錢嗎？

季薇：哈哈⋯不能這麼說，但是您也不算差得太遠啦，羅賓森先生。它之所以稱作「優惠」的原因，是因為跟普通的循環信用帳戶比起來，這個商品擁有較高的信用額度與較低的利率。

羅賓森先生：不是因為我們是妳比較喜歡的客人哪？

Mrs. Robinson: Oh, James. Stop **goofing around**. (Softly **nudges** her husband on the side.)

Chi: That, too. You're absolutely correct, Mr. Robinson. I should have mentioned that earlier! (Smiles and then continues.) It's a really good product. Not only you can use it as an overdraft protection, you can also use the line for your short term needs. Funds can be accessed by checks, on-line or in-branch transfers.

Mrs. Robinson: How much is our credit limit?

Chi: I'll have to put in an application to find out. And after we get the result, you and Mr. Robison can decide if you want to accept it or not. I would also like to let you know that there is a fifty-dollar annual fee, but the first year's fee is waived.

羅賓森太太：哦，詹姆士，你正經點好不好。（從旁邊輕輕地推了一下她先生。）

季薇：也是啦，您講的完全正確，羅賓森先生，我應該早些提到那一點才對！（微笑並繼續說話。）這真的是一個很好的商品，您不但能把它用來預防帳戶透支，也能用它提供的資金來滿足您短期的融資需求，取得資金的方法包括寫支票、上網或親自到分行轉帳。

羅賓森太太：我們的信用額度是多少？

季薇：我需要先把申請表送過去才能知道。拿到結果後，您跟羅賓森先生可以屆時再決定要不要接受銀行給您的額度。我也必須要提醒您，這個帳戶的年費是五十元，第一年免年費。

Mrs. Robinson: That's fine. We'll apply.

羅賓森太太：可以。我們就申請看看。

Chi: Thank you. Now if I may borrow your ID's and ask you both a few questions...

季薇：謝謝您。現在我能不能跟您兩位借用一下身分證，還有詢問您們幾個問題…

單字 Vocabulary

• **goof around** [ˋɡuf ə ˋraʊnd] **v.** 做出不正經或裝傻的行為、四處開玩笑
• **nudge** [nʌdʒ] **v.** 以手肘或握拳輕觸、小力地戳

日常用語 Common Expressions

You're not far off. 你（所講／做的事）也不算差得太遠。

職場須知 Business Know-how

Turn Customer Issues Into Sales 把危機化為轉機

Expect to get a few complaints periodically. It's part of operating a business. A customer's complaint can help you understand what he or she really wants and needs. Use this opportunity to further strengthen the relationship between you and your customers. Customers with resolved issues will return to you later with more business because they know you are reliable and resolute.

偶爾碰到客人抱怨是正常的，這是經營生意的一部分。客戶的抱怨能幫助你了解他／她真正想要和需要的東西。利用這個機會來進一步鞏固你和你客戶間的關係。如果你成功地幫助他們解決了問題，他們就知道你既可靠又有決心，客戶會回來找你買更多東西。

實境對話

A: I just got my statement and there is a ten-dollar fee on my checking account. Explain to me why you think you can just take my money whenever you feel like it. What is this nonsense? (Throws paper onto counter.)

我剛收到明細表，我的支票帳戶上出現了一筆十元的費用，跟我解釋一下為什麼你們可以隨時愛扣我的錢就扣我的錢，這到底是什麼鬼道理？（把紙丟在櫃台上。）

B: (Picks up the customer's statement.) It appears, sir, that your direct deposit didn't go in last month, so the system automatically posted a monthly maintenance charge.

（拿起客戶的明細表。）看起來，先生，像是您上個月的薪資沒有自動存進來，因此電腦系統就記入一筆當月的維護費用了。

A: That's not my fault. My company discontinued the direct deposit program. Now I only receive paper checks. You've got to fix this!

那不是我的錯。我的公司停止做薪資自動存款，現在我都拿支票，你一定要給我解決這個問題！

B: If you bring the balance up to fifteen hundred dollars, the monthly fee would be waived. If you increase your balance to ten thousand dollars, then we can upgrade your basic checking to a Gold account. Your personal checks and bank checks would be complimentary along with loan discounts and substantial savings on safe deposit boxes. There are additional benefits we could discuss if you like.

如果您將帳戶餘額增加到一千五百元就不會有月費。如果您把餘額提高到一萬元，那我們就可以幫您的基本支票帳戶升級成黃金支票帳戶，不僅您的個人支票和銀行本票免費，申請貸款有折扣，而且還能省下很多錢在保險箱的租金上。若您想要的話，我們可以討論其他的優惠內容。

A: Really? I could shift some funds over from Bank of America, but I'll have to speak with my wife first.

真的啊？我應該是能從美國銀行那裡轉些錢過來，但我必須先跟我太太談。

B: Of course sir. When would you like me to schedule your appointment? Might I suggest Saturday? That way we can sit down together undisturbed and hash this out.

那是當然的，先生。您希望我安排什麼時間和您會談？我建議星期六好嗎？這樣我們可以不受干擾地坐下來討論細節。

A: Yeah! That sounds good.

好！聽起來不錯。

B: Excellent. I'll call the day before to confirm.

太好了，我會在會談的前一天打電話確認。

07 Chapter

08 Chapter

09 Chapter

10 Chapter

11 Chapter

12 Chapter

13 Chapter

漫談循環信用帳戶

一般來說跟銀行借錢，途徑有兩種：一種是 *loan*，譬如個人貸款和汽車貸款等，另一種是 *line of credit*，也就是這篇文章所要談的「循環信用帳戶」。你可以用一個很簡單的規則來區分 *loan* 和 *line of credit* ─看它們的利率結構：*loan* 的利率是固定的，而 *line of credit* 的利率則是會上下浮動。

你或許會問：如果 *line of credit*（以下稱循環信用帳戶）的利率會變化，不是代表它的借款風險比 *loan*（以下稱貸款）高嗎？為什麼人們會想要使用這種商品呢？主要原因在於它的便利性。循環信用帳戶可以隨借隨還，沒有用就不會產生利息；而貸款只能用一次，不像循環信用帳戶，在客戶還款之後，額度又能恢復，能夠多次取用（這也是為什麼它被視為 *revolving account*的原因，*revolve*就是「循環」的意思）。

英文對話中的「優惠循環信用帳戶（*preferred line of credit*）」，與先前提過的循環信用帳戶（*line of credit*，見第五章的【什麼？透支了？】），都是可連到個人支票帳戶上，以防止透支與退票的商品，其運作過程為：當某一筆或多筆扣帳的總金額，超過當天帳戶內的存款餘額時，系統就會自動從相連的循環信用帳戶中提出不足的部份，將之轉入支票帳戶裡，以涵蓋所有的扣款。而優惠循環信用帳戶又比基本型的循環信用戶多了幾項優點：額度高、利率低，而且客人還能夠用特製的支票從帳戶裡領錢出來（有些銀行甚至提供金融卡）。大部份的金融機構只提供這種優惠型帳戶給信用等級較高的客戶，而客戶大多也都樂於接受，原因在於沒有人不知道自己什麼時候會需要用錢；未雨綢繆、提前建立好一個循環信用帳戶，在意外發生時（如失去工作或生病導致收入減少）就能有多一點的緩衝與支援。

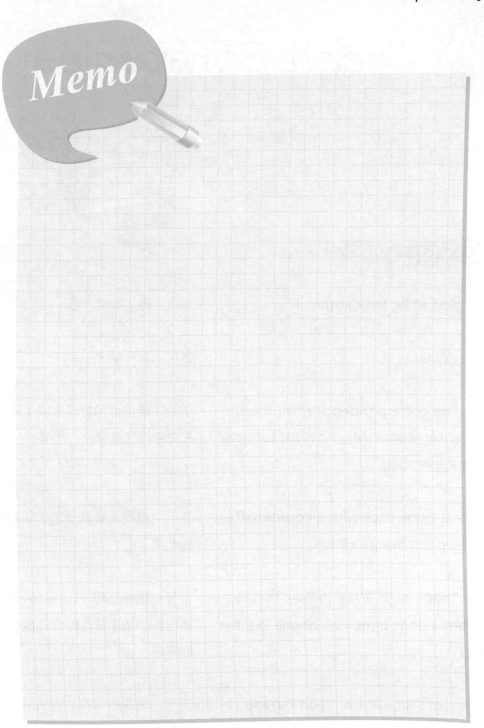

10.4 Credit Strategies

Chi: Hey, Mike, look at this.

季薇：嘿，麥可，看。

Mike: What?

麥可：看什麼？

Chi: The correspondence from the underwriter about Mr. Rodriguez's car loan application.

季薇：授信部門對羅德里奎茲先生申請汽車貸款的回覆。

Mike: It came back with a **counteroffer** of ten point five percent?

麥可：他們提議百分之十點五的利率？

Chi: That's high. Way higher than expected. I don't think he's gonna like the rate.

季薇：那很高耶，比估計的還高很多。我不認為他會喜歡這個利率。

Mike: Let's look at his credit **bureau** report.

麥可：讓我們看看他的信用評估報告。

Chi: (Opens up a new window, enters in customer's application number.) There.

季薇：（開啟一個新的視窗，輸入客戶的申請表編號。）喏。

Mike: (Reading the screen.) His score is seven hundred and ten. Not great, but acceptable. The score factors are: length of time accounts have been established, excessive revolving accounts, numerous credit inquiries in the last twelve months, and too many accounts with open balances. Mmm ...

麥可：（讀著螢幕上的資料。）他的指數是七百一，不算頂尖，但可接受。評估因素包括：帳戶建立的時間、過多循環信用帳戶、在過去十二個月內有多次查詢信用的紀錄，以及太多的帳戶內有餘額。嗯…

Chi: (Sighs.) That explains it. It's those store credit cards. He told me he signs up for whatever is offered to him so he can get discounts. I think he has like twenty or more of 'em.

季薇：（歎氣。）這就解釋了為什麼他利率會這麼高。都是那些商店認同卡啦。他告訴我只要買東西能打折，他就一律申請。我認為他大概有二十張信用卡或更多。

Mike: That doesn't sound good.

麥可：聽來不妙。

Chi: It's too late now. He said his car broke down a week ago and he needs a car to go to work.

季薇：太遲啦，他說一個禮拜前他的車壞了，而他急需一部車代步上班。

Mike: As of now he'll just have to deal with the **repercussions**. A lot of people don't realize how important a good credit score is until they need to borrow. Improving or maintaining good credit takes time and **perseverance**.

麥可：現在他就只得承擔後果了。很多人一直要等到有借錢的需要時，才瞭解信用指數的重要性。改善或維持一份良好的信用紀錄，需要時間及毅力。

Chi: What would you do if you were him? Would you start cutting up some cards?

季薇：如果你是他的話，你會怎麼做？你會開始剪卡嗎？

Mike: If I were him, I would start doing some trimming. However I would do it carefully. Closing many accounts at once can actually hurt your ratings. I would stop using about half of the cards, pay off the balances on the others, and then close them out gradually. I would keep the ones that have been opened the longest. However, there is one good thing about his report: he has been paying his bills on time and maybe that's why our underwriter is still willing to approve his loan at a higher rate.

麥可：如果我是他，我會開始削減一些卡片。不過我會很小心，一次關閉許多帳戶實際上可能損害你的信用評等。我會停止使用其中一半的信用卡，把剩下另一半卡上的餘額付清，然後逐漸地關掉那些卡。我會保留那些開得最久的信用卡。不過話又說回來，他的報告指出他作對了一件事：他一向都有準時繳款。這可能就是為什麼我們的授信部門仍舊願意以較高的利率批准他的貸款。

Chi: On top of that, I know he has been working with the same company for over five years. Doesn't that help?

季薇：除此之外，我還知道他在同一間公司裡做事超過五年了，那也有幫助，對嗎？

Mike: Definitely. Besides someone's credit score and what's in the report, underwriters also look at an applicant's income and work history in order to assess their ability to pay back the loan. A steady employment history says to the **creditor** that the applicant is reliable and is likely to fulfill the contract.

麥可：絕對有。除了客戶的信用評分，以及報告裡的內容，授信人員同時也就申請人的收入和工作紀錄評估他們償債的能力。一段穩定的就業歷史，對發放貸款的機構而言，表明了申請人不僅可靠，而且會履行契約的可能性高。

Chi: I guess it's now time for me to give Mr. Rodriguez a call. I wonder if he takes the offer?

季薇：我猜我現在該給羅德里奎茲先生個電話，不曉得他會不會接受這項提案？

單字 Vocabulary

- **counteroffer** [ˌkaʊntə ˋɔfə] **n.** 在原先的提議被否決後，略作修正再提出的第二份提案
- **bureau** [ˋbjʊro] **n.** （注意eau發音為[o]）收集並提供一般大眾資料（或服務）的機構
- **repercussion** [ˌrɪpə ˋkʌʃən] **n.** （通常用複數形 repercussions）餘波、事後的影響
- **perseverance** [ˌpɝsə ˋvɪrəns] **n.** 堅持、毅力
- **creditor** [ˋkrɛdɪtə] **n.** 提供貸款的人或金融機構、債權人

07 Chapter

08 Chapter

09 Chapter

10 Chapter

11 Chapter

12 Chapter

13 Chapter

職場須知 Business Know-how

How to Deliver Bad News Without Humiliating Your Client
怎樣告訴你的客戶一件壞消息，同時不令他們覺得困窘

Step One: Have your customer's goals in mind. Provide alternatives solutions in reaching those goals. Often news is only construed as disheartening if the customer perceives he or she has no control.

步驟一：記住你客戶要的是什麼，提供其他的途徑來達成那些目標。通常，一件消息之所以會被詮釋成壞消息，在於客戶覺得他們完全沒有控制權。

Step Two: Use a confident and soothing tone of voice. A calm steady delivery can ease its reception.

步驟二：使用帶有自信而又溫柔的聲音。冷靜穩定地傳達你的訊息，能夠緩和它帶來的衝擊。

Step Three: Utilize neutral words. For example, replace "problem," "bug," with "issue," or "situation." Stay away from emotionally provoking words, such as "I hate ... " and "It's bad." Instead say "It would be better if we avoid ... " and " It didn't meet the standard."

步驟三：利用中性的字眼。舉例來說，把「問題」、「困擾」換成「議題」或「情況」。盡量遠離挑撥情緒的字彙，像「我恨⋯」和「糟糕」，改成說「如果我們能避免⋯」跟「沒有達到標準」。

Step Four: Wait for a response. Give them time to mull it over. Listen to your customers, paraphrase their concerns to confirm that your understood them correctly and then find a solution together.

步驟四：等待回應。給他們時間反芻。聆聽你的客戶，重述一遍他們的疑慮，確認你了解無誤，然後一起找出解決方法。

實境對話

A: Hi, this is Chi calling from Best Bank. Am I speaking with Dave Rodriguez?

嗨，這是季薇從倍斯特銀行來電，請問是大衛・羅德里奎茲先生嗎？

B: Yes, speaking.

是。

A: Mr. Rodriguez, I have the result of the car loan. The underwriter would like to offer you the loan at a rate of ten point five percent.

羅德里奎茲先生，汽車貸款的申請結果出來了，授信部門提議給您百分之十點五的利率。

B: TEN POINT FIVE? That's really high! Is it because I don't have a good score?

百分之十點五？太高了吧！是因為我的信用指數低嗎？

A: Your score is fine. Our loan department also take other factors into account. Actually speaking of credit scores, once you pay off the car loan, your score would increase tremendously, Mr. Rodriguez.

您的信用指數還好，我們的貸款部門將許多其他因素都納入參考。事實上，講到信用指數，一旦您付完這筆汽車貸款，您的指數將會大幅提高，羅德里奎茲先生。

B: Would it? But ... ten point five! What's my monthly payment gonna be like?

會嗎？但…百分之十點五！這樣我每個月要繳多少？

A: Since you only need to commute to work, and the loan is ten point five percent then you might want to consider purchasing a smaller, previously-owned car.

既然您這部車只是用來上班通勤，這筆貸款又要百分之十點五，您可能會想考慮買小一點的二手車。

B: I'll need to think about it.

我需要好好想一下。

A: Definitely. I will e-mail you the revised payment amount and options. I understand you need time to plan it out. I'll call back this Thursday.

沒問題。我會用電子郵件寄給您修改過的繳交金額與選擇。我了解您需要時間來作規劃。這個禮拜四我會再打電話過來。

B: Okay. Thank you, Chi.

好的，謝謝妳，季薇。

影響巨大的三位數字

在美國，如果你想申請任何一張信用卡、貸款買車買房子、甚至租公寓—銀行或房東都會用這一組三位數的號碼來評判你的可信程度，這組號碼，就是我們今天要談論的「信用指數」或「信用評分」（*credit score*）。

信用指數通常介於 300 到 850 之間，數字越高，代表一個人的信用越好；大致說來分數在 690 以下算是不好的，介於 720 到 780 之間是優秀，超過 800 就近乎完美。這個指數有時也稱作 *FICO score*，*FICO* 的唸法為 [`faɪko]，這個字源自於 *Fair, Isaac and Company*：一九八九年，這間由工程師 *Bill Fair* 和數學家 *Earl Isaac* 創立的公司，設計出一種評估個人信用的模式，這個模組在金融商業界中被大量採用，企業團體開始憑藉由這個模式計算出的指數，來推測貸款給客戶的風險。

目前國內有三家主要的信用評等機構（*credit bureau*）：*Experian*、*TransUnion* 和 *Equifax*，它們從各處蒐集客戶借、付款的資料，以 *FICO* 的基本架構略作調整，針對每個人不同的情況做出評估報告並決定其信用指數。指數隨時都可能增加或下降，要看調出報告當時個人的償債狀況而定，但一般來說，這個數字的組成，大略是按照以下這五個條件的百分比來決定：

一、還款歷史（*payment history*）：佔 35%。如果客戶一直都有按時繳款，分數就會逐漸拉高，如果客戶有遲繳的情形，則按照拖欠的時間長短，分三十天、六十天及九十天以上不等的嚴重性扣分。

二、債務與所有可使用的信用額度的比例（*ratio of current debt to total available credit*）：佔 30%。客戶債務的總金額，最好不要超過所

有可使用信用額度的百分之二十五；這個標準也是為什麼許多專家不建議一下就把許多信用卡關掉的原因，因為這麼做的結果，是大幅降低個人可以使用的信用額度。

　　三、信用紀錄的時間長短（*length of credit history*）佔15%。一個人建立信用的時間越長，並且又能夠持續地按時繳款，顯示出他/她越能有效地經營財務。若是報告上顯示的多半是在短期內開過又關掉的信用卡，代表這名客人很有可能是以投機的心態來開戶，而非經營長期關係的客戶人選。

　　四、債務的種類（*type of credit used*）10%。如果你的報告裡不但有信用卡的使用紀錄、也有學生貸款、汽車貸款，再加上一個房屋貸款，乍聽之下，好像你這個人負債累累，但其實這在金融機構的眼中看來是個好現象，擁有不同形式的債務，說明了你這位客戶知道如何管理及使用各種金融商品。

　　五、最近申請信用貸款的次數（*recent searches for credit*）10%。若是你需要一筆貸款，請盡量把到處填申請表、比價的過程控制在一個半月內，因為每次在你的申請書送件後，銀行就會針對你個人的信用紀錄進行一次調查，而大約四十五天後，這些被調閱紀錄的過程，就會開始顯示在你的評等報告上，如果一年內調閱的次數過於頻繁，這樣的情況可能會被解釋為你因為週轉不靈，債務上開始出現問題而四處申請貸款，融資的銀行或機構多半會避免這種顧客。

Chapter 11

Wire Transfers
國際匯款

對話 Dialogue

Mike: Chi, would you like to come here? I want to show you how to send a **wire.**

麥可：季薇，妳想不想過來這邊一下？我想讓妳看看我們怎麼發國際匯款。

Chi: Awesome, I'll be right there!

季薇：好啊，我馬上過去！

(Chi walks over to Mike's office. A dark-hair, **chunky** girl is sitting at the desk.)

（季薇走到麥可的辦公室。一位頭髮深黑、身材微胖的女孩坐在桌子旁。）

Mike: This is Cherryl de la Cruz. She just bought a **condo** in her home town in the Philippines and she's sending her first payment.

麥可：這是雪柔・德拉克魯斯，她最近在菲律賓家鄉的鎮裡買下了一間公寓，準備要送第一筆貸款過去。

Chi: Wow, that's so cool. Congratulations, Cherryl.

季薇：哇，好酷喔。恭喜妳，雪柔。

Cherryl: Thank you.	雪柔：謝謝妳。
Mike: This is Chi. Chi is training to be a banker so she will be watching us put in a wire transfer request.	麥可：這是季薇。季薇正在受訓成為一位銀行業務人員，所以她會在旁邊觀察我們如何填寫匯款的申請表。
Chi: I hope you don't mind.	季薇：我希望妳不會介意。
Cherryl: Not at all!	雪柔：一點都不會！
Mike: Thanks, Cherryl. (Pushes a piece of paper towards them.) Basically, what we need from customers, to send out a international wire, includes either the **IBAN** or the **SWIFT code** of the beneficiary's bank, the name and address of the bank, and the name and address of the beneficiary, which Cherryl has provided us here. (Points at the neatly typed information on the paper and then opens a foreign passport.) We will enter the sender's ID information, and, (turns to the customer) Cherryl, you said you wanted to send out five hundred US dollars from your checking account, correct?	麥可：謝了，雪柔。（將一張紙挪近他們。）基本上，要送出一份國際匯款，我們需要從客戶那兒取得受款人銀行的國際銀行帳戶號碼，或是國際銀行代碼、銀行的名稱和地址，以及受款人的姓名和地址，這些雪柔都已經提供給我們。（指著紙上打得相當整齊的資料，接著翻開一本外國護照。）我們還要輸入送款人的身分證資料，還有，（轉向客人）雪柔，妳說妳想從妳的支票帳戶中匯出五百元美金，對嗎？

Cherryl: That's correct.

雪柔：正確。

Mike: Thank you. (Returns to Chi.) And the requested amount. Customers can choose to wire the money either in US dollar, or in foreign currency. (Begins to enter the data.) Cherryl, do you want to put anything in the memo line?

麥可：謝謝。（轉向季薇。）還有申請匯款的金額。客人可以選擇要以美金或外國貨幣匯錢。（開始輸入資料。）雪柔，妳想在備註欄內加入什麼事項嗎？

Cherryl: Can you please put my loan number in there? (Points to the number on the paper.)

雪柔：可以麻煩你把我的貸款帳戶號碼加進去嗎？（指著紙上的一組號碼。）

Mike: Sure. Anything else?

麥可：當然可以，還有其他的嗎？

Cherryl: That should do it.

雪柔：那樣應該就可以了。

Mike: (Nods and continues to explain the process.) Before we submit the form, we will print out two copies, one is for customer review, the other is for us to keep on file. Now, if you ladies may excuse me. (Stands up and re-trieves the paper work from the printer. Returns to the desk.) Cherryl, I would

麥可：（點頭並繼續解釋匯款的程序。）在我們送出表格前，我們必須列印出兩份複本，一份給客人覆審，另一份給我們自己存檔。現在，請兩位小姐包容一下。（起身到印表機取出文件。回到辦公桌旁。）雪柔，請妳在確認過資

like you to verify the information and then sign underneath.

Cherryl: Sure. (Compares the numbers on her document and the ones on the bank form.) Everything is correct. (Signs her name.)

Mike: Excellent. (Clicks on the "submit" button on the computer screen.) After I submit the wire, another authorized officer will go into the system and approve it. That means either Robert or Michelle can certify my wire. We've already requested to get you the authority for wire transfers. It should come to you soon through **interoffice mail** and tells you your authority limit.

Cherryl: Then you can start helping me with my wires, Chi. (Grins.)

Chi: Deal!

料後於底下簽名。

雪柔：好。（比較她自備文件上的號碼與銀行表格上印的號碼。）全部正確。（簽下她的姓名。）

麥可：非常好。（在電腦螢幕上按下「送出」鍵。）在我送出匯款後，另一位經授權的職員會進入系統內核准這份申請表，也就是說，不管是勞勃或是蜜雪兒都可以認證我的匯款內容。我們已經幫妳申請匯款的權限，它會以公司內部郵件的方式於近期內寄給妳，告訴妳妳的上限是多少。

雪柔：到那時妳就可以開始幫我做匯款了，季薇。（微笑。）

季薇：一言為定！

單字 Vocabulary

- **wire** [waɪr] **n. v.** 電匯、匯款。

（作者按：Wire 是 wire transfer 的簡稱。Wire 這個字原來是「金屬線」，十九世紀起，科學家發現他們可以利用金屬線遠距離傳送電流；一八四四年美國人山繆‧摩斯（Samuel Morse，即摩斯密碼系統的創始人之一）以控制電流的斷續，透過金屬纜線在遠端的紙上打印出點和線，送出第一封電報。之後這項技術被銀行界採用，不同的銀行間以電報溝通進行交易，此即 wire transfer 名稱的由來。）

- **chunky** [ˋtʃʌŋkɪ] **adj.** （身材）矮胖的、粗壯結實的

- **condo** [ˋkɑndo] **n.** 一種社區形式的連結公寓或屋宅。Condo 為 condominium [ˌkɑndə ˋmɪnɪəm] 的簡稱，其屋權分屬住戶所有，但土地權、公共空間與設施如屋外樓梯等，則由社區內所有住戶分享。

- **IBAN** [ˋaɪ ˋbæn] **n.** 國際銀行帳戶號碼。IBAN 為 International Bank Account Number 的簡稱

- **SWIFT code** [ˋswɪft ˋkod] **n.** 國際銀行代碼。SWIFT 是 Society for Worldwide Interbank Financial Telecommunication（環球銀行財務電信協會）的簡稱

- **interoffice mail** [ˌɪntɚ ˋɔfɪs ˋmel] **n.** 在公司不同部門或辦公室間遞送往來的郵件

職場須知 Business Know-how

Repeat Transactions Back to the Customer
複述客戶的交易內容

Taking an order is not as easy as one might think. Customers expect you to know what you are doing and to do it exactly like they tell you to. If there is more than one transaction, recite those

07
Chapter

08
Chapter

09
Chapter

10
Chapter

11
Chapter

12
Chapter

13
Chapter

transactions in the same order as the customer tells them to you. Reading a customer's request back to him or her assures accuracy and allows the customer make any changes before it is finalized.

接受客戶的指令，其實不如一般人想像的容易。客戶期望你熟悉你的工作內容，並精準地按照他們的指示完成任務。如果進行的交易不只一項，把那些交易按照客人告訴你的順序覆誦一次。將客戶的要求重新唸給他/她聽，不但能保證正確性，而且讓客人有機會在交易完成之前做任何的更改。

實境對話

A: I would like to transfer five thousand dollars from my savings to checking and then get a thousand in cash.

我想要從我的存款帳戶裡轉五千元到支票帳戶，然後取一千元的現金。

B: Are we taking the cash from your savings, sir?

先生，請問現金是從您的存款帳戶取嗎？

A: Yes, please.

是的，麻煩你。

B: So, we are going to transfer five thousand from your savings to checking, and then make a withdrawal for a thousand from your savings account. Is that correct?

所以我們準備從您的存款帳戶轉五千元到支票帳戶，然後從您的存款帳戶中領出一千元，對嗎？

A: Yes, that's correct.

對。

B: Right away, sir.

我立刻就會為您辦妥，先生。

IBAN 和 SWIFT code兩種代碼

　　到美國的銀行辦理國際匯款，行員第一個會跟你要的資料，就是受款人銀行的"IBAN number"或"SWIFT code"。究竟這兩種號碼有什麼不同？它們又是如何組成的？若是受款人的銀行根本沒有這些號碼，又要怎麼辦呢？以下讓我一一為您解釋：

　　一、IBAN：目前要辦理國際匯款，世界上的國家大致分成兩個系統，一派是使用 IBAN，另一派是使用 SWIFT code。用 IBAN 的國家包括了大部份的歐洲各國，如德、英、法，以及中東地區的國家如以色列和巴基斯坦等。IBAN 的特色是它的號碼很長，以表示國家簡稱的兩個英文字母開頭，後面接上一長串的數字。舉英國為例，它的 IBAN 格式大致長得像這樣：GB00WXYZ00000012345678，開頭的英文 GB 就表示 Great Britain，而受款人的銀行帳戶號碼 12345678 就包含在裡面。

　　二、SWIFT code：臺灣和美國就是 SWIFT code 派系之中的兩個國家。SWIFT code 通常是由八個英文字母和數字組成，如果你看到有十一個字的，後面多出來的三個數字代表分行代碼，可加可不加。以美國為例，通常 SWIFT code 大概會長得像這樣（以本書的背景倍斯特銀行為例）：BESTUS33，前面的四個英文字母代表銀行名稱，接下來的兩個英文字母 US 是國家，也就是 United States，而末尾的兩個數字或英文代表的是這家銀行在國內的地點。

　　三、什麼號碼也沒有的情況：中國就是一例。當碰到這種什麼代碼系統都不用的地區時，你唯一能做的就是儘所能填入越多資訊越好，包括受款人帳戶所在的分行名稱和詳細地址、以及受款人的姓名、連絡電話與住址。

07 Chapter

08 Chapter

09 Chapter

10 Chapter

11 Chapter

12 Chapter

13 Chapter

11.2 Mulligan

Title Note:

Mulligan發音為[`mʌlɪɡən]，在非正式的高爾夫球賽中，"mulligan"指「重揮一次桿（之前揮的那一桿不算）」、「重來」的意思。例句："He took a mulligan and tried again."（他引用了重來的規則而再試一次。）

對話 Dialogue

Mrs. Weis: (Frowning.) ... You said that normally they receive the money in three days and yet today's the fourth day, my niece still has not gotten the wire. I think it's better that we cancel the transaction.

威斯太太：（皺眉。）…妳説正常情況下他們在三天之內會收到錢，可是今天已經是第四天了，我的姪女還是沒有收到匯款。我想我們還是最好取消那筆交易。

Chi: You sure, Mrs. Weis? Robert suggests that we try to trace it first and see if the money is still on its way to your niece. As we discussed earlier, the fee

季薇：您確定嗎，威斯太太？勞勃建議我們先試著追踪這筆款項，看它是不是還在往您姪女的路上。就像我們先前討論

to **recall** a wire transfer is ten dollars. You've already paid forty dollars when you initiated the transfer, I hate to see you spend more money on this transaction.

Mrs. Weis: Um ... no, it's okay. I want to cancel it. I'll arrange another way to send her the money.

Chi: All right. Let me call the wire department.

Mrs. Weis: Thanks, Chi.

Chi: (Dials a series of numbers. After a brief moment, she begins to speak.) This is Chi Borst calling from University office. I would like to recall a wire that was sent to Germany four days ago. Yes. The transaction number is two zero, one four, zero three, three zero. Uh-huh, thank you. (Continues to hold the phone and listen attentively.) Yes? Oh, really? Good to know that. Yes, I'm ready. (Writes on her **notepad.**) Thank

的，取消一筆匯款的費用是十元美金，在您申請這筆轉帳時就已經付了四十塊錢，我不希望看到您在這項交易上面花更多的錢。

威斯太太：嗯…不，沒關係，我想把它取消。我會安排其他的方法將錢送到她那邊。

季薇：好吧，讓我打電話給匯款部門。

威斯太太：謝謝，季薇。

季薇：（按入一連串號碼。過了一會兒，她開口。）這是季薇·伯斯特從大學分行來電，我想取消一筆四天前送到德國的匯款。對，交易號碼是二〇、一四、零三、三零。嗯哼，謝謝您。（繼續握著話筒，並專心聽著。）是嗎？喔，真的啊？很高興知道這個事。是的，我準備好了。（在她的筆記簿上寫著。）十分感

you so much. No, that's it. Good-bye. (Hangs up the phone.) Mrs. Weis, the wire department will cancel the transfer. When it's finalized they will notify us then I will give you a call. Here's the **reference number** for the recall.

謝您。沒有了，就這樣。再見。（掛上電話。）威斯太太，匯款部門會取消這筆轉帳。所有的作業完成之後，他們會通知我們，然後我就會給您個電話。這個是取消匯款的查詢號碼。

Mrs. Weis: I'm sorry for all these trouble.

威斯太太：我很抱歉造成這麼多麻煩。

Chi: Don't mention it. Actually the wire transfer specialist I spoke with said it's better that you cancel the transfer now. Because once we find out that the money is credited to the wrong account, it would be very difficult to take the money back out. In order to take back the money, the receiving bank would have to contact the account owner to get permission to debit the account, which is difficult and time-consuming in most cases. I think you've made the right decision, Mrs. Weis.

季薇：不打緊。事實上，剛跟我對話的那位匯款專員說，您還是現在取消這筆匯款比較好，因為一旦等到我們發現錢放到錯的帳戶裡，要再把錢拿回來就變得十分困難。要把錢拿出來，受款銀行必須連絡帳戶持有人，以取得持有人同意從戶頭中扣錢，在大多的情況裡，這種過程不但費力且耗時。我認為您做的抉擇是正確的，威斯太太。

Mrs. Weis: Thank you. So, I'll wait for your call, right?

威斯太太：謝謝。所以，我就等妳的電話囉，對嗎？

Chi: Yes, you will hear from me in a couple of days for the confirmation.

季薇：是的，兩天內我就會與您確認交易取消。

Mrs. Weis: Got to go now. I have an appointment with my dentist in fifteen minutes.

威斯太太：我得要走了，我十五分鐘內要趕去看牙醫。

Chi: Drive carefully, Mrs. Weis. I'll talk to you later.

季薇：開車小心，威斯太太，下次再跟您聊。

Mrs. Weis: Okay!

威斯太太：好！

單字 Vocabulary

- **recall** [rɪˋkɔl, ˋrɪ-] **n. v.** 取消、撤回
- **notepad** [ˋnotˏpæd] **n.** （整疊紙張上方以膠條或螺旋併合，通常最後一張紙的後面附有厚紙板以利書寫，能一張張撕下來用的）筆記簿
- **reference number** [ˋrɛfrəns ˏnʌmbɚ] **n.** 供日後查詢之用的參考號碼、受理號碼

職場須知 Business Know-how

Keeping Track 記錄追蹤的重要性

When you have a transaction that requires more than one phone

call to handle or a transaction of significant value, it is imperative to keep track of them by asking for a reference number. In the case where a reference number is not available, the name, position and contact number of the person you're speaking with will suffice. Write down the date and progress of each encounter. A solid record of events should keep things from stalling or going awry.

當你需要打一通以上的電話來進行某項交易，或牽涉到的金額龐大，索取查詢號碼以利日後追蹤是非常重要的。若是對方沒有提供查詢號碼這項功能，記錄和你交談的人員的姓名、職銜與連絡電話也可以。寫下每次通話的日期及進度。一份紮實的紀錄應該能避免事情停滯不前或出錯。

實境對話

A: How may I help you today, Ma'am?

請問我能為您服務嗎，太太？

B: I'm calling because I just found out my reward points were not transferred to the new card that I received a month ago.

我打電話來的原因是我剛發現所有的紅利點數都沒有轉到我一個月前收到的新卡上面。

A: I apologize, Ma'am. We're aware of the issue and our technical department is doing everything they can to transfer card members' points to the new database. Your correct amount should show up within two statement cycles.

我十分抱歉，太太，我們的確有發覺這項問題，技術部門目前正盡全力將持卡會員的點數轉入新的資料庫。您的正確點數應該於接下來兩份對帳單的週期內顯示。

B: Can I please have a reference number for this call?

能不能請你給我這次通話紀錄的查詢號碼？

A: Most definitely. Your reference number is QU, one seven five, three eight, four five.

當然。您的查詢號碼是 QU、一七五、三八、四五。

B: Thank you.

謝謝你。

07
Chapter

08
Chapter

09
Chapter

10
Chapter

11
Chapter

12
Chapter

13
Chapter

國際匯款送出後可以取消嗎？

這個問題的答案要看情況。一般來說，在匯款申請書送出之後，到款項存入受款人的銀行戶口，這中間可分成三種不同的時段：

一、申請書送出後三十分鐘內：可以。依照美國現行法律，若是客戶在送出匯款後三十分鐘內反悔，所有銀行機構都必須將匯款金額，包括手續費，全數退給客戶。

二、申請書已送出超過三十分鐘，但匯款尚未進入受款人帳戶：大部份的情況下是可以的。在可以的情況下，客戶得以取回匯款，但是會損失大部份甚至全部的手續費，另外加上取消匯款的費用。銀行無法退回客戶手續費的理由包括本身匯款部門產生的費用，以及中間銀行（註）已收取的費用。不可以的情況則發生於受款人的銀行其實已經接受了匯款，預備將金額轉入受款人帳戶。

三、匯款已進入受款人帳戶：通常來說都是不可以。一旦匯款存入帳戶後即視同現金，受款人可立即領出，這也是為什麼多數設計跨國騙局的不法份子，都偏好使用國際匯款的方式來獲取受害者的資金，國際匯款於結帳後就被視為是一種不能變更（*irrevocable*）的交易，除非銀行能獲得帳戶持有人的許可，否則錢一般都是拿不回來的。

　　註：中間銀行的英文為 intermediary banks，是介於發款銀行和解款銀行（也就是受款人的銀行）間的中繼站。並非所有國際匯款都會經過中間銀行，只有當發款與解款的銀行沒有建立合約、缺乏互相轉帳用的帳戶時，才會經過中間銀行來進行匯帳。

07
Chapter

08
Chapter

09
Chapter

10
Chapter

11
Chapter

12
Chapter

13
Chapter

11.3 From Coast to Coast

Title Note: "From coast to coast"直接從字面上來看是「從一個國家的某一邊（海岸）到另一邊（海岸）」，也就是指「橫越國家的」或「全國性的」。

 **對話** Dialogue

A **filipino** girl approaches Chi at her desk.

一位菲律賓女孩走近季薇的辦公桌。

Cheryl: Hi, Chi. Are you available? I just have a quick question.

雪柔：嗨，季薇，妳有空嗎？我想問個問題，只要一下就好。

Chi: (Looks up from her paperwork.) Oh, hi, Cheryl. Sure, have a seat!

季薇：（從文件中抬起頭來。）喔，嗨，雪柔。當然，請坐！

Cheryl: Thanks.

雪柔：謝謝。

Chi: What's your question?

季薇：妳的問題是什麼？

Cheryl: My aunt wants to transfer some money to my bank account. She lives in North Carolina. What does she need to do?

雪柔：我的阿姨想轉些錢到我的銀行帳戶，她住在北卡羅來納州，她該怎麼做？

Chi: Um, her name is not on your account, is it?

季薇：嗯，她的名字不在妳的戶頭上面，是嗎？

Cheryl: No.

雪柔：她的名字沒有在我的戶頭上。

Chi: Does she has an account with Best Bank?

季薇：她在倍斯特銀行有帳戶嗎？

Cheryl: No. There's no Best Bank where she lives.

雪柔：沒有，她住的地方沒有倍斯特銀行。

Chi: She can mail you a check.

季薇：她可以郵寄支票給妳。

Cheryl: But that will take a while. I ... I kind of need the money right now.

雪柔：可是那樣要一段時間。我…我現在就需要那筆錢耶。

Chi: You could have her send you a domestic wire transfer. It'll get here almost **instantaneously**.

季薇：妳可以請她送國內匯款給妳，錢幾乎瞬間就可以匯到這裡來。

Cheryl: A domestic wire transfer? How do you do that?

雪柔：國內匯款？那要怎麼做？

Chi: She'll need your routing number, your name and your account number. I'll write them down for you. (Begins to write on a piece of paper.)

季薇：她需要妳的銀行代碼、妳的姓名和帳戶號碼。我會幫妳把這些資料寫下來。（開始在一張紙上謄寫。）

Cheryl: I appreciate it, Chi.

雪柔：我很感激妳這麼做，季薇。

Chi: No problem. And I just want to give you a heads-up, there's a incoming wire transfer fee of fifteen dollars which will be debited from the transfer amount.

季薇：沒問題。還有，我想先跟妳講一下，接受國內匯款的費用是十五元，這筆費用會直接從匯入的款項裡扣掉。

Cheryl: Okay.

雪柔：好。

Chi: By the way, when are you gonna send another wire to the Philippines?

季薇：另外還有一件事，妳下次匯款到菲律賓是什麼時候？

Cheryl: Around the fifth of next month.

雪柔：大概下個月的五號前後。

Chi: Basically you are sending to the same bank and the same beneficiary, correct?

季薇：基本上妳都是匯到同樣的銀行跟同樣的受款人，對嗎？

Cheryl: Yeah, that's right.

雪柔：對呀。

Chi: I can request a repeat code for you. That way you get a ten-dollar discount every time when you wire your house payment. Also, because most of the information is saved, it would be a lot quicker when we put in the requests.

季薇：我可以幫妳申請一組重複匯款碼，那樣一來，每次當妳匯妳的房貸時，妳可以少繳十塊錢的費用。並且，由於大部份的資料都會被儲存起來，我們以後申請匯款的時候速度就會快很多。

Cheryl: Really? That's great! Thank you, Chi.

雪柔：真的嗎？太棒了，謝謝妳，季薇。

Chi: (Smiles.) You're welcome. I'll let you know when I get the code!

季薇：（微笑。）不客氣。我拿到匯款碼以後會通知妳！

單字 Vocabulary

- **filipino** [ˌfɪləˈpino] **adj.** 菲律賓人的
- **instantaneously** [ˌɪnstənˈtenɪəslɪ] **adj.** 即刻地、立刻地

職 場須知 Business Know-how

Building Customer Rapport 建立你與客戶間的良好關係

Be genuine. Offer your clients something that is unique to you so they'll keep coming back to you. If you are meeting the customer for the first time, start the conversation with a light topic that's outside of the business. Chilly people get chilly reactions from other people. If you are relaxed and friendly, people will become relaxed and friendly, too. However, control the length of your chit-chat, being too agreeable or seeming subservient can turn off people and can also get you off track.

保持真誠。提供客戶一些唯有你才有的東西,這樣他們才會持續回來找你做事。在與顧客初次接觸的時候,試著以生意範圍之外的輕鬆話題展開彼此間的對話。態度冷淡的人,從別人那獲得的反應也會是冷冰冰的。你的態度如果是放鬆及友善的,人們也會跟著變得放鬆跟友善起來。不過,要記得控制你和客戶閒聊的時間,一昧地附和或顯得奉承不但會讓人倒胃口,也可能會導致你偏離正題。

實境對話

A: Thank you for calling Best Bank, this is Cindy Lawrence. May I please have your name, Ma'am?

感謝您致電倍斯特銀行,我是辛蒂・羅倫斯,請問您貴姓大名,女士?

B: Yes, my name is Teresa Weis.

好的,我的名字是泰瑞莎・威斯。

A: How are you doing this morning, Ms. Weis?

您這個上午過得如何呢,威斯女士?

B: Just fine. Thank you.

還好,謝謝妳。

A: I see that you're calling from New York. How's the weather over there? I used to live in upstate New York!

我看到您是從紐約州打電話過來的,那邊的天氣怎樣?我以前就住紐約上州呢!

B: You did? Um, we had some snow last night, but it didn't stick. Right now it's bright sunshine. I would say it's about fifty.

妳住過這裡啊?嗯,昨晚下了一點雪,但是沒多久就化掉了。現在是豔陽高照,我說大概是五十度左右。

A: That sounds really nice.

聽起來很舒服啊。

B: It is nice.

的確是很舒服。

A: So, Ms. Weis, what can I do for you in this wonderful day?

所以,威斯女士,在這麼美好的日子裡我能如何為您服務呢?

B: Cindy, right? Cindy, I would like to find out what my credit limit is, please.

辛蒂,對嗎?辛蒂,我想麻煩妳幫我查看我的信用額度是多少。

A: Absolutely, your credit limit is ...

沒問題,您的信用額度是⋯

不可或缺的銀行代碼

在本書第二章介紹櫃台交易系統（見 *Operating System Chi 2.0* 單元）的英文對話中，我有大略地提到過支票上的「銀行代碼」，今天，讓我們來進一步探討這組由九個數字合起來的號碼。

首先，如果你拿起一張支票來看，會注意到支票正面的底下有一連串的號碼，這些號碼可以分成三個群組：第一組就是我們這次要講的主題：銀行代碼，它由兩個這種模樣特殊的符號 ⑈：，一個在前，一個在後地與支票上其餘的號碼分開來；第二組是發票人的帳戶號碼（*account number*）；而跟在帳戶號碼後面那個長度稍微比較短的號碼，就是支票號碼（*check number*）。

銀行代碼的英文為 *routing number*，也有人稱之為 *routing transit number*、*transit number* 或 *ABA number*。*ABA* 是 *American Bankers Association* 的縮寫，銀行代碼最早就是由這個協會設計發展出來的。根據望文生義的道理，單字 *routing* 有「經由... 路線」的意思，所以按照這組號碼，我們就可以知道錢的來源是哪家銀行，或者錢要往哪裡送；而 *transit* 這個字則有「運輸」的含意，因此也代表了照著這個代碼走，就可以曉得錢該往哪裡運輸。

平常在網路上付帳單，或將薪資及退稅等收入設定成自動存款時，我們一般所使用的都是支票底下的那組銀行代碼；然而，碰到要申請國內匯款（*domestic wire transfer*）時，受款人一定要跟銀行問清楚他們國內匯款用的銀行代碼是什麼，因為根據各間分行的所在地不同，有些銀行用來辦理國內匯款跟用來做自動轉帳的銀行代碼是不一樣的，客戶如果提供了錯誤的代碼，不但匯款的速度會大打折扣，還有可能遭到退件的命運。

07
Chapter

08
Chapter

09
Chapter

10
Chapter

11
Chapter

12
Chapter

13
Chapter

11.4 Fast and Furious

對話 Dialogue

At a local **grocery store**.

在一家當地的超市裡。

Chi: (Noticing a familiar face by the Western Union service desk.) Mr. ... Rodriguez?

季薇：（注意到西聯匯款服務櫃台旁邊出現一張熟悉臉孔。）…羅德里奎茲先生？

Mr. Rodriguez: You're ... the lady at the bank!

羅德里奎茲先生：妳是…在銀行上班的那位小姐！

Chi: That's me, Chi.

季薇：對呀就是我，季薇。

Mr. Rodriguez: Chi. Nice to see you. You shop here?

羅德里奎茲先生：季薇，很高興看到妳，妳都是到這裡買東西嗎？

07
Chapter

08
Chapter

09
Chapter

10
Chapter

11
Chapter

12
Chapter

13
Chapter

Chi: I do. My apartment is just five minutes from here. You? Did you just get out of work?

季薇：是啊，從這裡到我的公寓只要五分鐘。那你呢？剛下班？

Mr. Rodriguez: Yeah. Actually today I came here to pick up a Western Union transfer.

羅德里奎茲先生：是。不過其實我今天到這裡是要來領一筆西聯匯款。

Chi: Western Union ... Is it good? How does it work if you don't mind I ask?

季薇：西聯匯款…？它的服務品質好嗎？如果您不介意的話，我可以請問它是怎麼個做法嗎？

Mr. Rodriguez: Sure. They are good. I've used their service for a while and I haven't had any problems. Their fees are cheaper than the bank's. (Chuckles.) The way I use their service is that, when I need to send money to Mexico, I take out cash from the bank, come here, fill out this form (picks up a blank form from the **kiosk** and shows it to Chi), show them my ID and they wire the money out for me.

羅德里奎茲先生：當然可以，他們的服務很好。我用他們的匯款服務已經有一陣子了，目前為止都還沒什麼問題。他們的費用比銀行來得便宜。（竊笑。）我的作法是，每當我需要匯錢到墨西哥時，我就先去銀行領錢，然後到這邊填這張表格（從架上拿出一張空白的表格給季薇看），出示我的身份證後，他們就會幫我匯錢出去。

Chi: So they only take cash?

季薇：所以他們只收現金囉？

Mr. Rodriguez: I think so. Another thing is you can set up an member account if you use their service a lot. One of the benefits of having an account is, every time you send money you get a certain amount of points, and when you have enough points in the account, you can use them to reduce future transaction fees. Another benefit is faster service. Two months ago they sent me a membership card, and now when I come here, I can just show them my card or they can look me up by my phone number, all of my information and past transaction history is stored and ready to be used for processing new transfers.

羅德里奎茲先生：我想是如此。另外，如果你經常使用他們的服務的話，可以去設立一個會員帳戶。擁有帳戶的優點之一，是每次匯款的時候，你都會獲得某些點數，累積足夠的點數之後，你可以用那些點數抵減下次的交易費用。另一個優點是更快的服務速度。兩個月前他們寄給我一張會員卡，現在，當我來到這裡，我只須出示這張卡，或者他們也可以用我的電話號碼進電腦查，我一切的資料跟過去的交易紀錄都有存檔，隨時能立刻叫出來辦理匯款手續。

Chi: How about receiving money? You said you're here to pick up a transfer?

季薇：那領錢呢？您説您今天來這裡是要領一筆匯款？

Mr. Rodriguez: Yeah, it's pretty easy, too. My brother would e-mail me a tracking number after he wires the

羅德里奎茲先生：對啊，那也很簡單。我哥在匯過錢後會以電子郵件寄給我一組追蹤號

07
Chapter

08
Chapter

09
Chapter

10
Chapter

11
Chapter

12
Chapter

13
Chapter

money. All I need to do is to give them the tracking number and my ID to receive the transfer.

碼，我只要提供他們追蹤號碼跟我的證件就可以領款了。

Chi: That sounds good. Thank you for the information. I learn something new today!

季薇：聽來真的不錯。謝謝您告訴我這些，今天又學到一樣了！

Mr. Rodriguez: Anytime. And thanks for your help with my car loan. Will I see you at the bank tomorrow?

羅德里奎茲先生：隨時都行。還有我要謝謝妳幫我辦汽車貸款，妳明天會在銀行裡嗎？

Chi: I'll be there!

季薇：會的！到時見。

單字 Vocabulary

- **grocery store** [`grosərɪ `stor] **n.** 超市。（作者按：單字 grocery 如果寫成複數形 groceries，意思為「生鮮蔬菜等食品及雜貨」。）
- **kiosk** [`kiɑsk] **n.** （商場或街道中）獨立的小販售亭

日常用語 Common Expressions

I learn something new today! 我今天又學到一樣了！

職場須知 Business Know-how

Know Thy Enemy 了解你的敵人

If possible, shop your competitors discreetly on a regular basis to study their operations firsthand. There is no need to copy what your competitors do. Because if you try to copy everything that they do, you will always be one-step behind. Instead, focus on your strength and strive to provide greater value. Never bad-mouth your competition. Respect your competitors, since they are the ones who determine your prices, your profit margin, and, most importantly, your very survival.

如果可能的話，固定每一段時間去暗中查訪你的對手，親自了解他們的經營方式。無須拷貝他們的作法，因為若是你拷貝他們每一樣作法，你永遠都將落後他們一步。把重心放在你的強項上並努力提供更高的價值。避免說你競爭對手的壞話。對你的敵手抱持崇敬之心，因為他們的存在決定了你的產品標價、你的獲利空間以及，最重要的，你能否繼續在這個行業中生存下去。

實境對話

A: I saw your TV commercials. I would like to know more about your personal checking. Do you have one that has no maintenance charge?

我有看到你們的電視廣告，我想更深入瞭解你們的個人支票帳戶。你們有免維護費的帳戶嗎？

B: Absolutely. (Takes out a brochure.) These are the personal checking accounts we currently have. (Points to the middle section.) This one is our most popular account: Convenience

Checking. As long as there is more than a hundred dollars in the account, you won't have any monthly maintenance fee.

當然有。（取出一份小冊子。）這些是我們目前有的個人帳戶種類。（指向冊子中間的區域。）這一個是我們最受歡迎的帳戶：便利支票帳戶。只要戶頭裡的餘額超過一百元，您就不須付月費。

A: That means it has a minimum balance requirement.

意思是說它有最低餘額的要求。

B: Correct.

正確。

A: Do you have an account that doesn't?

你們提供無最低餘額限制的帳戶嗎？

B: Yes, our Simple Checking. It has a low monthly fee of six dollars. No minimum is required.

有的，我們的簡易支票帳戶。每月只需繳六元的月費，沒有最低餘額的限制。

A: I see.

我了解了。

B: You can take this pamphlet with you and think about it if you'd like. My direct phone number is on the front.

如果您想要的話可以拿這份手冊回去仔細考慮。我的直撥號碼就在正面。

A: That would be great! Thank you for your help.

那太好了！感謝你的協助。

跨國匯款的另一途徑：西聯匯款

　　在山繆·摩斯（*Samuel Morse*）成功地發出世上第一封遠距電報後的數年間，大大小小的電報公司如雨後春筍般相繼林立，其中之一，就是西聯匯款的前身：紐約與密西西比峽谷電報印刷公司（*New York and Mississippi Valley Telegraph Printing Company*）。一八五五年，它與埃茲拉·康乃爾（註）所創立的紐約和西聯電報公司（*New York & Western Union Telegraph Company*）合併，更名為西聯電報公司（*The Western Union Telegraph Company*），「西聯」這個名稱從此就一直沿用下來。

　　西聯電報公司原以拍發電報為主要業務，在一八七一年它展開了匯款的服務，此後匯款即逐漸成為其重要的收入來源。二○○六年，西聯正式宣布結束電報事業，全力朝向匯款事業發展。

　　今天，西聯在全球各地有超過五十萬個據點，憑藉著收費低廉及取款快速的優勢，成功地吃下了小額匯款的市場（大筆金額的國際匯款還是使用銀行的服務比較划算，也來得安全，客戶不須攜帶鉅額現金於西聯據點和銀行間來往奔波），最近並開始提供客戶在網路和自動櫃員機上進行匯款的功能，可說是一家實力不容小覷的國際匯款機構。

　　註：埃茲拉·康乃爾（Ezra Cornell，Ezra發音為[ˋɛzrɑ]）不但建立了西聯匯款，也是美國東岸名校康乃爾大學的的創始人之一。

07
Chapter

08
Chapter

09
Chapter

10
Chapter

11
Chapter

12
Chapter

13
Chapter

Chapter 12

Personnel Changes

人事變化

12.1 Second Life

對話 Dialogue

Chi walks into the branch and sees a large poster pinned to the wall. On top of it, there is a scroll with a ribbon and a black **graduation cap** made with cardboard. Michelle is taping a balloon to the corner of Mike's station, while Kris pumps out another silver blue balloon.

季薇一走進分行就看到一張大型海報釘在牆上。海報上方黏著綁著緞帶的紙卷與一頂用硬紙板做成的學士帽。蜜雪兒正將氣球貼在麥可工作間的一角，克莉絲則把另一個銀藍色的氣球灌滿氣。

Chi: Michelle ... Kris ... How sweet of you two!

季薇：蜜雪兒…克莉絲…妳們兩個好貼心喔！

Kris: What do you think?

克莉絲：妳覺得怎樣？

Chi: I think it's wonderful. Who made the poster? It's so **neat**!

季薇：我覺得這真是很美好。海報是誰做的？做得好精緻！

Kris: (Looks past the balloon.) Michelle did. Hey, you want to make some coffee? Robert brought cookies. We should set up a table next to the poster with a couple of **markers** so people can sign it.

克莉絲：（越過氣球看去。）蜜雪兒做的。嘿，妳可不不可以去泡點咖啡？勞勃帶了餅乾來，我們應該在海報旁邊設立一個桌子，放幾支麥克筆讓大家在上面簽名。

Chi: Okay! (Turns around and sees Mike walk through the **vestibule**.) Michael!!!!

季薇：好！（轉身見到麥可正走出玻璃穿廊。）麥可！！！！！

Mike: What? What did I do wrong? Whatever they say I did, I didn't do it.

麥可：什麼？我做錯了什麼？不論他們說我做了什麼事，我真的沒有做。

Chi: Today's your last day!

季薇：今天是你在這裡上班的最後一天耶！

Mike: Oh, yeah. (Glances around.) Are these all for me?

麥可：喔，對噢。（環顧四週。）這些全都是為我做的？

Michelle: No, it's for someone else. OF COURSE IT'S FOR YOU, **DUMMY**!

蜜雪兒：不，是為另外一個人做的。這些當然是為你做的，傻瓜！

07 Chapter

08 Chapter

09 Chapter

10 Chapter

11 Chapter

12 Chapter

13 Chapter

Robert: (Comes out from the back room.) What are we going to do without you, Mike?

勞勃：（從後面的房間裡走出。）沒了你我們要怎麼辦啊，麥可？

Kris: Aw, I'm gonna miss you!

克莉絲：噢，我會好想念你！

Mike: (Points at the poster.) So people are going to sign on the poster? Can I take it home after?

麥可：（指著海報。）所以大家會在上面簽名是嗎？之後我可以把它帶回家嗎？

Michelle: Of course. It's yours. Since we all have been telling customers about your leaving, I think there will be a lot of them coming here today to say goodbye.

蜜雪兒：當然啦，它是你的。我想今天很多人會來跟你道別，我們一直都有在告知客人你要離開的消息。

Robert: Pierre and Colleen will be here later. We should grab a drink after work.

勞勃：皮耶跟柯琳稍晚會到。下班後我們應該去喝一杯。

Mike: That's cool with me.

麥可：我沒問題。

Chi: I'll be there!

季薇：我要去！

Kris: Me, too. Michelle, you're going?

克莉絲：我也要去。蜜雪兒，妳也會去，對吧？

07
Chapter

08
Chapter

09
Chapter

10
Chapter

11
Chapter

12
Chapter

13
Chapter

Michelle: I'll call Ron and tell him to come and pick me up. I'll go.

蜜雪兒：我要打個電話給榮恩跟他講到酒吧接我。我會去。

Mike: Sounds like someone will be drinking tonight.

麥可：聽起來某人今晚準備好要喝酒了。

Michelle: Yep, this old lady and, (points at everyone around) this big family!

蜜雪兒：沒錯，就我這位老女人還有，（指著周圍所有人）這個大家庭！

單字 Vocabulary

• **graduation cap** [ˌgrædʒʊ ˋeʃən ˋkæp] **n.** 學士帽
• **neat** [nit] **adj.** 精巧的、極佳的
• **marker** [ˋmɑrkɚ] **n.** 麥克筆
• **vestibule** [ˋvɛstə ˌbjul] **n.** 銀行入口處的穿廊，通常以玻璃隔間。在建築物內附加這一種類似玄關的空間，主要目的是減低室內的冷氣散失；有些銀行甚至會在這裡設置自動取款機，當大廳的營業時間結束後，人必須先刷卡才能進入，提供了顧客一個兼顧安全和隱私性的提款環境。
• **dummy** [ˋdʌmɪ] **n.** （口語）笨蛋、傻瓜。Dummy 這個字原指「假人」、「人體模型」，由於假人偶不會思考，因此引伸出「傻瓜」的意思。

日常用語 Common Expressions

Aw. 噢、哦。

（作者按：Aw 是一種表示輕微沮喪、同情、甚至是見到可愛的小孩或動物時，感到極度的愛憐或不捨所發出的聲音，唸起來類似ㄡˇ，美國人經常把這個字的音拉長來強調其情緒的投入程度，因此很多人會寫作 "Awww"。注意不要跟另一個字 "Ah" 混淆

了，Ah 的用法和唸法近似我們的「啊」，用以表示驚訝、抗議不滿或突然發現某事物等的情緒。）

**場須知** Business Know-how

Go the Extra Mile in Bidding Someone Farewell
多花心思來安排歡送會

We spent most of our waking moments with our colleagues. In a way, they are more like family than we realize. When someone is leaving the company, do your best to make the parting of ways special. Organize a potluck, throw a surprise party, or even invite a few unexpected guests. New things can be scary. Let them know that change is healthy and good. Ease their transition into the next phase of their life by showing your support. You may have lost a co-worker, but you've gained a lifelong friend.

每天我們睜開眼睛的大部份時間都是跟我們的同事在一起。在某方面來說，他們還更像是我們的家人。當某人準備要離職時，盡你的可能把離別的時刻變得特別起來。安排一場各人自備菜餚的聚餐、設計驚喜派對、甚至邀請祕密賓客都好。新事物可能令人恐懼不安，告訴他們改變是健康及有益的。表現出你的支持，以協助他們踏入人生的另一階段。你也許失去了一位工作夥伴，但獲得了一個永遠的朋友。

實境對話

A: (Inconspicuously passing a card under a manila folder. Speaks in a quiet voice) Chi, sign the card when Mike is not looking.
（暗中地把卡片藏在一份文件夾裡傳遞過來。低聲地講話。）季薇，趁麥可沒在看的時候在卡片上簽名。

B: Got it.

知道了。

A: Robert suggests that we each chip in five bucks to get Mike a Staples gift card. You know, so he can use it for school supplies and stuff.

勞勃建議我們每個人出五塊錢，集中起來買張 Staples 的禮物卡給麥可。妳知道，這樣他可以用來買上課用的文具跟其他東西。

B: Good idea. Who's collecting the money?

好主意，誰在負責收錢？

A: Michelle. Pass the card to her when you're done.

蜜雪兒。妳簽完了就卡片把傳給她。

B: Okay!

好！

該回學校唸書嗎？

　　到社會上工作了一段時間後，面對每天固定朝九晚五的工作內容，許多人這時會開始興起回學校唸書的念頭。是的，記憶中的大學生活是那麼多彩多姿、無憂無慮，有機會的話，誰不會想重溫那段美好的時光呢？但是，成人回學校讀書，跟青少年時期的就學有很大的不同，人們這時多半經濟已經獨立，結了婚、甚至已經有小孩，重新當學生的決定不再只是自己一個人的事，這個決定會影響到周遭的許多人，在這種關鍵時刻裡，你會問：到底是我的興趣／轉換跑道／更好的升遷機會重要呢？還是維持一份穩定的收入重要？

　　也難怪「中年危機」這個名詞會被創造出來，這世界上太多人有同樣的感受了。

　　要回答標題內的問題，首先你必須通過三個測試：第一、你要問自己：挑選的學科是你喜歡的嗎？在做這件事情時你會獲得成就感嗎？務必誠實地回答這第一個問題，因為如果你挑的學科對自己來說沒有意義，那麼我保證你，當你在研讀的過程中碰到挫折時會很難堅持下去，因為你沒有辦法從裡面獲得樂趣。

　　第二個測試是你的經濟能力許可嗎？很多人由於考量這項因素而選擇白天上班、晚上跟週末唸書的作法，這樣做當然也可以，只是這種生活形態非常辛苦，要有打長期抗戰的心理準備；不過如果你要唸的學科會對你目前的工作有直接的幫助，許多公司會補助學費，所以可以跟你的上司還有人事部門詢問清楚。其他打算辭去目前工作、回學校做全職學生的人，可以考慮用學生貸款支付學費，輔以少量的兼職收入以維持生計的方法來完成學業。

　　最後一個測試是，你的配偶或任何與你分擔家計的人，能夠體諒並支持你嗎？在跟他們解釋你的決定之前，想好你要回學校唸書的理由、支付學費及生活費的計畫、以及完成學業的決心，呈現給他們一個有希望、有未來的藍圖。親愛的另一半與家人，在你意志消沈或遲疑不決的時候，會成為你最好的啦啦隊。

通過以上這三個測試以後，如果你決定回學校唸書是最好的選擇，那麼就勇敢的向前去吧！*Good luck and enjoy it!*

12.2 Competition

對話 Dialogue

It's Monday morning. Chi is unlocking the vault with Robert; she hears a knocking on the door across the lobby.

星期一早上，正當季薇和勞勃在開金庫時，她聽見從大廳的另一端傳來敲門聲。

Robert: That must be Cynthia. (Steadies the vault door.) You okay, Chi?

勞勃：那一定是辛西亞。（穩住金庫的門。）妳沒問題吧，季薇？

Chi: Yep, I got it. (Robert nods and turns to the front door. A gentle breeze **whisks** through the office. A professionally dressed woman gracefully steps inside. Robert holds the door for her.)

季薇：沒問題。（勞勃點點頭，轉身向正門走去。一陣微風穿過辦公室，某位穿著專業的女人優雅地踏進來，勞勃為她扶著門。）

Cindy: Dear, it's so nice to see you!

辛蒂：親愛的，見到你真好！

Robert: Come on in. Has been a long time. Our morning **huddle** will start soon. You can put your personal belongings in the break room. This way, let me show you.

(A few minutes later, standing in the middle of the lobby, Robert signals everyone to gather around.)

Robert: Before we begin today's huddle, I would like to introduce to you all: Cynthia Lawrence. Mrs. Lawrence has seventeen years' worth of banking experience under her belt. As you all will soon find out, she is an incredibly knowledgable and capable person. While we look for a replacement for Michael, Mrs. Lawrence will be helping us.

Cindy: My God, Robert. Did you have to mention "seventeen years"? It makes me sound old! (Turns to the crowd.) I am very flattered when Robert asked me to come here and work with you

勞勃：歡迎，好久不見了。我們的晨間會議很快就要開始，妳可以把個人物品放到休息室，往這裡走，我帶妳去。

（數分鐘後，勞勃站在大廳的中央，打手勢要大家集合。）

勞勃：在開始今天的晨間會議前，我先要給你們介紹：辛西亞‧勞倫斯。勞倫斯女士具有十七年的銀行做事經驗，我保證你們接下來很快就會發現，她是一個知識豐富並十分有能力的人。在我們找尋麥可接班人的這段期間裡，勞倫斯女士會在這兒幫忙。

辛蒂：我的天，勞勃，你非得提到「十七年」嗎？把我講得好老喔！（轉向群眾。）當勞勃問我能不能來這裡與你們共事時，我感到十分地榮幸。你

guys. You can all just call me Cindy. Drop the "Mrs. Lawrence" crap. (Group giggles.)

們叫我辛蒂就好，別叫我什麼「勞倫斯女士」。（眾人竊笑。）

Robert: (Coughs.) Ahem. And today, "Cindy" of course will help us **kick off** our new savings program: Best Savers. Every time when you see a customer without a savings account, you will talk to them about starting one. The program offers customers an **incentive** that, when they open a new savings account with a initial deposit of one thousand dollars, they will receive a fifty-dollar gift card in six weeks. (Group gasps and murmurs.)

勞勃：（咳嗽。）咳，今天「辛蒂」會協助我們展開新一波的儲蓄活動：「存錢我最行」。當你看到哪個客戶沒有儲蓄帳戶時，你就跟他們講要開一個起來。這個活動獎勵客戶的方式是，如果他們以一千元開立新的儲蓄帳戶，六個禮拜內就會收到五十元的禮金卡。（眾人驚歎並低聲竊語。）

Cindy: Fifty dollars' free money from the bank? I like it! (Grins.)

辛蒂：銀行免費送出五十塊錢？我喜歡這個點子！（露齒而笑。）

Robert: I'll have Michelle print out **coupons** for you to give to your customers. Let's have a good week!

勞勃：我會請蜜雪兒印一些優待券讓你們發給客戶。加油！

(Group **disperses**. Robert approaches Chi and pulls her to the side.)

（眾人散去。勞勃走向季薇並把她拉到一旁。）

Robert: Chi, I know you are applying for the RM position. And I want you to know that you're at the front of the line. I don't want you to think that Cindy is stepping on your toes.

勞勃：季薇，我知道妳在應徵客服經理的職位，我想讓妳知道妳是我們優先的人選之一。我不希望妳認為辛蒂是來侵犯妳的領域。

Chi: I understand.

季薇：我了解。

Robert: You'll like her. Cindy and I used to work together at Chase. She is very good.

勞勃：妳會喜歡她的。辛蒂跟我以前在大通銀行一起做事，她非常棒。

Chi: She seems cool. Um, Robert?

季薇：我感覺她是滿酷的。嗯，勞勃？

Robert: Huh?

勞勃：嗯？

Chi: About how long do you think it's gonna take for them to decide on the new RM?

季薇：你想他們大概需要多久時間決定新的客服經理人選？

Robert: Normally around a month. We still have a couple more candidates to interview.

勞勃：正常來說大約一個月，我們還要再面試幾位候選人。

Chi: (Nods.) Thanks for letting me know.

季薇：（點頭。）謝謝你讓我知道這些情況。

Robert: Not a problem.

勞勃：沒問題。

單字 Vocabulary

- **whisk** [wɪsk] ㉖ 快速地移動、拂動
- **huddle** [ˋhʌdḷ] ㊀ 美式橄欖球選手們集合在攻防線後面的戰略磋商。這個名詞經常被引用到商業中，意指「（快速的）會議」。
- **kick off** [ˋkɪk ˋɔf] ㉖ （足球和美式橄欖球中的）開球。引伸為「開始」的意思。
- **incentive** [ɪn ˋsɛntɪv] ㊀ 誘因、獎勵
- **coupon** [ˋkupɑn] ㊀ （供顧客兌現獎品或獲得折扣的）優待券、折價券
- **disperse** [dɪs ˋpɝs] ㉖ 散開、解散

片語 Phrases

under someone's belt 擁有（某項成績或經驗）。

（作者按：Belt 原指「腰帶」，在這句慣用語裡，「在某人的腰帶下面」意思就是「到了某人的肚子裡」的意思，當某件事被你吃到肚子裡面去時，即代表你已獲取某樣經驗。）

step on someone's toes 侵犯某人的領域

07
Chapter

08
Chapter

09
Chapter

10
Chapter

11
Chapter

12
Chapter

13
Chapter

好 用句型 Useful Sentences

使用worth的講法

Seventeen years' worth of banking experience

十七年（份量）的銀行任職經驗

（作者按："Worth" 在這裡的意思是「份量」、「總值」，seventeen years' worth 直接翻譯成中文就是「十七年的份量（或總值十七年）」的意思。 注意在這個句子裡，我們必須把時間，也就是「年」加上所有格，十七年是複數，所以省略符號「'」要打在s的後面。依此類推，如果連接 worth 的時間或金錢是單數，那麼省略符號就打在s的前面，例如下面的第三個例句："A month's worth of groceries"（一個月份量的生鮮雜貨）。）

你還可以這樣說

Two days' worth of work

A hundred dollars' worth of quarters

A month's worth of groceries

例句

A: I would like to take out five thousand dollars from my line of credit. How much is six months' worth of interest at my current rate?

我想從我的信用循環帳戶裡提出五千元。按照我目前的利率，六個月份量的利息是多少？

B: Let me see. (Types in the numbers.) Okay ... Five thousand for six months at five point nine-nine ... Your total interest would be one hundred forty seven dollars and fifty seven cents—about one hundred and fifty, sir.

讓我看看。（鍵入數字。）好的…五千元，期間六個月，利率五點九九…您的利息總共是一百四十七元五角七分一大約一百五十元，先生。

經營職場中的人際關係

從學校畢業後踏入工作職場，大多數人會逐漸發現這兩種環境裡面的人際關係截然不同。在學校裡，很多時候，你可以選擇只跟你志氣相投的同學一起唸書、做報告或聊天；但是在職場裡，每天與你相處的人，並不是憑你喜好挑選的人，他們有些是原來就待在公司有一段時間的老將、有些是老闆應徵進來的新人、有些甚至是人事部門指定的空降部隊。

由於人類自然的本性與直覺，我們還是會不由自主地在群眾中找到跟自己合得來的人，並花較多的時間和這些人相處，所以理所當然的，你也會在公司裡發現這些份子。但是，在那些難得的「啊哈，真高興你也在這裡！」幸運時刻外，大部份時間，我們也必須與跟我們個性及做事方式截然不同的人維持一份和諧的工作關係。

記住在職場中，你不能只挑那些會服從你或喜歡你的人來跟你共事；真正有能力的人，可以影響具有各種態度、風格的同事一起往相同的目標努力。保持幽默感、尊重彼此的想法差異、關心他人在公事以外的其他生活層面如家人健康或嗜好等、適時地提供協助，這些作法都能 *"grease the wheels"*（在人際關係間加入潤滑劑），讓辦公室裡的氣氛更融洽、大家的心情更好、更能達成你想要的結果。

07
Chapter

08
Chapter

09
Chapter

10
Chapter

11
Chapter

12
Chapter

13
Chapter

12.3 Mixed Signals

對話 Dialogue

The month has passed quickly. While the staff at University branch has become accustomed to the presence of Cynthia, Chi notices this morning she is arranging several personal items around her desk.	一個月很快就過去了。正當大學分行的職員逐漸適應了辛希亞的存在，這天早上季薇注意到她在辦公桌周圍擺放數件個人的物品。
Kris: (Notices Chi's absent-mindedness.) Hey, what are you thinking?	克莉絲：（注意到季薇心不在焉。）嘿，妳在想什麼？
Chi: I … am … thinking I probably didn't get the job.	季薇：我…在…想我大概沒被選上。
Kris: What are you talking about? You know all the customers here. Why wouldn't they give you the job?	克莉絲：妳在說什麼鬼話啦？妳認識這裡所有的客戶，他們怎麼可能不選妳？

Chi: Yesterday Cindy asked me to order some binders and a **desktop planner** for her. I bet next she will ask me to order her new business cards.

Kris: Have you talked to Robert? When was the last time you two spoke about the job opening?

Chi: A while ago. Speaking of job opening, let me check something real quick ... (Chi clicks on webpage of the internal job postings. She holds her breath and stares at the screen.) It says, "The position has been filled."

(They look at each other in silence. A few seconds later, Robert comes out of his office and approaches Chi's window.)

Robert: Chi, can I borrow you for five minutes?

Chi: Yes, of course. (Robert waits while Chi closes up her station. The two walk

季薇：昨天辛蒂要我幫她訂一些資料夾和一份桌面計劃表，我打賭接下來她就會要我幫她訂新的名片。

克莉絲：妳跟勞勃談過嗎？上一次你們倆個談到這個職位空缺是什麼時候？

季薇：有一段時間了。提到職務空缺，讓我來查一下…（季薇點選發佈公司內部職務的網站，接著她屏息並張大眼睛瞪著螢幕。）它顯示：「這個職位已找到適合的人選。」

（她們沈默地相互對視。幾秒鐘過後，勞勃從他的辦公室出來並走近季薇的窗口。）

勞勃：季薇，我可以跟妳借五分鐘說話嗎？

季薇：好，當然可以。（勞勃等候著季薇將她周圍的東西鎖

together into his office and sit down across the desk.)

進抽屜裡。兩人一起走入他的辦公室，並在桌子的兩端坐下。）

Robert: Chi, I would like to personally give this news to you: I've accepted the district manager's position so I will be leaving the branch next week.

勞勃：季薇，我想親自告訴妳這個消息：我已經接下了區域經理的職位，所以我下個禮拜就會離開分行。

Chi: What?

季薇：什麼？

Robert: I had an interview with Diane Dean on Wednesday and I was offered the position this morning.

勞勃：我星期三跟黛安・狄恩面試，今天早上收到錄取的通知。

Chi: Oh, Robert, that's good news! You're promoted!

季薇：噢，勞勃，這是好消息！你升官了！

Robert: I figure that I have been managing the branch for the last ten years, it's time for me to do something a little different.

勞勃：我想我經營這間分行也已經有十年，是該做點其他事的時候了。

Chi: But ... who is going to be the new manager here?

季薇：可是…接下來新的經理是誰？

Robert: Colleen. You know Colleen. She will be here tomorrow.

勞勃：柯琳。妳認識柯琳啊，她明天會到這裡。

Chi: What about the RM position?

季薇：那客服經理的職位呢？

Robert: We have other plans for you. Currently there is a opening at **Newark** office. Go and try that, I think you'll be a good fit.

勞勃：我們對妳有其他的計畫。目前在紐華克辦公室有一個空缺，去試試看，我認為妳會很適合。

單 字 Vocabulary

- **desktop planner** [`dɛsk͵tap `plænɚ] **n.** （通常一個月一頁、可整頁撕去，附有日期以供使用者紀錄每天待辦事項的）大型桌面計劃表
- **Newark** [`nju͵wɚk] **n.** 紐華克市。位於舊金山灣的東南邊，四週被佛利蒙市包圍的一個城市。聯合市、佛利蒙和紐華克市組成所謂的「三連市（Tri-City）」。

職 場須知 Business Know-how

How to Present a Potentially Upsetting Message
如何傳達一份可能使人沮喪的訊息

Change is sometimes challenging and may entail work, pain, and uncertainty. However, there are (or will be) times when you need to tell somebody that an inevitable change is on the way. Pay close attention to the following four key elements so you can lessen the

emotional impact when presenting a potentially upsetting message:

變化，有時不是那麼容易能夠讓人接受，它可能帶來更多的工作量、不適與對未來的不確定感。然而，有時候（或遲早）你必須告訴別人某種無法避免的改變即將到來，所以當你在表達一份可能會使人沮喪的訊息時，請特別留意以下這四個關鍵因素，以緩和它對當事人情緒上的衝擊。

1. Your attitude when delivering the news. Put yourself in the other person's shoes. Imagine how you would react if you were in his or her position. Be calm, honest, and professional.

   你的態度。設身處地，站在對方的角度來想你會如何反應。保持沈著、誠實和專業。

2. The clarity of the message. Think about what you are going to say. Practice. Be clear and to the point.

   清晰地表達這份訊息。先想好你要說什麼。練習。清楚明白並切中要題。

3. Privacy. A private setting allows your audience to respond freely and express their emotions safely.

   隱私性。選擇在私下的場所傳達訊息，可以讓聽眾自由地反應並安全地表達他們的情緒。

4. Your ability to answer questions. Identify possible solutions before you meet with the other person. Your ability to answer questions demonstrate your professionalism and shows that you are focused on moving forward.

   你回答問題的能力。在跟對方面談前先找出可能的解決方案。你回覆問題的能力展現出你的專業精神，並顯示你專注於持續往前的決心。

實境對話

A: I would like to advance five hundred dollars' cash from my checking account, please.

我想從我的支票帳戶中預借五百元出來，麻煩你了。

B: Definitely, Ma'am. And, since you use this product, I would like to remind you that we're discontinuing account advances, starting August 1st.

沒問題，太太。還有，既然您有在使用這項產品，我要提醒您八月一日起，我們就要停止提供帳戶預借現金的服務。

A: What? Why? I use it almost every month!

什麼？為什麼？我幾乎每個月都會用到耶！

B: The bank's goal is to simplify our product line. We offer other products, such as credit card and line of credit, that can also satisfy your short-term cash needs. I have a brochure here. (Takes out a blue pamphlet and highlight a few sections.) You can take a look and see which product best suits you.

銀行的目標是簡化我們的產品線。我們其他的商品，像是信用卡與循環信用帳戶，也能夠滿足您短期內的現金需求。我這裡有一份手冊。（拿出一本藍色的本子，並以螢光筆強調出其中的幾塊區域。）您可以拿去看看，找出哪種商品最適合您。

A: You said starting August?

你說八月開始？

B: Yes, August 1st. I'll write it down here, along with my phone number in case you have any questions. I'll do my best to help you during this transition period.

是的，八月一日。我會把這個日期跟我的電話號碼—萬一您有任何問題的話—都寫在這裡，在這段過渡期內，我會盡我所能地協助您。

A: Thank you. I appreciate it.

謝謝你，我很感激。

07 Chapter

08 Chapter

09 Chapter

10 Chapter

11 Chapter

12 Chapter

13 Chapter

應徵工作然而沒有獲得錄取

電影《戰爭遊戲》（*Ender's Game*）中，主角安德一心渴望獲選進入戰爭學校，以帶領人類擊退外星異族的入侵。他與眾不同的表現與氣質引起總司令官葛拉夫的注意，但葛拉夫的副手安德森少將懷疑安德可能跟他哥哥一樣具有暴力傾向，並非擔任領導的最佳人選。於是他們故意安排將安德頭上的監視器拔除，不提供任何的解釋就遣送他回家，這時扮演司令官葛拉夫的哈里遜福特在鏡頭前，說了一句十分耐人尋味的話：*"Let's see how he handles rejection."*（讓我們來看看他在落選的情況下會如何反應。）

這句話之所以耐人尋味，是因為它點出了一個事實：原來，真正要判斷一個人，不能光看他在順境裡的行為，還要看他在逆境中如何控制自己的情緒、怎麼樣應付挫折和難題。英文裡的 *"rejection"*，中文的直接翻譯是「拒絕」，*getting rejected*，也就是被拒絕；落選、被人拒之門外、遭到淘汰... 被拒絕大概是最折磨人的情緒之一，因為它傷及到我們的自尊心，表面上它似乎在對我們說：你不能有這個東西（無論這個東西是什麼），因為你不夠好。

其實，如果我們深入分析自己被拒絕的原因，不是因為我們不夠好，而是因為雙方不適合。

每一天，我們都在拒絕、淘汰，或對某人或某個東西說「不」，這個過程是人類社會的一部分，不管是某位條件極佳的結婚對象、一件熱列促銷中的商品、甚至是待遇優渥的工作機會，這個揀選的過程幫助我們做出最佳的決定、挑出最適合我們需求的產品。即使對方的各種條件再好、商品價格再低、職務薪水再高，如果它們不適合我們，我們還是不會接受。

同樣的道理反映在人員的甄選上，公司進行面試也是希望能找到「最

12.3 **Mixed Signals**

07
Chapter

08
Chapter

09
Chapter

10
Chapter

11
Chapter

12
Chapter

13
Chapter

適合他們需求的人」，而不是「最好的人」。如果你應徵某項工作卻沒有獲選，這並不必然代表你能力不足，而是因為你不適合那項工作跟它周遭的環境及文化，所以，放開手，看清鬆點，保持樂觀的態度，繼續往下一個職位空缺前進，假以時日，你一定會找到那個最適合你的工作！

12.4 Towing the Line

Title Note: 片語 "tow the line"的意思是「遵守並執行規則」。例句："You need to tow the line by not skipping the steps."（若要按照規則來做的話，那麼你不能抄捷徑、省略步驟。）

對話 Dialogue

Chi arrives at the Newark office five minutes early. The branch door is locked. There are two customers waiting for the bank to open. She politely nods at them and approaches the door. After a few knocks, she can tell that the employees inside seem to have noticed her but no one has come to the door.

A smiling woman came out and unlocks the door at precisely nine o'clock.

季薇比預定的時間還要早五分鐘抵達紐華克分行。分行的大門仍是鎖著的，外面有兩名顧客正等待銀行開門營業。她禮貌地朝他們點頭，接著朝門接近，在敲了幾次門後，她感覺裡頭的員工似乎有察覺到她的存在，但沒人來應門。

九點鐘一到，出現了一位笑盈盈的女人將門鎖打開，她愉快

She cheerfully greets everybody on their way in.

地向每個走進來的人打招呼。

Mary: You must be Chi. Hi, I'm Mary. Right this way! (Accompanies Chi to an office in the back.) I saw you but I didn't want to frustrate our customers if I only let you in. I hope you understand.

瑪麗：妳一定是季薇了。嗨，我是瑪麗，請往這邊來！（陪伴著季薇一同走到後方的辦公室。）我有看到妳在外面，可是我不想使客人覺得我只讓妳一個人進來，我希望妳能夠理解。

Chi: I do.

季薇：我了解。

Mary: Would you like to have some coffee? It's chilly this morning.

瑪麗：妳想不想要來點咖啡？今天早上滿冷的。

Chi: I would love to.

季薇：好啊。

Mary: How do you like your coffee? Cream? Sugar?

瑪麗：妳的咖啡要加鮮奶油跟糖嗎？

Chi: Just cream. Thank you.

季薇：鮮奶油就好，謝謝。

A minute later Mary reappears with two cups of coffee. She puts one in front of Chi.

一分鐘後瑪麗端著兩杯咖啡現身，她把其中一杯放在季薇面前。

Mary: Starbucks is right across the hall-way from us. We only buy our ground coffee from them. (Sipping.) Thank you for coming in.

瑪麗：星巴克就在大廳的另一邊，我們只跟他們買研磨咖啡不跟別人買。（啜飲咖啡。）謝謝妳過來面試。

Chi: Oh, thank you for having me, Mary.

季薇：喔，謝謝妳邀請我來面試，瑪麗。

Mary: When you are ready, we can start the interview.

瑪麗：妳準備好了的話，我們就可以開始今天的面談。

Chi: Please go ahead! (Smiles.)

季薇：請開始吧！（微笑。）

(Mary asks a few questions about Chi's background, training, and skills. Then she presses her last question.)

（瑪麗詢問了幾個有關季薇背景、受訓過程和技能的問題。然後她拋出最後一個問題。）

Mary: What would you do if there's a conflict between you and your manager?

瑪麗：如果妳和妳的上司之間產生衝突，妳會怎麼做？

Chi: (Slightly puzzled.) Um, I can't think of an incident when that happens. My manager and I have always worked quite well together.

季薇：（有點困惑。）嗯，我不記得曾有那樣的情況，我的上司跟我相處一直都很融洽。

Mary: How about **hypothetically**?

瑪麗：譬如說假設呢？

Chi: I believe we will be open and **candid** about it. Together we'll work out a plan to resolve the conflict. However, if the issue is concerning bank security or **compliance**, I won't **budge**.

季薇：我相信我們會開誠布公地談。我們會一起研究出一套計畫來解決這樣的衝突。不過，若是問題牽涉到銀行的安全性或是該不該遵守法律，我則不會讓步。

Mary: I understand. So that **wraps up** our interview today. I'll call you later on with the results.

瑪麗：我了解。我們今天的面試就到此為止，我稍晚會打電話通知妳結果。

Chi: Great! I look forward to hearing from you.

季薇：好極了！我期待妳的來電。

單字 Vocabulary

- **hypothetically** [ˌhaɪpə`θɛtɪkəlɪ] **adv.** 假設地、假定地
- **candid** [`kændɪd] **adj.** 坦白的、直言無隱的
- **compliance** [kəm`plaɪəns] **n.** （對法令、規定的）遵守、服從
- **budge** [bʌdʒ] **v.** 動搖、移動
- **wrap up** [`ræp `ʌp] **v.** （口語）結束、完成

職 場須知 Business Know-how

The Art of Speaking Succinctly 說話扼要的藝術

When you practice speaking, imagine you are in front of an audience. Your goal is to be understood perfectly. Be mindful of your tone and rate of delivery. Speak boldly and with authority at a steady yet comfortable pace. This will help solidify your message. Be brief, direct, and utilize simple terms that anyone can understand. Chunk your information into bite-sized bits while taking breaks in between in order to verify that your audience has retained it. Repetition of key points is a powerful tool in ensuring continuity between new ideas and your earlier statements. End all dialogs with a clear summation of benefits to its participants.

當你在練習講話的時候，假想你面對著一群觀眾。你的目標是讓觀眾清楚地瞭解你說話的內容。注意你的聲調和速度。大膽、帶有權威性、並以穩定而舒服的步調來講，這麼做可以使你要傳達的訊息更有說服性。扼要、直接並使用任何人都能理解的簡單辭彙。把資訊切成小塊小塊的，而且每隔一段時間就暫停一下來確認觀眾已聽懂。重複關鍵的要點是一件有力的工具，這項工具可確保先前的言論與接下來要提到的新觀念間的延續性。在談話的最後把這項資訊為參與者帶來的福利，作一個清晰的總結。

實境對話

A: Chi, Mr. Klein returned your call and placed an order of fifty gift cards. Put them in your referrals!

季薇，克萊先生剛才回覆妳的電話並訂購了五十張禮金卡，把那些卡片記錄到妳的轉介客戶名單下！

B: He did? Fifty cards?

他真的訂了？五十張？

A: Yes. Good Job. But …next time when you leave a message, you'll want to speak slower. He said you talked really fast and he wasn't sure about what he had heard on the phone. So I explained the discounts we currently offer to him again. I guess you were nervous.

是啊，做得好。不過…下次妳留言的時候最好講慢一點。他說妳說話說得很快，他不懂妳在電話上說什麼 ，所以我又跟他重複解釋了一次我們這回給他的折扣。我想妳大概是緊張。

B: Oh, I was. Thanks for letting me know, Robert. I need to slow down next time.

噢，我的確是滿緊張的。多謝你讓我知道這一點，勞勃，下次我得講慢一些。

A: Not a problem!

沒問題！

建立你的人格與行為準則

今天我們要來談談兩個英文字：*Character* 和 *Integrity*。

第一個字，*character*，指的是人外顯的個性和取向。這個字也有「角色」的意思，所以你可以把它跟戲劇聯想在一起，一個人的個性，他的 *character*，就像他在舞台上扮演的角色一樣，這個角色具有獨特的性質和風範，這些性質和風範讓他與別的角色有所區別，令觀眾很容易地把他從一堆人中分辨出來。

再來是 *integrity*，這個字常用來指「正直」。除了正直外，*Integrity* 還有另一個含義：「完整」，也就是說，一個人要做到正直，其中非常關鍵的一點是他必須保持自我的完整，就算在不同的情境中也不會改變他的信念及作為。

相信每個人在踏入社會裡一段時間後，跌跌撞撞地都悟出了一些道理，這些道理漸漸形成人們的行為準則。你的準則是什麼？在情況變得異常困難時你還能不能維持那些標準？拿暢銷小說《飢餓遊戲》（*The Hunger Games*）中的主角凱妮絲來說，這個角色之所以受到廣大讀者的愛戴，不是因為凱妮絲知道如何射箭打獵，也不是因為她贏得殘酷的電視競賽，而是因為她不論敵人如何強大、環境再如何惡劣，都能始終如一地展現出仁慈的心地、向弱勢族群伸出援手。

建立一套你相信並能夠接受的人格特質（*character*），努力保持這套特質的完整性（*integrity*）。就像美國人說 *stay in character*，意思是某人不管面前有沒有觀眾、不管你的觀眾是誰，都不要分心、跳脫出角色來；因為一個只知一昧應和、沒有準則的人會失去他的獨特性，這樣的人與其他的角色間界線很模糊，容易被人忘懷。相對地，一個堅守原則、言行一致的人則會帶給人深刻的印象，並受到尊敬與信賴。

07
Chapter

08
Chapter

09
Chapter

10
Chapter

11
Chapter

12
Chapter

13
Chapter

Chapter 13

Epilogue
尾聲

13 Looking to the Future

對話 Dialogue

At home.

在家裡。

Paul: Check your phone! Someone was trying to call when you were out. It <u>went off</u> twice.

保羅：去看妳的手機！妳外出的時候有人打給妳，手機響了兩回。

Chi: (Putting the groceries in the refrigerator.) It did?

季薇：（把生鮮蔬果放入電冰箱。）是嗎？

Chi walks over to her handbag and takes out a cell phone. The screen shows "one message."

季薇走到她的手提包旁，拿出一只手機，手機螢幕上顯示「一則留言」。

Chi: (Presses "Dial" and listens attentively.) It's Mary from the Newark branch!

季薇：（按下「打出」並仔細地聆聽。）是紐華克分行的瑪麗！

Paul: That's the branch you had a interview a few weeks ago, right?

保羅：那是妳幾個禮拜前去面試的分行，不是嗎？

Chi: (Heart pounding.) Right! I'm calling her back. (Replays the message and write down a phone number.)

季薇：（心跳加重。）是啊！我要回她電話。（再次播放留言，並寫下一組電話號碼。）

A moment later. On the phone.

一分鐘過後，在電話上。

Chi: Hi, Mary, this is Chi returning your call.

季薇：嗨，瑪麗，我是季薇，回覆妳的來電。

Mary: Hi, Chi! How are you? Sorry if I have interrupted your day off.

瑪麗：嗨，季薇！妳好嗎？不好意思打擾妳休假。

Chi: Not at all. What can I do for you?

季薇：不會。有什麼我能為妳效勞的地方嗎？

Mary: Chi, I would like to offer you the relationship manager's position at my branch.

瑪麗：季薇，我想請妳到我分行擔任客服經理。

Chi: Oh, I'm thrilled! Mary, thank you for this opportunity. You won't be disappointed!

季薇：噢，我真是太興奮了！瑪麗，謝謝妳給我這個機會，妳絕對不會失望的！

07
Chapter

08
Chapter

09
Chapter

10
Chapter

11
Chapter

12
Chapter

13
Chapter

Mary: I'm glad to hear that. I've talked to Colleen and I would like to have you start on Monday.

瑪麗：很高興聽到妳這樣說。我跟柯琳談過了，我希望妳星期一開始上班。

Chi: Monday? Okay.

季薇：星期一？好。

Mary: Excellent. I'll let Robert know that you'll be here next week. On Monday, can you be here at eight fifteen? That way I'll have time to get you **situated** and then we can attend the corporate's call together.

瑪麗：非常好，我會告訴勞勃妳下禮拜就會到我這裡來。星期一那天，妳能不能八點十五分進辦公室？那樣我比較有時間幫妳在新辦公室裡安頓下來，然後我們可以一起參加公司的電話會議。

Chi: Sounds good. I'll be there. Thank you again, Mary.

季薇：好主意，我會準時到。再次謝謝妳，瑪麗。

Mary: You're welcome. Happy to have you on board. I'll talk to you later. Enjoy your day off.

瑪麗：不客氣，很高興妳能加入我們的團隊。我們以後再聊，好好休假吧。

Chi: Thanks. Talk to you later, Mary. (Tabs on "End Call.")

季薇：謝謝，我們再聊囉，瑪麗。（輕敲「結束通話」。）

Paul: That's my baby! Congratulations on the promotion! (**Cups** Chi's face and presses a loud kiss on her cheek.)

保羅：我真是以我的寶貝為榮！恭喜妳升職囉！（托著季薇的臉並在她的頰上大聲地親了一下。）

Chi: (Lets out a huge breath.) I thought they'd never call!

季薇：（吐出一大口氣。）我以為他們不會打給我！

Paul: Of course they would call. You're such a capable employee. You're more than qualified. We should celebrate!

保羅：他們當然會打給妳，像妳這麼有能力的員工，妳的資格超過他們的標準太多了。我們應該要慶祝！

Chi: Hooray!!!!!

季薇：好耶！

07 Chapter

08 Chapter

09 Chapter

10 Chapter

11 Chapter

12 Chapter

13 Chapter

單字 Vocabulary

· situated [ˋsɪtʃʊˏet] **adj.** 被安置成某種狀態的
· cup [kʌp] **v.** 以手掌包圍、用手托著

片語 Phrases

go off 爆發、發出很大的響聲

日常用語 Common Expressions

Hooray! 好棒啊！好耶！
（表歡喜、鼓舞、贊成等，亦可拼成 "hurray"。）

好 用句型 Useful Sentences

Happy to have you on board.

很高興你能加入我們的團隊。

你還可以這樣說

Great to have you on our team.

Glad that you can join us.

Delighted to have you as part of our Newark family.

例句

A: Wait a second, Justin ... So you knew that Mary was gonna hire me, but you didn't say anything—even when you came over to help out that week?

等一下，賈斯汀…所以你知道瑪麗準備要雇用我，可是你什麼都沒說—即使在你過來幫忙的那一整個禮拜內？

B: Yeah ... I didn't want to ruin the surprise. Didn't want to spill the beans for yah!

是啊…我不想破壞驚喜，不想要太早洩露機密！

A: And I thought the reason you didn't say a word about Mary's pending decision was because I wasn't picked! I was so disappointed.

我還以為你對瑪麗的決定一字未提，是因為我沒被選上！我那時好失望喔。

B: It was not easy. I wanted to tell you the whole time. Ha, now you know! I'm so glad that you can join us. It's going to be great!

那可不是件容易的事，我從頭到尾一直都想告訴妳。哈，現在妳終於知道了！我很高興妳能加入我們的團隊，接下來一定會很棒！

接下來呢？

　　恭喜，恭喜！你終於拿到期待已久的職位！

　　嗯…那接下來呢？

　　接下來，我要告訴你，有三件很重要的事你一定要做：第一，感謝在這個過程中曾經幫助過你的人。邀請他們共進午餐、送份禮物、打個電話… 等等，通知他們你晉升的消息，與他們分享你的喜悅。世上沒幾種情況比知道自己教導、培養和推薦出來的學生，終於也獲得其他人肯定還來得令人欣慰及驕傲的，讓你的恩人與伯樂曉得他們沒看錯人，而你感激他們在你身上投注了許多心血，並在你需要時拉你一把。

　　第二，吃好睡好，保持精力充沛。新的職位代表改變的來臨，以及更多的責任，你需要有清晰的頭腦和健康的身體來應付這些挑戰。所以，儘可能保持規律的生活作息，做適量的運動，有空的話去買幾件新的套裝跟配飾，可以讓自己看來更加容光煥發。

　　到目前為止，前面兩件事聽起來都還滿容易的，對吧？好了，最後的一件事就有一點點難了：第三，重新架構並加強你的人際關係。聽好，職位越高，你的人際關係也越形重要；特別是在目前的這個時刻，當你拿到升遷的機會，意思是另外有一些人失去了相同的機會，這些人可能是你以前的同事、可能是你現在的同事、甚至還有可能是你新的下屬，你應該要給他們空間去平息見到你被拔擢（而不是他們！）所帶來的挫折感，千萬不要咄咄逼人、時時刻刻在人家面前晃來晃去，提醒他們自己失敗的事實。我希望你能保持謙虛的態度，讓所有身邊的同事感到被尊重、被欣賞。作家 *Kate Stull* 曾寫過這麼一句話，而我衷心地贊成：*"The more you are someone who makes other people happier and more successful,*

the more successful you will be."（如果你能讓其他人更快樂和更成功，你就會變得更加成功。）

　　然而人際關係不僅僅是靠幾段對話就能建立起來的一尤其在工作的場合。在公司裡，你需要以專業的表現贏得新同事的尊敬和信賴，這些表現包括了：有效率地完成工作、將出錯的機率減到最低、準時、以及樂於助人。

　　新的頭銜與職位，代表你又回到上班的第一天，不過不同的是，這一次你已經具備這份新工作需要的絕大部份知識，你現在對自己更有把握，你的自信流露於談笑之間。加油，祝你一切順利！

07 Chapter

08 Chapter

09 Chapter

10 Chapter

11 Chapter

12 Chapter

13 Chapter

好書報報

心理學研究顯示，一個習慣養成，至少必須重複21次!
全書規劃30天學習進度表，搭配學習，
不知不覺養成學習英語的好習慣!!

圖解學習英文文法，三效合一!
　　◎刺激大腦記憶 ◎快速掌握學習大綱 ◎複習迅速
英文文法學習元素一次到位!
　　◎20個必懂觀念 ◎30個必學句型 ◎40個必閃陷阱

流行有趣的英語!
◎「那裡有正妹!」
◎「今天我們去看變形金剛4吧!」

作者：朱懿婷
定價：新台幣399元
規格：368頁 / 18K / 雙色印刷 / 軟皮精裝

文法再弱也有救! 只要跟著解題邏輯分析句子，
釐清【文法重點】找出【判斷依據】並運用【關鍵知識】
《英文文法有一套》讓你一套走天下，三步驟有答案!

【一套邏輯】
　文法重點= 常考、愛考、一直考的文法
　判斷依據= 題目中足以判斷「文法重點」的依據
　關鍵知識= 不受誘答選項影響，正確答案立即浮現的
　　　　　　「關鍵文法知識」
【十大主題】
　10大考官最愛文法主題 建立考生精準文法觀念
【三步驟解題】
　先10題範例: 3步驟 全面掌握解題邏輯
　再10題練習: 3步驟 完全熟練必考重點

作者：黃亭瑋
定價：新台幣369元
規格：372頁 / 18K / 雙色印刷

好書報報

Leader 006
銀行英語

作　　者／季薇‧伯斯特、Paul James Borst
發 行 人／周瑞德
企劃執行／劉俞青
封面設計／高鍾琪
內文排版／菩薩蠻數位文化有限公司
校　　對／徐瑞璞、陳欣慧

印　　製／大亞彩色印刷製版股份有限公司
初　　版／2014 年 11 月
出　　版／力得文化
電　　話／（02）2351-2007
傳　　真／（02）2351-0887
地　　址／100 台北市中正區福州街 1 號 10 樓之 2
Ｅ ｍ ａ ｉ ｌ／best.books.service@gmail.com
定　　價／新台幣 380 元

港澳地區總經銷／泛華發行代理有限公司
地　　址／香港筲箕灣東旺道3號星島新聞集團大廈3樓
電　　話／（852）2798-2323
傳　　真／（852）2796-5471

國家圖書館出版品預行編目(CIP)資料

銀行英語 /
　季薇‧伯斯特, Paul James Borst著
　— 初版. — 臺北市：
力得文化, 2014. 11
　面；　公分. —
　ISBN 978-986-90759-5-4(平裝)

1. 英語 2. 銀行業 3. 會話

805.188　　　　　　　　　　103020879

力得文化
Leader Culture

Lead your way. Be your own leader!

力得文化
Leader Culture

Lead your way. Be your own leader!